PRAISE FOR ROSE GIRL

"*Rose Girl* is a stunner. Holly Payne takes us into the yearning at the heart of the mystic's search. She turns the Sufi quest for connection with God into a human drama that is both moving and soaring."

—TAMIM ANSARY, author of *Games Without Rules: The Often-Interrupted History of Afghanistan*

"In *Rose Girl*, Holly Payne has deftly captured the magic, beauty, and ecstatic energy of the Sufi's ancient sema dance with her story about a girl, Damascena, whose life transcends her own world, and ours. The prose transports the reader creating astonishing characters and at times, a thriller-like plot, carrying us into a world that is part hallucination and part real as Payne weaves in themes of loss, beauty, devotion, evil, struggle, magic, and, ultimately, love."

—DAVID EWING DUNCAN, best-selling author of *Experimental Man: What One Man's Body Reveals About His Future, Your Health, and Our Toxic World*

"*Rose Girl* is a captivating read, with a beautifully satisfying ending. In her meticulously researched novel, Holly Payne's expertly crafted prose captures not only the souls of her characters but the essence of Rumi's wisdom: that life's shattering experiences can break our hearts open, ultimately compelling us to receive the love intended for us. I loved this book."

—KRISTEN HARNISCH, author of *The Vintner's Daughter*

"Holly Payne lives inside her characters. Seeing through their eyes and feeling with their hearts, she illuminates the soul personality in each portrayal. Ms. Payne is an intuitive writer who lets life rip through the pages. *Rose Girl* is storytelling embedded with timeless wisdom."

—FRANCESCA MCCARTNEY, PhD, author *Body of Health: The New Science of Intuition Medicine®*, Founder, Academy of Intuition Medicine® & Energy Medicine University

"Read *Rose Girl!* Love will come alive for you in the life of Rumi. Holly Payne is a wildly gifted writer serving the great cause of love with discerning devotion, insight and lyrical prose."

–DR. MARC GAFNI, author *Your Unique Self, The Radical Path to Personal Enlightenment*, Co-Founder, Center for Integral Wisdom

"Holly Payne's latest novel touches Jelaluddin Rumi's essential beauty within the fragrance of 13th century Turkey and the rich tapestry of his life as a mystic, poet and honored scholar. Payne exposes the very human challenges Rumi encountered as he grew into one of the greatest poets of all time."

—MURSHIDA MARIAM BAKER, author of *Woman as Divine: Tales of the Goddess*, senior teacher, Sufi Ruhaniat International and the Mevlevi Order of America

"This is one of the most gorgeous novels I've ever read. Payne's research was so thorough. It makes me want to learn more about the dervishes, their religious practices, and about Rumi and his achingly beautiful poetry. The themes of forgiveness, spirituality and all the different forms of love resonated with me on every page."

—LAURA MARQUEZ, Emmy Winner and former ABC News Correspondent

"Meet the astonishing rose girl. She begins life orphaned, a mystery to herself, and grows to become a sainted figure, acquainted with miracles, schooled by one of the greatest and most beloved poets of all time, Rumi. In lush prose, with deep wisdom and knowledge, Holly Lynn Payne's wonderful novel captures the extraordinary life of a young woman seeking truth through the transcendent spiritual practices of 13th century Turkey. Rose Girl is a dramatic tale of healing and transformation. Immersive and wise, this story will expand your mind and open your heart."

—KATE MANNING, author of *Gilded Mountain*

ROSE GIRL

A TALE OF RESILIENCE AND RUMI

HOLLY LYNN PAYNE

ROSE GIRL
A TALE OF RESILIENCE AND RUMI

Skywriter Books
Sausalito, California

This is a work of historical fiction. Names, characters, places, and incidents either are the product of the author's imagination or are used fictitiously. No portion of this book may be used or reproduced in any manner whatsoever without written permission from the publisher except in the case of brief quotations embodied in literary articles and reviews. Your support of the author's rights is appreciated. For more information, contact Skywriter Books, P.O. Box 2630, Sausalito, CA 94966.

ROSE GIRL: A Tale of Resilience and Rumi

Copyright © Holly Lynn Payne, 2023
All rights reserved.

Published in the United States by Skywriter Books, Sausalito, California
www.skywriterbooks.com

FIRST EDITION
September 2023

Payne, Holly Lynn.
Rose Girl: a tale of resilience and Rumi/
Holly Lynn Payne.

p. cm.

Paperback: ISBN: 978-0-9822797-6-2
Ebook: ISBN: 978-0-9822797-1-7

1. Jalal al-Din Rumi, Mevlana, 1207-1273—Life—Fiction. 2. Roses—Cultivation—Fiction. 3. Sufi—Customs—Sema—Fiction. 4. Turkey—Konya—Fiction. 5. Orphans—Fiction. 6. Religion—Islam—Sufi—Fiction. 7. Spirituality—Fiction. I . Title.
PS3616.A97 D36 2014
813'.16-dc22   2014905295

Printed in the United States of America on Forest Stewardship Council (FSC) paper

Grateful acknowledgement is made for the following permission to reprint previously published material: translations of Rumi and Shams of Tabriz. *The Essential Rumi* translations by Coleman Barks with John Moyne, Harper Collins, copyright © Coleman Barks, 1995. *The Call to Love: In the Rose Garden with Rumi* translated and edited by Andrew Harvey, Sterling Publishing, copyright © Andrew Harvey, 2007. *Me & Rumi: The Autobiography of Shams-I Tabriz* translated, introduced and annotated by William C. Chittick, Fons Vitae, copyright © William C. Chittick, 2004. *Nightingale Under The Snow* by Annemarie Schimmel, Khaniqahi Nimatullahi Publications, Nimatulliah Sufi Order, copyright © Annemarie Schimmel, 1994. *The Way of the Sufi* by Idries Shah, Arkana Penguin, copyright © Idries Shah, 1968.

Interior design by Tom Joyce
Cover design by Scott Larson / Tom Joyce
Cover photo of girl by Mou Aysha

For Gracelyn Rose

and in loving memory of
Hilary Blake Hamilton,
our resilient rose girl

A NOTE TO THE READER:

The story of *Rose Girl* is a work of fiction inspired by the poet and Sufi teacher, Jalala-al-din "Mevlana" Rumi, the Afghan refugee born 800 years ago in the early 13th century, famous for his masterpiece collection of 27,500 love poems and his deep faith in the spirit world. The name Rumi had been given to Jalala-al-Din after he died in 1273; however, for the sake of modern readers, who know him primarily as Rumi, I refer to him as such throughout the manuscript.

The novel centers around two historical mysteries involving Rumi's beloved friend and spiritual companion, Shams of Tabriz, a controversial and elusive figure, from whom Rumi received the spiritual insights that made him famous. Rumi spent only three years in the presence of Shams, from the age of 37-39; however, his life changed forever as a result of Shams' tragic disappearance. Many theories exist: Rumi's own son killed Shams, Rumi's jealous disciples stabbed Shams outside Rumi's house, or Shams drowned in a well in Konya. To this day, nobody knows for sure, though several countries claim to be the resting place of Shams.

The second mystery, and perhaps the most significant inspiration for this book, involves an Afghan girl, believed to be the first influence on Rumi's profound faith. According to the tale, Mongols invaded and terrorized Balkh, Rumi's birthplace in what is now Afghanistan. Rumi's father insisted the family flee before the Mongols destroyed the city. On the day of their exodus, apparently young Rumi saw the beautiful girl praying, surrounded by Mongol soldiers. Nobody knows what happened to the girl, but those who have written about Rumi believe the power of her faith made an indelible impression on his heart. *Rose Girl* is a fictional continuation of the girl's family lineage and the spirit of Shams.

Holly Lynn Payne, Sausalito, California

And the day came when the risk to remain tight in a bud was more painful than the risk it took to blossom.

—Anais Nin

PROLOGUE
Konya, Turkey 1270

On the third day of spring, Jalal al-din Mevlana Rumi woke with a quiver in his stomach. He lay in bed, feeling heaviness in his heart, reluctant to visit the caravanserai. The sugar merchants had found a girl wrapped in a wool cloak. Her body had been charred. They had taken her for dead and called on *Mevlana* Rumi to perform the girl's funeral.

Rumi rose slowly from his bed and stepped into the triangle of light coming in from the window. He crept to his closet, hoping not to wake his wife when the wooden doors creaked on their hinges. She was still a beauty at 40. Her thick hair was dark and shone so much in the morning light it looked like she had stepped out of the bathhouse—cheeks flushed, skin dewy, lips full and turned up in a half smile. He regretted that she tasted pleasure only in her dreams these days, and he had the impulse to go back to the bed, bend down and kiss her cheek when the words struck.

> *Be silent,* he heard.
> *Spring is here.*
> *The rose is dancing with its thorn*
> *Beauties have come from the invisible*
> *To call you home.*

He stood there, unable to move while the poem moved through his body and pounded him to the floor. He had no control over when the poetry would happen, like an invisible flood inside his house. It often made a mess of things—mostly his relationships. He told his disciples it felt like a hard rain; and it had given him even more compassion for the earth.

He would have liked to remember this small poem. It spoke to him of something fragile that he could not name but wished to know. He drew in a deep breath and waited for more words but nothing came. And without speaking the poems aloud as he heard them, he would almost always forget, especially now at the age of sixty. Without Hosam or other disciples near him, the poems would go unrecorded. It was not as if he could write them all down himself; it was impossible to keep up with the torrent of poetry that had flooded him for the last ten years. The compulsion to write had become a sort of madness, and although he was relieved to stop today, he did not favor a funeral.

Rumi savored the walk through the streets at this early hour. It was already unseasonably warm for March, and the spring sun had melted the snow on the high plain almost overnight. The heavy scent of the *igde* tree filled the air but did not override the smell of roses that perfumed the city and kept everyone in suspense. Not a gardener in Konya had seen their roses blossom yet. It was too early. Perhaps it was the earth's way of welcoming the girl to Konya's soil, making room for her.

Beauties have come from the invisible to call you home.

Fragments of the poem whirled in his head as he walked past the citadel on the western side of the city and followed the old city wall, toward Sultan Alaeddin Kaykobad's palace, its marble portal gleaming in the eastern light. He climbed the hill to step inside the Alaeddin Camii, the old Arabic designed pillared mosque, where he prayed to know what the poem meant.

He stood under the forty-two antique columns supporting the mosque's huge wooden ceiling and touched his lips and limbs to the floor, feeling a knot in his stomach. He hoped the girl had not died in fear, but had anticipated her death as a chance to meet the Beloved. He had spent his lifetime teaching others to love God, not from fear or hope, but because of all the beauty in the world that is God. Tears ran down his cheeks when he considered the possibility that the girl did not understand this.

Morning light poured through the rounded arched galleries of the caravanserai and across its open courtyard, where camels stood like golden statues tethered by long hemp ropes, their drivers against the walls, slumped and drooling, still asleep.

Rumi followed a group of small boys tending to the men just waking, delivering coffee in small white cups and tea in tulip glasses. The clanging of cups and small nickel saucers, teaspoons and sugar bowls, sounded like music. It was the first time in a decade that he had not come here seeking news of his beloved friend Shams. He missed the energy of the caravanserai and marveled at the distances these men had traveled, transporting sugar from Egypt, silk from Iraq, cinnamon and cumin from India. Stacks of silver candlesticks and chessboards carved from mother-of-pearl glinted in the early light.

A boy in a colorful wool cap carried a copper tray of fresh *simet*. He stared wide-eyed at Rumi and rushed toward him. "Fresh, fresh, *Mevlana*. You will like them very much. My mother baked these this morning," obligating the old man to buy a stack of sesame rings. Rumi dug into his pocket and gave the boy a gold coin. He bit into the savory, ring-shaped pastry and thought he cracked a tooth. The *simet* had been over-baked, the sesame seeds toasted black but he swallowed it all and laughed.

"I am sorry it was a bit scorched. Is it bad?" the boy asked.

"No. Do not be sorry."

The boy stared at him, perplexed.

"It is a good reminder of all that burns and nourishes," Rumi said and took another *simet* from the boy's tray and continued through the square-shaped building, passing small shops, guest rooms, and elaborate baths. The whole place felt more familiar than his home, and he shared an intimate understanding of its details. He took in the sweetness of the air, filled with the scent of fresh hay and the smoke of mint tobacco bubbling up from the hookahs of men seated cross-legged on bright red and blue carpets. In his deepest despair, he always appreciated the companionship of the merchants, even if they had had no news to share about Shams of Tabriz. He still refused to believe his friend had died, but now the merchants delivered news of the legendary girl saint from the mountain monastery in Bulgaria. A girl whose body had been wrapped in black wool.

A young boy carrying a shiny samovar of Turkish tea nudged Rumi's leg.

"*Great Mevlana*," he whispered and pointed. "Go. They are waiting for you."

Rumi looked down at the boy who had already set the samovar on the ground and prostrated himself. Rumi bent down and kissed the boy's head then walked to the center of the inner courtyard where a cluster of merchants gathered around the sugar wagons.

They stopped talking and parted when Rumi appeared. Grown men, like the boy, immediately prostrated themselves to the old man. Rumi gently tapped them on the shoulders, resisting the urge to sigh. He was not weary of their reverence; he only wished it were for God, not him. "Please stand," he said, gesturing for them to get up off the floor. "You will ruin your knees on me."

There was only one man among them who did not get on his knees. A man, his face unshaven, dirt-smeared, stared transfixed at the girl wrapped in black wool. His head was shaved and he wore the threads of what appeared to be a monk's dark brown robe that had been cut and frayed.

Rumi recognized him as a Christian without the arrogance of a crusader. He was moved by the monk's connection to the girl, as if they had known each other for lifetimes and shared the same heart. The monk trembled when Rumi stepped toward him.

"Do you know her?" Rumi asked, looking down at the body in black wool.

The monk lifted his head to the old man. His mouth opened but no words came. Rumi looked into his mouth and saw that his tongue had been partially cut out. His teeth had rotted and a foul smell wafted out of the blackened cavity.

Rumi met the monk with a gentle gaze.

"Did you travel with her?"

The monk nodded.

"Is she your sister?"

The monk looked wide-eyed, stricken.

"She is your Sister," Rumi concluded gently. Aren't we all spiritual siblings, he thought? "She is my Sister too," he said, and studied the girl, doubtful the monk had given her the cloak. The black wool cloak was not part of the order of any monastery, only the Sufi orders, which was why Rumi, of all people, had been called to help with her funeral.

He lifted the black wool cloak, seeing the blistered skin on her left leg and arms, the oozing wounds on her hands and wrists. She was barefoot and the melted stubs of her left toes stuck out beneath the edges of the cloak like the nubs of wasted candles.

"My God," he muttered. He had never seen anyone burned as badly as the girl. Her hair was completely singed and lay in dark clumps under the cloak, as if she had been rolled in dead leaves and twigs. He was surprised the monk and the girl had made it through the Rhodope Mountains. Surely they knew the perils of such a journey. Death was a risk every man in the caravanserai had taken for the chance to explore the world and expand their minds, second to the thrill of scandal, intrigue and thievery along *ipek yolu*, the Silk Road that defined this greatly traveled trade route.

"Welcome to Konya, my sister," Rumi said, his voice soft yet reverberating. *May you be free of pain in your death*, he thought, feeling the rhythmic wave of words wash through him again. He lowered his head and sang aloud the poem he heard in Persian, a ballad of longing and separation. His voice mimicked the somber tone of the reed flute.

> *Bahar amad bahar amad bahar-I mushkbar amad*
> *an yar amad an yar amad an yar-I burd-bar amad ...*
>
> *The spring has come, the spring has come,*
> *the spring with loads of musk has come,*
>
> *The friend has come, the friend has come,*
> *the burden-bearing friend has come.*

Not a merchant moved. They sat, enchanted, and listened.

Rumi crouched to perform an ablution. He rolled up his sleeves and washed his hands and face in the basin of lemon water under the sugar wagon. He dipped his hand in the water and stroked the girl's face, then withdrew it immediately and lifted it to the sky, hearing small gasps from the merchants who understood that he was about to perform *sema*. He did not apologize for making the sacred dance public. He pointed his left hand down to the earth then walked around the girl, slowly at first, until the rhythm of the poem altered his cadence and he was twirling around her like a child playing barefoot in the streets after a storm.

> *Biya biya dildar-i man dildar-man*
> *dar a dar a dar kar-i man dar kar-i man*
> *Tu-i tu-i gulzar-i man gulzar-i man,*
> *bi-gu bigu asrar-i man asrar-i man*
>
> *Come, come my beloved, my beloved,*
> *Enter, enter into my work, into my work!*
> *You are, you are my rose garden, my rose garden:*
> *Speak, speak my secrets, my secrets.*

The words came faster and when he circled the girl for the third and last time, the scent of a rose sweeter than he had ever smelled filled the air. It was the kind of scent that could intoxicate even the purest among them. The boys with the samovars and *simet* stumbled like old drunks, pawing at each other's bony shoulders for support.

The monk let out a cry. Not a man spoke except for Rumi.

"The girl does not need a funeral," he announced.

A young sugar merchant spoke out. His voice echoed in the stillness.

"But you gave us your word, *Mevlana*," he said, igniting uproar among the other merchants. Tea cups rattled. Fists pounded the dirt floor.

A man with a fiery beard stood—a Gallic Turk with a temper.

"Have mercy on your brothers who have been so kind to sit with the girl and keep her spirit company. For all we know it has already departed in your absence."

Someone booed. Rumi turned his left hand toward the ground. He had always appreciated a good debate. Let them talk, he thought. The sugar merchant turned to him.

"Please help the girl, *Mevlana*."

"I can not help her with a funeral," Rumi said.

"What? You think your dancing is what she needs?"

"The girl does not need dancing or poems! She needs a funeral!"

"God is counting on you to deliver the girl's soul!"

Rumi nodded and bowed. *"Khamush!"* he whispered in Turkish. Quiet. He felt light-headed and drunken, slightly intoxicated by the scent of roses. He steadied himself against the sugar wagon, his gaze on the girl. The air flickered with anticipation.

"Take in her scent," he commanded. "Does it not console you?"

The merchants turned to each other, perplexed when Rumi lifted both hands and opened his palms to the sky, offering gratitude for the miracle he was witnessing: the girl had just then blinked and opened her eyes—revealing two luminous blue green pools that seemed to glow in the dim light. She was not dead. She did not need a funeral.

When the girl met his gaze, Rumi recognized her instantly as his final companion.

PART I

The rose speaks of love silently, in a language known only to the heart.

—Unknown

ONE
Rila Mountains, Bulgaria 1256

The girl was born beneath the shadow of a dance on the sixth day of the sixth month in the year 1256. Hers was the first birth in the monastery and it riled the young friar, Ivan Balev, to have to clean up her mother's blood. He stood inside the chapel door with a mop and bucket, fingers stiff with the chill of dawn, and he could hear, between the woman's screams, the laughter hissed by the monks who had assigned him this duty.

He was eighteen and assumed they wanted to test him, to see if his massive body stiffened when he saw her breasts. He felt nothing more than astonishment and disgust—not at her body, but at what her body could endure. He had known no man, other than Jesus Christ himself, who had suffered more, and he wondered if giving birth was akin to a crucifixion. If it was, he wanted to know why there was only a son of God. He figured there ought to be a daughter of God, too, if she had to go through this.

The woman buckled and pawed the base of the baptismal fountain. Her wet hands slipped and left bloodied prints on the marble. She tilted her head and threw her arms into the air, gasping something indecipherable, most likely a curse, at the ruby flame burning inside the lantern dangling from the ceiling.

Ivan's own stomach cramped when she pushed out the baby. She moaned, beat the air, punched the floor and pushed until a small bald head, not much bigger than the palm of his hand, emerged between her legs. Her voice softened and grew hoarse as she pulled the wrinkled bag of skin and bones from her body. She held the baby against her chest and cried and laughed and cried again.

At first, Ivan wanted to alleviate her pain and offer the kind of relief that the saint after which he was named might have brought. But Ivan Balev was not like the mystical hermit Ivan Rilsky—who became a priest at the age of twenty-five, after spending years in a cave near the monastery. Young Ivan Balev was an archer, whose bow could travel nearly three hundred fifty yards, rivaling the longest range of Mongol warriors. He had been trained since childhood and had the strength to draw the bow fully up to one hundred pounds since he was twelve.

Why Ivan's mother had named him after the most respected saint in Orthodox Christianity, a man known as 'the revealer of heavenly mysteries,' was perhaps the greatest mystery of his life. Ivan had never felt his mother's respect. He knew nothing about heaven, aside from what he had heard, and he did not like mystery.

Ivan Balev had no curative powers, no hands that could heal, no true way of knowing if he could ever bless anyone, and for this he felt like less of a man watching the woman struggle with her baby. He wanted to carry her out of the chapel and into a proper bed, but he could not move. Not because he was terrified of what he had just witnessed, but because the moment the baby entered the chapel, the smell of roses leaked from its walls. He pressed his nose against the door and smelled roses in the wood. He tested the sleeve of his robe, expecting the smell of dirt and sweat, but it, too, smelled like roses.

Roses did not typically grow so high in the Rila Mountains of Bulgaria. They grew in the valleys between the Balkan Range and this one, and in his mother's home garden in Sofia, but not at nearly a thousand meters above the sea. He turned to see if anyone was watching, but saw only a passing cloud that flashed red when he looked at the sky, where a stork made circles above the chapel, throwing shadows against the glass.

These were strange things to witness, even in a monastery where Saints had performed miracles and spirit guides appeared. But a red sky, a stork, and the mysterious smell of roses spooked Ivan Balev, who had, only days before, studied with the abbot from the book of Revelations. He was too young to experience the end of the world. If Ivan could have moved, he would have run—not just to his room—to his mother's house in Sofia, but he could not turn away from the baby or her mother.

The woman moaned, wiped her brow, lifted her pelvis off the floor and sat up with the baby at her breast. Her hair was soaked with sweat. Ivan thought whoever said birth was beautiful was lying. Even the rose-smelling baby, who suckled at her mother's breast, looked like a wrinkled old woman who had seen too much of the sun.

The mother ran her finger along the length of the baby's umbilical cord, studying it in the light as if it were made of the finest silk. She reached behind her for a small knife and sliced through the gray cord, depositing it into one of two small pouches dangling from the thin copper wire around her neck. She rolled the stub of the cord from the baby's belly into a knot, then stood in the pool of her own blood.

Suddenly, the flames above the baptismal fountain flickered and the tapestries billowed from the stone walls, though no wind was blowing from the mountain. It felt as though a strange force had entered the chapel just then, and to Ivan's astonishment, the woman extended her arms, as if to touch whatever it was—and let go of the baby.

Ivan shrieked. The woman was clearly possessed, which was the only explanation he could give for the way the baby appeared to be floating in mid-air. He expected her to fall to the ground but she circled her mother once, then without dropping out of the air, she moved around the chapel in a wide arc as if she were flying on the cape of the Devil.

Ivan dropped the mop and bucket and tore through the front door, slid across the bloody mess, and snatched the baby out of the air. He had never held an infant, and he trembled feeling how light she was in his arms. And the smell! My God. He had never smelled anything as sweet as this child.

She cried. He tried to shush her by humming then turned to her mother, desperate for the woman to take her baby back. She seemed distant, her gaze transfixed on the front door. Her face was neither contorted with regret, nor blank with apathy, but something far more subtle and harder to detect, though Ivan caught the tear welling inside her eye.

She walked toward him. "You know, don't you."

Ivan shook his head. He knew nothing. He watched her hands carefully, expectant, anxious. She unhooked the second pouch from the copper wire around her neck and handed it to him. He felt something smooth and round through the thin silk sack. At first, he was unsure if the smell of roses was coming from the pouch or the baby.

"What are they?"

"Rose hips. From the *rosa damascena*."

The woman lowered her gaze to the floor, reached out to Ivan and laid her bloodied hand on his, curling her long fingers around the pouch of rose seeds.

"Damascena," the woman said. "You will call her Damascena."

The baby opened her eyes, hearing her name.

Ivan swallowed. He felt a strange pulsing, as if the whole chapel shook. A current charged the air. He smelled lightning and heard a trickling, like the cascade of a waterfall in spring.

The woman lifted her bloodied hands from his and stepped away.

"Can you keep a promise?"

Ivan nodded, moored in his trance.

The woman continued. "Grow cuttings from the seeds and plant them on the first full moon. If she wants to know where I am, tell her I will always be in the roses."

The baby lifted her small wrinkled arm off Ivan's shoulder and groped the air as if to protest, while her mother turned and quickly walked out the chapel door and down the dirt road outside the monastery—then disappeared into the morning light.

TWO

For weeks after the birth, Ivan prayed that an angel would come and take the child. Every morning, he rose early, not to pray, but to run to the end of the road hoping to find the woman returning for Damascena. He chased the phantasmal forms of fog that wrapped themselves around the trees. On his knees, he bargained with God. He did not need a baby added to his burdens.

He cursed his own mother for wanting to "fix him" by sending him to the monastery in the first place. He was certain she would assure him that the baby was God's answer to his own unique sexuality. She had hurled his clothes out the window the morning after he was caught, then hissed her final words in a whisper: "The sailor came to ask about you and I told him you had married God." Since then, he begged for mercy, but mercy was no more part of the plan than convenience or luck or relief.

Ivan pleaded with the abbot; he was no more prepared to parent a child than he was ready to parent himself. A huge oak desk separated them in the abbot's office, a dark, musty room that smelled of brandy and snuff and vibrated with the abbot's throaty timbre.

A shard of light cleaved through the only window, a narrow pane of glass, no wider than the abbot's arm, and fell across the Bible on the desk.

"Maybe that is the point, Ivan."

"There is no point, abbot! There is only a crisis," Ivan said and stomped his foot, raising his shaking hands. Ever since he had touched the rose hips, he had developed a palsy, and even in his deepest meditations, the shaking never stopped. It had already compromised his aim with the bow, and he feared he would lose his greatest skill. He longed to be back in Veliko Turnovo, shooting birds and other game for the king of the Second Kingdom, not the monks in this lesser fortress.

The abbot directed his gray eyes on Ivan's face, refusing to look at his hands.

"Ah, if you see a crisis, then there is a crisis. But this is God's will. It is up to you to see the opportunity," he offered. "Perhaps you have lost focus? Or faith?"

Ivan didn't want to hear such theories. He had not lost faith. Looking after the baby was distracting him from hunting. He could not imagine the abbot wanted anyone to starve to death. Without his help hunting game, they would have nothing but bread to eat.

He loathed that they loved his sudden transformation into a parent. It spurred him to fling dirty diapers out the window of his room and bark, "I'm no miracle worker. You can't turn shit into wine!" When their howls echoed up to him from the transept, he'd slam the shutters on their mocking, "At least her shit smells like a rose!"

Ivan became their court jester, hands full of feces, soft foods, spittle dried and caked on the collar of his robe. And the lullabies.

God have mercy on him. He should have never opened his mouth to sing, but it was the only way to keep Damascena from crying. It was not easy, and he wondered how anyone could do it alone. He bemoaned the Lord, the father of mankind, for giving this kind of responsibility to any human being.

Ivan Balev wore his disdain in the droop of his lips, and the slope of his shoulders that were slung with Damascena. When Ivan turned to the abbot, desperate, the abbot assured the young friar that there was nothing out of the ordinary about his new role.

"You've become a father," he said and shrugged, looking out at the granite cliff though the window behind his desk. "Stranger things have happened on Lozen Mountain. This is your service, Ivan Balev. Remember, St. Ivan never wanted to come out of his hermitage, but it was God's will for him to do so." He chuckled, "Consider yourself a most blessed young man, for God could have asked you to marry a woman."

"I assure you this was no mercy. This child was sent to punish me," Ivan said, standing in the doorway of the abbot's office.

"If that's your belief. I hope it is not the way you will explain it to Damascena."

Ivan looked up and caught the abbot's unsteady gaze. He had not considered that he would have to explain anything to the girl, and he wiped his cheek as if this string of responsibilities had landed there as a clump of phlegm.

"How can I explain when I don't fully know myself?" Ivan asked, too afraid of ridicule to tell the abbot what he had seen in the chapel on the day of her birth.

"You will ask God for understanding. That is our job, Ivan. To help others understand the tragedies of life. To give them faith despite their misfortunes. Heaven is not on earth, of this I am most certain."

The abbot stood and patted him on the back, not hard, not lightly, and his hand lingered longer than Ivan expected. Besides the baby's small hands, this was the only touch Ivan had received from anyone since he arrived one year ago.

Ivan wanted to press that same, heavy hand against his chest—any hand would do, but the abbot flicked his eyes away from Ivan, then waved him off when he heard the baby's familiar wailing. She was hungry. Again. Ivan excused himself, hating that he ran.

In the first three months, Ivan had managed to decipher Damascena's octaves of outrage, so distorted and exaggerated in infancy. He wondered how a person so small and inexperienced in life could have so much power over someone eight times her size. Or why someone his size didn't kill her. He had considered drowning her by disposing of her in the well. It was not like the abbot and the other monks would miss her. Aside from the way she smelled at birth, her novelty had worn off, eclipsed by their duties to God.

This did not surprise Ivan. What startled him were the instincts Damascena stoked inside him: cradling her soft head, making sure her milk was not too hot or cold, and that she drank enough of it, carrying her on his shoulder while she slept and filled his ears with the sound of her breathing.

And this secret. Behind closed doors, closed shutters, closed mouths, when Ivan Balev looked into Damascena's eyes, the color of a blue-green tourmaline, half sea, half lake, and as luminous as the sun, he found a reason for his own existence. Even his ailing father had never made him feel as needed as the baby did when she gazed up at him, pleading, begging for his mercy to keep her alive another hour. Another day. Another month.

He had no such luck with his father, the kingdom's legendary archer who could hunt on a horse with such prowess that he acquired the moniker, the Tall Mongol. Even with those same skills, Ivan could not hunt down his father's illness like a deer or a bird, and his mother never let him forget it. He was six years old and his mother blamed him for his father's death. "All because you wanted to hunt in the rain!" she said. She refused to touch him as he wept by his father's grave, apologizing for the storm, the illness and all the things he could not control—why his mother struck him and turned his cheeks purple. "Why do you hate me?" he asked, years later, when he had grown taller than her.

She had turned to him, startled. "My son, I do not hate you. I hate that you destroyed my love! I begged you to stay home that day, to wait for the storm to pass, but you insisted, like a spoiled child, and your father indulged you like he always did."

There were countless things Ivan regretted about the baby, too, but she trusted him, and for this reason, he liked Damascena. Though he suffered many sleepless nights, he had taken an odd comfort in his purpose, even if he could not fully understand it.

The abbot had given them a small first floor apartment with their own outhouse and a pipe to the well, another godsend, considering how many times Ivan had to change the girl's rags. They had a window overlooking a massive green hill, and beyond that the ridgeline of mountains—the stage for the shadows of clouds to enact an etheric theater of light. The first time he saw the monastery, he mistook it as a fortress with its twenty-four meter stone walls, hundreds of arches, colonnades and carved verandas. Ivan Rilsky's vision was far more elaborate than the simple cave in which he mediated. The monastery seemed to be in a constant state of development, with artisans and craftsman coming in and out so often that they outnumbered the one hundred monks who dwelled there.

Soon, Ivan Balev fantasized about hiding Damascena in one of the carpenter's bags, hoping someone would fall in love and take her to their village. He welcomed any plan other than the one God dictated. As the days turned to weeks and the weeks to months, and the new seasons dictated the life of the monks, Ivan worried not so much about the health of the girl, but of the rose hips that he failed to plant on the first full moon after her birth.

Time was running out for Ivan Balev. He had to plant the rose hips before the girl learned to talk. He prayed that a rose garden, God willing it took root in the mountains, would prevent Damascena from asking the question he dreaded most—why her mother left.

How would the girl ever believe that she would find her mother in the roses?

Day and night, Ivan calculated the severity of the truth and could find no words to soften it. His mother taught him that women were cruel and more powerful than he would like to admit. He had seen it with his own eyes, God damn them. If all else failed, Damascena would have to understand that misery and joy often share the same face.

❀

After six months, there was a change in Damascena. She no longer responded to Ivan's care. No matter how bright the lantern that Ivan set beside her, she lived inside a perpetual darkness. She lay listless for hours, staring through the slats of the bassinet, eyes lifted to the window, as if she was waiting for her mother to appear.

Ivan thought that the rose hips might help to stimulate her, but when he dangled them above her, she grabbed at the pouch and whimpered. She would not sleep on those nights, as if by holding the pouch of rose hips, she had smelled her mother again.

The monks believed she would soon die of a broken heart. Ivan stood over her powerless, uncertain he could do anything to stop her sadness, until one day, her eyes fluttered open when a stork flew to the window and perched on the ledge. The bird caught Ivan's gaze and he stiffened, seeing human eyes looking out from the bird's. He felt a chill through his whole body, wondering if it was the same bird he had seen on the day of Damascena's birth. The huge white creature seemed to calm the baby immediately, and she fell asleep in its presence, as if she understood it had been sent to watch over her.

THREE

When Damascena started to crawl, the bird never left her window, soliciting curiosity and awe among the monks. The storks of Bulgaria sought the warmer climates of the valleys, not the cold mountain air enveloping the monastery. Not a single stork had ever built a nest there, at least not to their knowledge, so no one could deny the phenomenon.

The monks attributed the stork to Damascena's arrival, reviving their interest in her and giving thanks to God for their good fortune. Even Ivan believed the legend associating storks with good health and prosperity—the coming of spring, even though it was the dead of winter with snow as thick as wet flour.

Soon, the monks snatched Damascena out of Ivan's arms in the rectory and kissed her cheeks, chanting, *Blessed is the baby who smells like a rose and brings storks. May she be healthy. May she be happy.* They offered to babysit, noticing the beleaguered face of the young friar. You're exhausted, they told him. Take respite. Sleep awhile. We can look after her now.

Ivan grabbed the baby, left his soup to chill and stormed out of the rectory, vowing from that moment forth, he would eat alone and keep Damascena from everyone. They did not deserve her blessings. In the first few weeks, he would have gladly accepted help, but it was too late after nine months.

He'd be damned if he needed assistance now. He would prove to everyone, including his mother, he was capable of caring for the baby.

The rose seeds continued to haunt the young monk, exhausting him more than the baby. He had heard about bleeding crosses but had refused to believe such phenomena until he discovered blood dripping from the pouch of rose seeds. He panicked, assuming Damascena had cut herself crawling. He followed the trail of blood on the floor of the apartment to the silk pouch she had reached up and grabbed off the table beside his bed.

"Give me that!" he shrieked. As he snatched the pouch from the baby's bloody fingers, he heard a man's voice.

To go guided by fragrance is a hundred times better than following tracks.

The words seized his heart and his body trembled.

"Who speaks?" he said, panicked, but the voice did not speak again.

Ivan wiped the baby's fingers with the sleeve of his robe and cleaned up the floor. He did not sleep that night but stayed up praying with the rose seeds in his hands. They bled again at dawn, and this time the voice returned with the wind from the mountain.

If you do not plant the rose seeds, you will meet a wretched fate.

Terrified, he turned to the abbot for help, praying the rose seeds did not bleed again. He did not want the abbot to blame him, should the rose seeds invite misfortune to the monastery. He had waited long enough to plant them, but despite the resentment he had toward her mother, Rasa, he would oblige her request only to stop the horrible mess.

The abbot explained that roses do not actually grow from rose hips exactly, but from the cuttings that grow from the seeds inside the hips. Ivan's guess was as good as any on how to open the rose hips and get the rose seeds to sprout.

"Then how will I ever get the roses to grow?" Ivan asked.

"Start believing in miracles," the abbot suggested and handed Ivan a letter.

"What is this?"

"A letter from Rasa. It arrived by pigeon carrier this morning."

Ivan snatched the letter, feeling a pang of relief and panic. He removed the seal and opened it, fingers trembling as he read. Rasa was sorry she had not returned for her baby. She had been in bed for months from birth complications. She would not be able to make the journey from Veliko Turnovo until the fall. The king refused to shorten the indenture. He looked up at the abbot, perplexed. "The woman is a servant to the king?"

The abbot nodded. "That is why we agreed to allow her to give birth here."

Ivan took a deep breath, incensed. He felt as though the whole world had conspired against him. He continued to read, finally understanding why Rasa and her baby looked so foreign. Her mother had survived her family's assailants in Khorosan only to surrender to the Second Kingdom. Apparently, two days before Rasa was born, the king's men hung her own father in Baldwin's Tower, simply because he was competition for the men in his own court. He shuddered, reading the letter.

"*We have been working ever since to pay back the debt of having our lives spared and my mother has never once complained. The king's men have done awful things to us but she gives thanks every day for our lives. When we found out I was with child, we prayed that the king would permit me to keep the baby. We were not so fortunate, but my mother had a vision of a mountain hermitage where I would be safe to give birth, believing it was a sign that the secret of the rose was meant to continue.*"

Ivan's hands trembled, detesting what he now knew of the baby and her mother.

"My mother received God's word: Damascena would be blessed with the gift of life as long as the roses grew. I will be forever indebted to you for caring for her all these months. I pray for both of your health every day. Please tell Damascena that I am coming soon and that I love her very much. May God's grace shine upon you, Ivan Balev."

That night, Ivan broke open one of the rose hips and scattered the seeds into a shallow hole he dug with his bare hands. But rain came and turned the soil to mud.

Ivan needed a gardener to show him what to do. On his knees with stones under his shins, he closed his eyes and prayed for this miracle, since there was no gardener at the monastery. *I will give you my life*, he promised, and when he opened his eyes, he saw the stork standing in front of him.

Ivan refused to believe that the stork was any indication that the Heavenly Father of All Beings heard Ivan Balev's plea. Ivan considered giving up. So what if he never told Damascena about the roses? So what if he told her that her mother was dead? The words sounded smooth in his mouth, about the creamiest of lies he'd ever tasted.

No one would ever know. Or care. Her mother was a whore.

On his walks through the woods outside the monastery, Ivan imagined all the ways her mother could have died or should have died by now. On the days when Damascena was fussiest, when nothing could quiet her, he allowed his mind to roll around muddy thoughts, how, if the girl's mother was still alive and ever returned, he would murder her.

One night, when the stars of winter filled the sky like chunks of ice, the threat of Rasa's impending return darkened Ivan's mind again. Though the nightmare would end in six months, Ivan was certain a new one would begin. After all this time of exhaustion and worry, it struck him that if he lost Damascena, he would lose her love. He could not handle that kind of heartache again, not after his mother had driven away Petur.

Rasa was only proving what he knew to be true of the women in his life; he refused to let her take away the only love he had left. Damascena had been teething and feverish, and he had carried her for hours, walking back and forth trying to get her to sleep, when it struck him that *he*, not her mother, was her master. He startled her awake with his voice.

"I make the rules from here on out! Do you understand? You will listen to *me*."

"Bird," she cried, her tiny voice struggling beneath her sobs.

Ivan grabbed her small chin and slapped his hand over her mouth. The girl shrank under his touch. "*Bird*," he hissed, regretting the girl's first word and the pure love with which she spoke of the stork. It was the bird she called out to in the middle of the night. The bird she demanded first thing in the morning. The bird she played with, the bird who amused her and shaded her from the harsh sun with it wings. After everything he had done for her, he wanted her first word to be Ivan, not bird. If he didn't believe in the ancient legend, he would have destroyed the stork's nest and turned the bird into stew—but he feared the misfortunes that would befall him. God had already taken away his father, his lover and made his mother cruel. He could not imagine life getting any worse.

"The bird will not save you and neither will these!" he screamed, ripping the pouch off his neck like a leach that had sucked his skin. He shook the rose hips in front of Damascena's eyes, and just as he flung them through the trees and into the snow—the stork suddenly flew out of the tree above him, as if it had been watching all along.

That night, Ivan dreamed of roses and slept until sunrise for the first time since the girl's birth. In his dream, he saw beams of sunlight reflecting off delicate pink petals. The rose grew by itself on a lonely rock outcrop, pinned against the stones by the wind.

It was cold inside the dream and Ivan shivered in his sleep. He reached out to touch the lace-like frost that had wrapped itself around the leaves, then slid his finger down the stem, so deeply frozen that it shattered beneath his touch.

When wood smoke filled the air in September, Ivan spent hours hunting. He was not looking for game like his father had taught him, he was searching for signs of Rasa. For the first time in his life, he wished to use his own hands, rather than a bow, to seize his prey.

Each day, he waited by the river, knowing she would have to cross it in order to continue on the sinuous trail to the monastery. He left Damascena to nap in their quarters and hunkered down among the bushes. The snap of a twig was all he needed to know her mother had arrived. No other animal would have followed the trail with the scent of his piss. He had marked it to be sure that he did not mistake Rasa for any other creature.

He was surprised that she looked so well now. Gone was the protruding belly. She was lean and strong, her shoulders and neck gilded with sweat. Her green eyes glowed in the diffuse light through the trees. She was one of the most beautiful women he had ever seen. No wonder the king had indentured her to the needs of his own men. The thought disgusted him, and he spat on the ground. He would make sure she returned ugly and of no use to them, or anyone else, especially her daughter.

Ivan waited until she approached the river to make his move. Rasa stared across the water, as if strategizing her way across the rocks. He wondered how she had ever crossed it when she was with child, with all the snowmelt flowing in the spring. He crept up behind her while she took off her shoes, and pinned her on the ground.

Rasa lay on her back, startled.

"Ivan? It's me. Rasa! What are you doing?"

"Making sure you never see Damascena again!"

She let out a whimper.

"Please, don't hurt me! I came to take my daughter home!"

"She is home. You made her home with *me*, and you will never see her again."

She stared at him, shocked. "Why?" she asked, eyes spilling with tears.

His plan was simple. He would maim her first, then drown her. He slapped his hand over her mouth and raised the knife, slashing into her left cheek. She howled, writhing on the ground, kicking him away. When he pulled the knife out of her flesh, he suddenly felt the claws of a bird digging into his eyes. He saw a mash of white feathers and shrieked, trying to get the stork off him. Wretched bird, he thought. Storks have no voice. He had not heard it sneak up. He batted at the creature, trying to tear off its wings, but the bird thrust its talons into his arms, until he dropped the knife, and Rasa fled.

"You don't deserve her love!" he cried into the woods, hearing her footfall, while the stork continued to circle, preventing him from any attempt to chase her.

FOUR

For years, Damascena dreamt of roses in a vast and infinite plane. She ran through the rose fields to a small white house surrounded by storks and fountains. She plunged her hands and arms into the water to wash away the blood from the thorns that had scratched her, when she noticed the shadow of an old man dancing. She recognized something in the reflection of his dance, for it was the only thing she remembered about her birth. It felt like a huge cloak and she wrapped herself in its warmth. She cast her eyes on the valley of the roses that rolled on like a wave, feeling the irresistible invitation to stay there forever—because she had never seen a real rose outside the dream.

When she first asked Ivan about roses, he forbade her from speaking of them.

"They are the work of the Devil," he said.

Damascena was six years old then and did not want to believe him.

"How can the Devil make such beautiful things?"

"Beauty is cunning, that is why the truth can often be very ugly."

Ivan also prohibited her from mentioning her mother. As long as Damascena did not ask the kind of questions to which Ivan Balev had "no good answers," she was free to ask anything else. To keep her mind busy, he asked the abbot to prescribe a rigorous course of study, including memorizing the Bible in Latin and becoming a respectable chess player among the oblates, but her inquiries into Ivan's history continued.

She knew where Ivan had come from. That he had no siblings. That his mother was prone to fainting spells and that his father was dead. She knew he was allergic to dogs, liked dark cherries and snored when he slept on his back. His hand shook all the time and he shivered in his sleep. She had grown used to covering him with the blanket that he kicked off his bed during one of his many fitful moments. She knew that he had a friend named Petur, because when he spoke in his sleep, he repeated his name. She once asked if Petur was a horse and Ivan grew red-faced and spat on the ground. "No!"

"Then who is he?" she asked one night, sitting up from her own bed.

"He is … a sailor. And a very good friend."

Damascena's eyes blazed with joy. "I didn't think you had any friends."

"Enough, child," Ivan had said, pulling up his blanket. "Do not be rude."

"If Petur is your friend, why has he not come to see you?"

"He is at sea. And he will never visit, Damascena. Not with you in my life."

She would have liked to invite Petur to the monastery to prove to herself that Ivan was capable of being more than miserable.

One day, close to her twelfth birthday, Damascena sat in the chapel, preparing for her writing lesson. Moon-eyed, she sat in a pew and watched the installation of a rose window inside the nave, fascinated by the woman in the central rosette. The window had been commissioned by the abbot who had seen a similar one in the abbey of Saint-Denis: a massive circular window divided by rose-petal spokes, radiating from a central rosette so huge that it could fit a man upright. The complex design depicted every saint in multi-colored glass, a meditation on the virtues and vices of mankind.

Damascena spent her mornings watching as each petal was placed, waiting for the moment when the light would bring the woman in the central rosette to life in the glass. She wanted to tell Ivan how the woman came to her in her dreams, but he stormed into the nave to collect her for her writing lessons and he had no time to talk.

"You're late," he snapped.

"Isn't she beautiful?" she asked and pointed to the window, ignoring his sour mood. Ivan stared up at the woman in glass; a crooked smile spread across his lips.

"They should have made her a man," he said and latched his hand onto Damascena's elbow. She pulled away, resisting his touch. He let go and took a step back from her to stare, mouth gaping; she had never defied his authority.

She looked up at the rose window. "She could help you."

"Help me?"

"Maybe she can make your hands stop shaking. If you ask her. If you pray."

He stood there, staring at his palsied hands. "I've not always been like this."

"You were well once?" she asked, doubtful.

"Yes. Before I came to this place," he grunted. "Now come. Discussing this … *woman* in the glass is not as important as your writing lessons."

"I see a woman like her in my dreams."

Ivan scowled, staring up at the window, perplexed. He whispered, his voice flinty with anger, wondering who had spoken to the girl.

"*Who* do you see in your dreams?"
"A woman—who grows roses."
"There is no such woman!"
"She visits me every night."
"She visits?" he said, high-pitched. "Why?"
"To tell me about roses and love. She says she is …"
Ivan clutched his heart. His head throbbed.
"What? Tell me, child. What could she be to you other than a distraction?"
The girl shook her head. "My mother," she said, immediately regretting the word.

❀

Damascena's writing teacher was strict, one of the oldest and most famous monks in the monastery, having taught hundreds of men how to write and bind books in leather. He oversaw the production of countless manuscripts throughout his life and contributed to the burgeoning library at Rila. He took his calling seriously and demanded punctuality of all his students, but he did not fault Damascena for her tardiness that day. He saw her bloodshot eyes and sensed her sadness. "What's wrong?" he asked.

"My dreams," she said and sat beside him, casting her eyes on the ground.

"At least you have them, Damascena. I cannot recall a lick of my dreams these days. I remember what I ate for lunch ten years ago, but not the dream I had last night. The last dream I remember I was running in a field with a farrier and his bride. It was very strange. His horse ran through me. Yes, dreams can be scary but never wrong."

Damascena sighed and ran her fingers through her long, dark hair—as shiny as a raven's wing in the mid-day light. It was hard to believe she was almost twelve and on the edge of becoming a young woman; only her full lips still held a heart shape from infancy. She had grown taller each year, thin and strong, and though her affection had grown quiet, he appreciated the clear communication they still shared. He often wished there had been others girls to teach there through the years. She rarely spoke with the other monks and had learned to keep to herself, but he was glad she sought his counsel.

"My dreams make Ivan angry."

The old monk laughed, hoping the girl would, too, and wiped the spittle from his beard. "Ivan thinks the whole world is wrong. He probably even thinks God is wrong."

Damascena looked up and caught his eye. "Maybe he is. What Heavenly Father would ever keep a girl from her mother? I have found more comfort watching the men install the rose window than believing God might ever help me understand why she left."

"Maybe you are not meant to know just yet."

The monk laid his hand on the girl's shoulder, feeling the warmth of the sun. In all his years teaching, he had never come across a more intuitive child and he marveled at the wisdom she seemed to posses. He wanted to tell her what he remembered of that devastating beauty that was her mother, how she survived on root vegetables in the smokehouse, how they found her when the roof collapsed under a late spring snow, eight and a half months pregnant and as wide as a moon, hands clasped in prayer. She had claimed God had sent her there to give birth.

He wanted to tell her this, but Ivan had threatened them all with their lives; he refused to hunt and vowed to starve them to death if they ever told the girl anything about her mother. It was difficult to ignore the letters she sent each month, the letters Ivan tossed into the fires that cooked their food—the game he shot week after week. No one had the courage to stop him. Despite his palsy, he broke the arm of a monk twice his age, bullying anyone who appeared to help the girl other than her appointed teachers.

It pained the old monk to keep Ivan's secret, but he believed that teaching Damascena to write had reduced his share of shame over the years, even if he gave her no ink or paper per Ivan's instructions. "She comes from filth," Ivan had bellowed. "Let her then speak the language of the soil. Teach her to write in the dirt."

The old monk handed her the writing stick.

"Have faith you will understand some day."

"I am tired of waiting for God."

The girl turned and locked eyes with the old monk. She picked up the stick, glanced across the transept to see if anyone was watching or close enough to listen, then wrote in the dirt, forming each character in Cyrillic, slowly and precisely.

Tell me her name.

The old monk sighed, feeling a sudden breeze grace his cheeks, as if the girl's request had already disturbed the spirits on the mountain.

The girl handed him the stick, pressing it gently into the palm of his hand until his grip was firm, but he handed it back.

"Let us begin your lesson."

Damascena listened, compliant as he rattled off the words she was meant to practice; seasonal fruits and vegetables to warm up, then Bible verses from Revelations. When the clatter of cookery from the kitchen finally called them to lunch, Damascena dropped her stick and stood.

"Sit, Damascena. We are not done," the old monk said.

The girl turned back, seeing the old man pick up the stick and write in the dirt.

His hands shook as he wrote the characters R A S A.

Damascena looked at him curiously, feeling a tightness in her stomach.

"My mother?" she whispered.

The monk scratched his neck and lowered his voice, disgusted that he had kept Ivan's lie. "Yes," he said, knowing his days were numbered. He had lived a good life. If Ivan did anything to him now, he would at least die in peace knowing Damascena had learned about her mother.

She took the stick and wrote.

What else do you know?

The old monk glanced at the chapel.

"You were born there on the sixth day of June, and you smelled like a rose."

The words fell away like stones, heavy, thudding in her inner ear like thunder. The old monk dropped the writing stick on the ground and it fell across her mother's name as if to divide it; then before Damascena could ask him anything else, he dragged his foot across the characters, leaving nothing but dirt.

Later that night, Ivan found Damascena in the chapel again, sitting beneath the rose window. She had fallen asleep and her cheek was pressed against the pew. It wasn't that she was early for evening prayers that vexed him, it was her muttering her mother's name. "Rasa, Rasa," she said in her sleep, the word floating up to the chapel ceiling, haunting him again. He marched into the pew.

"What is that you say?" he bellowed, noticing a few oblates turn at the door.

Damascena sat up and stiffened. "Rasa," she whispered, feeling her body go cold. She had learned to tolerate his flashes of impatience and mild violence, but something inside Ivan had exploded that night. His eyes twitched and she could see the throbbing vein in his neck like a thick blue rope about to snap.

Ivan slammed his fist into the back of the pew. "Who?" he screamed.

Damascena lifted her eyes to the woman in the glass. She stood slowly from the pew, feeling suddenly protected. "Rasa is my mother," she finally said.

Ivan stiffened. "Who taught you that?"

Damascena said nothing, fearing for the old monk.

Ivan drew in a breath and spat on the floor.

"Is that who you see in your dreams?"

"Yes," she said, her voice barely audible.

Ivan gasped and held up his hand as if the girl's words had assaulted him.

"Enough! Tell me who told you!" he bellowed and dug his nails into her shoulder.

She wished to leave but turned to him, jaw clenched as the words escaped and the truth ripped open her throat. "It should have been you!"

Ivan stood there frozen, strangely composed, despite the trembling in his hands.

FIVE

That night, Damascena felt nothing but a chill when she found the door to their room open and blood dripping down the wood grain. She moved into the darkness and took the lantern from the table, then followed the speckled trail across the stone path in the courtyard to the rectory where she could see in the moonlight, beyond the fogged glass, Ivan pinning one of the oblates to the table. The right shoulder of Ivan's robe had been ripped and smudged with blood. Ivan's nose dripped over the young oblate and his hands trembled when he spoke.

"How many times have I told you she was not to know?"

"But I told her nothing, Ivan."

Damascena recognized him as one of the chess players.

"You spoke nothing of her mother?"

"No. I swear on God's name!"

"What about the letters?"

"Damascena has never read them! I swear."

"I trusted you!"

"I have kept my promise, but she keeps writing more letters."

"Because you encourage her! You indulge that whore."

"I have not. I swear, Ivan. You must believe me!"

"You think of me as some idiot do you? I've heard you. I've heard what all of you say behind my back. I watch how you ply for the girl's attention when you think I'm not looking.

But I see everything. You will not win her affection by telling her the truth!"

Damascena wondered how much Ivan had kept from her all this time. He looked like a dog, mouth foaming as he paced, grunting and slamming his fist into the table. The young oblate cried out when Ivan's fingers gripped his throat. The boy gasped and grabbed at Ivan's sleeves, kicking the legs of the table.

"Ivan, stop! Stop!" he cried. "Someone ... help ... me!"

Damascena dropped the lantern on the ground and grabbed her throat, feeling the oblate's pain as if it was her own. The young monk lay limp on the table, wide-eyed, staring through the window at her. She gasped and shivered, feeling the weight of a hand on her shoulder, as if he had reached out to touch her. When she turned, she saw nothing but the flicker of lanterns inside the rose window of the chapel, where the other monks had retreated for evening vespers. Even stranger, beneath their chanting was a faint hum, low-throated and drum-like, coming from the oblate before death sealed the sound.

Ivan felt it, too, the prick of cold on the back of his neck, and a momentary relief that comes only after confronting a fear. He had never killed a man. He gasped, hearing the meow of a cat that had suddenly trotted in through the door.

"Jesus Christ!" he spat into the darkness. "The boy is dead!"

He wiped his cheeks with his wrists, then hugged the sleeves of his robes, resisting the urge to be sick. He closed the oblate's mouth, dismayed that the boy had not fought harder to save his own life. He paced in front of the body, wading in and out of the moonlight, wondering if he should have killed *himself*. His misery would be over. He would no longer have to care for Damascena or keep his secret about the rose seeds.

He dug through the oblate's robes searching frantically for the letter from Rasa, tearing back the cloth as if lodged in the fibers was any evidence to indict him. He found nothing but a pilfered dinner roll and a stick of cinnamon, which he hurled across the room at the cat. He shoved his right fist into his mouth and clamped down hard until he tasted his own blood.

Damascena remained pressed against the wall outside the rectory window, trying to keep her body from shaking, feeling trapped by the weight of the invisible hand on her shoulder. She fixed her gaze on the oblate and held her breath, watching what looked like a vapor of light trailing above him and Ivan. It moved toward her, swimming in the darkness until it glided through the window and over Damascena's head, then disappeared into a dark quiet corner of the sky above the monastery. A flicker of light, then blackness.

She flinched, feeling her right hand being lifted and placed over her heart. She tried to pull it away, but the force of whatever stood in front of her would not let her remove it. She felt the pounding beneath her sternum, and the prickle in her throat, trying not to cough, or make a sound. Something told her that Ivan might like to put his hands around her neck, too, if she screamed. She could see the storm still raging inside him as he slammed his fists on the table, making the oblate's body jump.

Ivan paced the floor of the rectory, tousling his hair with bloodied fingers. He walked toward the door, then paused, turned, walked back to the oblate, ripped open the other half of the oblate's robe, exposing a scarred, lean chest, and this time, took what appeared to be a letter. He shook the piece of parchment in front of the young boy's face, proving to the dead that he had been right. The oblate *had* intercepted the latest letter from Rasa. He tore the parchment into small flakes then tossed them into the fire on the hearth, where they curled and hissed and burned black. "Go to hell, Rasa."

Damascena shuddered and clutched her heart. Her stomach churned and she backed away from the window to retch beside the rosemary bush growing beneath it.

She grabbed a sprig of pungent needles and breathed in the oily fragrance until she caught her breath. She had not come to the oblate's rescue when he called for help, and for this reason only, she wished she would never have the chance to meet her mother and reveal that her daughter was a coward.

Damascena lay in her bed that night, sweating through her sheet, wishing for the stork, but it was nowhere to be found. The air was hot and still, and carried the stench of Ivan's breath, acrid with the burn of alcohol and the soot of his lantern. She hated that they still shared the same room. She had asked for her own room, but he said families slept under one roof.

He blew the lantern out and lay on the floor, clamoring for the coolness of the stones, whimpering whenever he rolled on his shoulder. Damascena sat up in her bed.

"Are you hurt?" she asked.

Ivan groaned. "How much did you see?"

Damascena swallowed hard. "It was dark."

"You watched us. Why did you not stop me?"

She could not tell him about the hand on her shoulder and the force that had pinned her to the window. "I was scared," she said. "I could not move."

"Scared? Of what?" Ivan roared and slapped the floor. "Were you scared of me? Or the truth about your mother!"

"I was scared," she began slowly, "Of what the letter might say."

Ivan stiffened. "*Might* say? The oblate did not read it to you?"

Damascena rolled her head across the pillow, eyes wide, glued to the sudden vision of the stork in the window. In an instant, it turned into an old man wearing a white robe with a hood pulled over his face.

"No," she said, rubbing her eyes.

Ivan cleared his throat. His words were scratchy and barely audible.

"And if he did read to you, what would you have wanted to know?"

His question was heavy and felt like a hot rock in her belly.

"I would want to know if my mother loves me."

Ivan flashed his teeth in the dark, but she understood it was not a smile.

"She left you. That's all you'll ever need to know about your mother's *love*."

At first, his words felt like a needle in her lungs. She could not breathe and the room grew narrow and cloudy, as if she were being squeezed through a hallway. The vision of the old man was gone, and the stork flew down and nestled above her head. She let the tears fall into its feathers, unable to sleep, struck by Ivan's admission; it was the first time he had acknowledged she had had a mother at all.

SIX

The abbot woke the girl the next morning. She would have rather been left to sleep for the rest of her life than to find any evidence of last night's events. Blood splattered the floor and door of the apartment. When Damascena paused to touch the stain on the wood grain, the abbot pushed her into the courtyard. She searched for signs of Ivan.

"Where is he?" she asked, hearing the caw of vultures circling overhead. A most awful, fetid smell wafted in the warm breeze blowing across the transcept walkway.

The abbot swallowed and his cheek twitched. Damascena followed his gaze to the group of monks leading a small procession out of the rectory, a body shrouded in cloth. Then a horse appeared between the guesthouse and bathhouse, led by two oblates. She turned to the abbot and squinted, looking up at him from the ground. He seemed more tired than usual, and the rings around his eyes reminded her of dark moons.

"Is Ivan leaving?" she asked. A group of monks opened the heavy iron gates and the hinges screeched in the still morning air.

"No. You are," the abbot said, swinging his jaw back and forth as if it had also come unhinged. The girl stepped back, realizing that the horse had been sent for her.

"Do not be afraid, Damascena. She is a good horse and will take care of you."

She swallowed, feeling the immensity of the animal and its black shadow pooling around her. Its huge hoofs and long neck looked like a tree trunk. She had never been invited to ride and did not trust she had the skills. The oblates hoisted her on top of the copper mare, and handed her a small satchel of clothing. She clutched at the saddle.

"Go," the abbot said and handed the reins to the oblates. "Let them lead you."

The abbot explained that Damascena should be delivered to his cousin's house. He instructed them to go around the river, not risk crossing it, and that at no time should the girl ever dismount the horse, until she arrived safely at her destination.

"Why do I have to leave?" she said forlornly, stroking the coppery mane.

"There's been an illness. We don't want you to catch it and get sick."

She turned, catching one last glimpse of the shrouded body, as the pallbearers rounded the wall by the monastery guesthouse. She looked down at the abbot.

"The boy died," she said without reserve. "He doesn't have flu."

The abbot swatted the air with his hand and nudged the horse forward.

"You need to go until it's safe to come back," he said quietly and locked eyes with the 12-year-old girl, beseeching her understanding. "It won't be that long. We'll send someone to get you soon."

Just then, the horse lifted its tail and dropped a mound of manure on the ground. The abbot pawed the deepest pockets of his robe, feeling for the flask of brandy, wishing to send the girl on her way so that he could have a drink, in the shade, before vespers.

"What if I like it?" she asked. "What if I want to stay?"

"Stay?"

"I want to stay away from Ivan," she said, eyes searching everywhere for fear he would appear at any moment, storming through the open cloister to kill her.

The abbot reached up and put his hand on Damascena's thigh. She felt his thumb dig into the flesh as if he were trying to push back something that had sprouted in her, a truth he wanted to bury.

"You must promise me you will never tell anyone what you saw."

She nodded slowly.

"I promise, abbot," she said, then whispered, "It is my fault that the boy died."

"No. It is not, but if anyone finds out what happened here, we might lose our lives. You don't want that to happen do you? You don't want the people who have taken care of you to perish?"

"No, abbot," she said and wiped her cheek quickly with her wrist.

"Good girl, Damascena. Go with God."

The oblates pulled the reins and led the girl and the horse down the path from the cloister, toward the great iron gate that opened to a world that Damascena knew very little about. She turned one more time with a thought that hung heavy in her heart.

"Abbot? Does my mother write?"

The abbot tossed a quick glance at the oblates.

"Does your mother write what?"

"Letters," she said, feeling the furrow between her brows. A trickle of sweat slid down the back of her neck in the heat.

The abbot shifted on the hot stones in the walkway and tapped his toe.

"On occasion."

"For how long?"

The abbot coughed. He had cleared them off his desk and handed them to Ivan, fearing for his life should he ever dare to tell the girl what he had read about her mother.

"Ever since you were born."

The girl swallowed, registering the betrayal, a storm of stones crushing her heart. Ivan had raised her, but she was uncertain now if she hated his lies or the whole of his being more. She turned from the abbot, and cast her eyes at the rose window in the chapel, already missing the woman in the glass. She clutched the reins and uttered one final prayer before she left— to never see Ivan Balev again.

SEVEN

Through the warm, heavy rain of twilight came the shimmer of the first lake, The Tear. Damascena had nearly fallen asleep on the back of the horse with her nose buried into the copper mane when the rain woke her. Spread before her like an unstrung necklace was a series of seven blue alpine lakes lying in ascending succession of niches in the mountain called Ezeren. No monk had made the journey in less than six hours, and to complete the trip in one day was a feat so rare it was construed miraculous.

Not even Ivan had made it this far, and he had tried, once, before the girl was born. The men who stayed too long witnessed strange events—lightning strikes, visions of flying objects, sightings of wolf-like humans. Plenty of superstitions had emerged over the centuries about the confluence of saints and demons there. But the girl did not feel afraid. Instead, she felt an overwhelming sense of peace, as if she had been carried home, though she could only see rock and sky and lake.

The oblates led the horse and the girl to the edge of the lake and gulped water. They argued over the directions that the abbot had given them—whether or not they could permit the girl to get off the horse. It had been six hours and the girl had not asked them once to stop to relieve herself, though they had done so many times, and often in plain sight of her. She appeared to be asleep, and they seized the opportunity to explore.

Damascena watched them skip off, the youngest limping with a blistered heal, the oldest loping along scree fields, oblivious to the lightning. She expected the oblates to keep their eyes on the sky, hoping, like she did, to glimpse St. Bartholomew, the ruler of hailstorms and thunderstorms. She fisted the reins and looped them around her arm, pulling the spooked horse's head to her, stroking its neck with her other hand. It neighed and twisted its neck in long, deep swoops, eyes bugged and bulging. She heard a voice.

To go guided by fragrance is a hundred times better than following tracks.

She let go of the reins and dismounted, then got on her knees and plunged her hands into the glacial waters, only to glimpse the reflection of a hooded man looking over her. She felt a rush in her heart and turned, expecting to see the man's face, but she saw only the swish of the horse's tail and the damp sides of its belly. There was no man. No cloak. No face. When she turned again to be sure, she saw the hook of the moon rising into the inky sky, then froze, feeling the hand on her shoulder in the same place, and with the same weight that she felt outside the rectory window. This time, the force of whatever was there pulled her back immediately. Her words came in a flutter.

"Please don't hurt me," she whispered, but the rain muffled her voice and in the space between the thunder she heard another voice.

There is nothing there to hurt.

"Who is speaking to me?"

A friend.

She turned her head quickly and stood, only to be flung back on the horse with such force that she felt queasy and dizzy. She pressed her cheek against the horse's mane and her hands slid down its wet neck, grasping to hold on. She opened an eye and looked across the first lake, searching for any sign of the oblates because at that moment, she would have told them she was scared. Her knees shook, knocking the sides of the horse so hard she thought it would turn and bite her.

She felt a sudden rattling inside her, shaking her core and she found she had lost her voice. No matter how much she tried to call out, her words vanished into the rain-soaked air. The man in the hooded cloak appeared before the horse and led the girl away from the lake to another trail of rocks that flashed silver in the lightning. The man did not speak. All Damascena heard was Ivan's voice above the horse's hooves on the rocks and the constant patter of rain.

She left you. That's all you need to know about your mother's love.

It was dark when Damascena opened her eyes. At first, she saw the twinkling of stars through the canopy of trees arched over the trail. She could make out the sliver of moon and the silhouette of a stork that flew just then across the night sky.

"Bird," she called out, her voice strained, throat dry.

She pushed herself off the ground and sat up, feeling dizzy and disoriented in the darkness. She closed her eyes, feeling the familiar weight of a hand on her shoulder and froze, taking in the musky, sweet scent. When she opened her eyes, she saw the hooded man standing before her. The horse was gone.

"Where are you taking me?"

"Home," he said. His voice was flat and direct, quite different from the lyrical whispers she had heard coming from another man.

"I have no home," she said, unwilling to explain anything to the stranger.

"Everyone has a home, child. I will help you find it."

He extended his hand and she took it, trying to glimpse his face beyond the shadows of his hood. She caught only the flash of teeth when he smiled, then the flash of the lightning in the threads of his robe. It looked like it had been woven with the storm.

Damascena had no idea how long she had traveled or where she was. She saw a forest and beyond its thick canopy, the land rolled away from a small white house in the clearing. She swallowed, wondering if this, too, was part of some trick; for the white house in the distance was different than the white house in her dreams. It had no roses.

"Who are you?" she demanded.

"A friend," the stranger said again, this time aloud, and his voice sounded old, like he'd come from another time.

"How can you be my friend when I don't even know you?"

He flashed another smile beneath his hood. "You must trust me."

She shifted her eyes from him to the white house. "Is it my mother's house?" she asked, and her voice quivered, and the tears she had held back for days slipped free.

"No. It is not your mother's house," he said, unsure of how much more he could or should say to the girl. There was nothing but a field when he had planted the rose seeds here more than a decade ago—after seeing the young monk scatter them in the snow. He was disappointed no roses had grown, and he blamed Ivan's negligence.

"But it is yours," he said. "For now."

Damascena stared at the small white house, transfixed. It appeared to have been abandoned for some time. Grass hung over the roof and vines blocked the windows. But she liked that it was hers. She had never possessed anything. Not a piece of clothing or a sheet from her bed. Not even a sock was hers to keep. Even the pewter cups from which she drank, and the wooden plates from which she ate, belonged to the monastery, and ultimately, to God. "Everything is borrowed," Ivan Balev had told her. "Even kindness and time." He had also told her never to expect favors from anyone without the debt of repaying them. She believed him.

"Don't you want to see it?" the hooded man asked and extended his hand.

Despite every instinct to refuse his help, Damascena flung her hand into the stranger's and followed him across the clearing to the white house. So what if his hands were cold, she thought. He had given her something to hold.

The hooded man stood in front of the door and placed the girl's hand on the cool metal knob, then made a grand sweeping gesture with his arms.

"Your fortune," he said.

Damascena grinned. She pushed open the door, hopeful, peering inside.

Moonlight flooded the empty square of stone, divided into two small rooms by a thin mud wall where a table, two benches, and a small bed sat draped by sheets.

It was cool and she shivered, feeling the breeze. Clay teacups and a small pot crowded the windowsill in the second room, where a huge cavity had been cut into the wall, smudged with the soot from previous fires. The room was no wider than ten of her steps. She walked over to inspect the fireplace, and the hooded man closed the door.

She shifted her gaze to the other room, to the wooden beams in the ceiling and a small lantern and several graduated clear glasses hanging on hooks. A skein of wool shifted in the crossbreeze and a small wooden spool sat on the shelf beside it. She wondered if whoever had lived here had been a weaver. If it had been her mother, Damascena would have liked to know that she could make the things that would keep her warm at night, a thick blanket to bring her comfort in the darkness.

She reached up and fingered the wool with her eyes closed, imagining the softness of her mother's hands. She could almost feel in the yarn the warm fingers curled around her. She preferred them to the hooded man's cold hands and did not wish to let go, but when Damascena opened her eyes and readjusted to the darkness, she withdrew her hand from the skein of wool and shuddered, seeing something through the open window.

"My God," she said, entranced by the glimmer of a dewdrop so huge that it appeared to be a jewel. She ran to the backyard, not moved by the brilliance of the dewdrop, but by its very setting: a rose bud growing in loamy soil and a ring of weeds.

On her knees, numb to the discomfort of crushed stones in her shins, Damascena leaned into the grayish pink bud, overcome by its delicate scent. It was as if within its voluptuous curves another world and another life existed exclusively for her, a world filled with beauty and protection. The beauty confounded her, but no matter how closely the girl inspected the bud, her mother's absence was apparent.

She remembered the woman in the rose window, but felt lost and confused by her words. Hadn't she heard the woman say, "You will find me in the roses some day"? Had she imagined those words? Had she created a fairy tale to soothe her heart? If this was so, she had caused another to lose his life because she had blabbered about her visions.

In that moment, Damascena's dream faded. It was as if the hope she had held had been snuffed by circumstances beyond her control or comprehension. All she felt was the deep pain of being separated from her mother, and she crushed the rose under her fingers, pricking herself with a thorn.

She took in a deep breath and invited the hooded man to join her. He sat on the ground, and she had the strange and sudden impulse to lean against his shoulder, something she had never done with anyone. She soaked his old robe with mixed tears of gratitude and regret. She was relieved to be far from Ivan, but she didn't know if the hooded man was her friend or her enemy. She did not know many things that night, but when she cast her eyes back on the rose bud, she knew why the thorn grew beneath it.

"There is only one rose," she said and pulled the hooded man's robe into her fist to wipe her cheeks, then surprised herself again when she lay her head on his lap.

"There will be more roses, child. Where there is one, there can be many."

The girl lifted her head off the man's lap and, weary, stared up at the moon.

"But my mother isn't in any of them, and she never will be."

"She *is* there. You just don't have the ability to see her yet."

"But where? When will I see her?" she asked.

"When it is meant to be," he said. "I am your guide, not a soothsayer. Your training will require time, as it does with all mystics."

"Mystic?"

"You must trust the visions in your heart. Do you see a rose garden there?"

"You have not even told me your name."

The hooded man collected the petals off the ground.

"My name is Shams. But you can call me the Friend."

"And where does the friend come from?"

"Many places. I was born in Tabriz but I have traveled far from home."

"I have never been to Tabriz, but I have been alone…like you."

"Then we shall make good travel partners," he said.

"We are partners?" she asked, unsure.

"For now."

"*Shaaams?*" the girl asked, feeling her throat quiver with the 'ahhh' of his name. She circled him with her eyes, feeling the urge to lift the hood and see his face fully.

"Then I ask you, my friend, Shams, to trust *me* this time."

She flung the rose petals in her fist into the ring of weeds.

"I never want to see another rose for the rest of my life," she declared, then buried her face in the friend's leg and muffled sobs that made even him shiver. He rocked her gently and rubbed her back to quiet her, then passed the girl one more secret.

EIGHT

Damascena did not remember sleeping that night, but her heart heard the rose speak of love. In the morning, when she lifted her head to sniff the air, she felt a sharp pain in the back of her neck and her hair was tangled with thistles. In the diffused light, the hooded man, who called himself Shams, approached with two clay cups and a small metal pot. Her stomach gurgled smelling the sweet steam of whatever he had brewed.

"You don't need to sleep on the ground. You can have the bed next time," he said and motioned for her to sit at the table he had brought out of the house. A small mound of sticks and dirt lay by the walkway where he had swept.

"Next time?" she said. "Where will you sleep?"

"I am old and do not sleep much at all. The bed is all yours."

"I am not staying here."

"Where will you go?"

She stared at him, jaw stiff with frustration, unable to answer.

Shams plucked two peaches from the tree above him and hurled one at the girl.

She caught it and met his gaze.

"Why did you do that?" she asked, her voice sharp.

"To test you."

"Test me?"

"It is not your hands that will be the hardest to train. You are raw, weary, disturbed by secrets. You must open your heart again—and you are safe to do so here."

"Safe?" the girl asked, startled. "With you?"

Shams drew in a deep breath. "If you leave, where do you plan to rest at night?"

Damascena kicked the rose bush. "Under the trees, since this is only temporary. I don't plan to remain long under your tests and training."

Shams bunched up his robe and sat, gesturing to the hot pot on the table.

"Come have some tea while it is warm," he said and poured her a cup.

"I am not thirsty," she said, but her throat was parched.

"At least eat your peach before you go on your way."

She held the peach to her nose. Her stomach growled. Her mouth watered. As much as she wished to clench her jaw forever, she marched to the table, sat across from Shams and bit into the fruit with such ravenous delight that she didn't stop eating until all that remained was the stone and the juice dripping from her fingers.

Shams rolled his peach across the table toward her.

"Have mine, too."

The girl lifted her chin, wet with peach juice, and stared.

"What will you eat?"

Shams nodded toward the sun. Damascena searched beyond the shadow at his back, seeing nothing but a well and a flock of ravens scattered in the distant fields.

"You eat black birds?"

Shams held back a smile.

"As long as the sun shines, I do not have to eat."

Damascena cocked her head and pulled a thistle from her hair.

"You eat the light?" she asked, testing him. "You are very strange."

Shams nodded. "Even Rumi would say so," he said aloud.

"Who is Rumi?"

Shams hesitated to speak again but simply said, "An old friend from Konya."

"Does he also think you are a strange bird?" she asked.

"Bird?" he asked and straightened.

He was certain that Rumi would not recognize him now, especially in the forms he had taken to help the girl. He did not recognize his body when he passed his reflection in glass. He was far taller than he had been and he had lost his bushy beard.

"I made him burn his books once," Shams said. "Some people find that strange."

Damascena set her cup on the table and looked at him perplexed.

"Why would you do that to a friend?"

Shams shrugged. "He did not need his mind to know the truth. None of us do."

"You are both odd birds," she said, confused.

"Perhaps," he said. "You should eat some more."

Shams gestured for her to pick up the peach. She held up her hand, refusing it, turned her face toward the sun instead and opened her mouth, mocking him.

"Why do you want to help me, Bird?"

Shams smiled and pulled the cloak tighter around him.

"There are many forms of assistance in the world. And mind you, not all of them are construed as help. Let me just say that I have been sent to guide you."

Damascena blew on her tea, enchanted by the sweet smell wafting from the cup. She met Shams' gaze. "To what?" she asked.

"To learn the secret of the rose."

Damascena decided to stay for one day. She avoided the rose bush and explored the property boundaries instead, singing low sad hymns. She spent her time alone, in the shade of fruit trees, discovering two pears, one cherry, three apples ripe for picking, berry bushes, too, and rabbits from which she made a hearty stew. Ivan had demanded she find her own meat and had taught her how to hunt—practicing with sling shots before she mastered the bow.

She offered Shams a bowl the next night.

"*My* secret," she said and smiled.

Shams sniffed the boiled meat. "Then I shall not ask who taught you to make it."

She handed him a small wooden spoon. "Very good idea. Go on. Try it."

He obliged her request and sipped the stew. "It is delicious. As good as light."

She nodded, satisfied to see he emptied the bowl, something Ivan had never done.

For the first five days, Shams watched the rose bush carefully when the leaves started to yellow, indicating insufficient iron. Lack of water. He wondered if the only evidence of the girl's mother would last long enough for her to witness it. For the rose was suffering, too, from the girl's neglect.

However, on the sixth day, Damascena paused beside the rose bush. "It is dying," she said, crouching to inspect its yellowing leaves. "What should we do, Old Bird?"

Shams pursed his lips, quelling a smile. He pulled his robe tighter against his chest, worried he might blind Damascena with the light beaming from his heart.

"There is only one thing to do," he said. "You must bring the rose back to life."

Shams began Damascena's studies with separation. Not just as a symbol. As a tool. She needed a good knife to make cuttings from the rose. Early the next morning, he gave her a few bronze coins he found in the soil with a dowsing stick and instructed her to buy the best knife she could find—twice the size of her hand and no longer, with a decent sheath and a handle that would last, preferably made of bone, not wood or metal.

"I already have a knife," she told him.

"This one is not meant for rabbits. It's for the roses. To make cuttings."

"Cuttings?"

"So that you will have more than one rose."

Damascena swung her legs over the edge of the bed, rubbing her puffy eyes, uncertain she was ready for any new teachings, especially those that involved weapons.

"Where do I find a knife around here?"

"In the village."

Damascena laughed. They were no closer to a town than she was to finding her mother in the grasses that grew as high as her waist.

"What village?"

Shams pointed out the window. "Krun. Through the trees. Beyond the orchard."

Damascena stood wide-eyed. She had never considered neighbors. The vastness of the land had sucked her into a kind of sweet oblivion during her first week there.

"Is Krun where you go at night?" she asked, curious about his frequent disappearances. Whenever she woke up to relieve her bladder, he was nowhere to be found. It scared her at first and made her homesick for the stork.

Shams, who had taken to sitting by the window while the girl drifted off to sleep, pivoted toward her on a small stump of walnut tree he had brought in from the yard. Behind him, storm clouds left streaks in the sky.

"You know where I go," he said, meeting the girl's eyes in the dim light that filled the room. "I am always with you."

"Then come with me to the market, " she pleaded.

"My feet hurt," he said.

Damascena could see he was old and weary, but there was nothing about their long journey over the mountains that suggested Shams couldn't endure a walk to the village—a short distance from the white house which he obviously knew. His actions belied his age. He moved more swiftly and adeptly than Ivan or the monks ever had.

"Then let's go tomorrow. Or the next day. When you're feeling better."

"The market will be closed and the rose will suffer for another week."

She pulled her shawl tighter around her shoulders, noticing the long, oily tresses that had grown matted in the summer heat and humidity.

"I do not like knives," she said, wondering if he intended for her to cut her hair.

"You will discover their usefulness," he said, then he recited a verse without speaking, preferring to transmit most teachings in silence: *From the worm they make silk with the passing of days. Make slowness your trade, show patience.*

Damascena turned to him and glowered.

"Are you the man who whispers to me?"

Shams met her cold stare.

"I know the voice of which you speak, but it is not me."

"Then who? Why can't he just speak out loud?"

"You will know soon enough. Now go before the rain starts," he said. "And buy some bread with the change. You'll need more than fruit for the work that lies ahead."

Damascena did not move. "This is your idea of teaching me?"

"No," he said and turned his eyes toward the window. "The lessons are not mine. They belong to the rose, the true teacher here. And she is literally dying—to teach you."

PART II

Your task is not to seek for love, but merely to seek and find all the barriers within yourself that you have built against it.

—Jalal al-din Mevlana Rumi

ONE

Damascena walked to the village of Krun with long, heavy steps, clothes sticking in the humidity. Her thoughts drifted upward where the dark sky swept shadows off the ground. Was she Shams' student or servant? Had he come into her life to teach her, or did he simply want her to teach herself? She had seen no evidence of instruction in the white house. The old man must be a fool, she thought. A flower could not teach her anything.

She hiked her skirt up to cross the stream beyond the orchard, feeling tenuous with every step she had taken away from Shams. Although she was many hours from the monastery, she felt the panic in her throat, fearing that Ivan might find her in the market. Something else bothered her about this task to get a knife, but no words came to mind, only the tightness she felt in her belly.

❀

Damascena walked with her head down, eyes cast on the road. Each time a carriage or wagon passed, she heard the shift in the rhythms of the horses' hooves hitting the ground, slowing down, then she felt the heavy gaze of its occupants. They snickered and coughed. Some giggled and spat.

"Girl," they cackled. "What happened to your shoes?"

Damascena felt her jaw tighten and fixed her eyes on the grooves left by the wagon wheels, wishing she could roll up inside them and hide. Shams had said nothing of wearing shoes to the market. He didn't seem to mind that she traipsed around the property barefoot. In fact, when her skin made contact with the earth, she felt a lightness in her being and a strength she didn't know she had when she had worn shoes. She simply left the shoes under the bed. She never considered the trouble of walking without them.

Damascena entered Krun through a series of narrow streets where the buildings nearly touched overhead, leaving little air to circulate. It was hot and crowded with people and animals, and the girl paused several times to catch her breath, having held it to avoid the stench of open gutters. She pressed herself against a butcher shop window on the north side of the street, mistaking the dung-heaps oozing between her toes for mud until a well-dressed woman wielding a ham hock walked out and saw her.

"Do not play on our property, child."

Damascena turned to the woman, already feeling awkward as a small crowd of passersby paused to gawk. "I'm not playing," she said. "I'm going to the market."

The woman eyed the girl's threadbare dress and the leaves and twigs woven into her hair. She was dressed like a creature of the woods, belying the angelic features of her face. "Like that? I should hope not. Where's your mother?"

The girl said nothing and lifted her eyes to the small crowd, glimpsing the flushed faces of children younger than she staring in awe and disgust at her feet. They pointed and squealed at the excrement.

Damascena trembled, catching sight of a group of monks walking in the opposite direction, faces shrouded in hoods, each bearing Ivan's stern countenance.

"Child. Answer me. Where is your mother?" the woman asked, studying the girl's tangled hair and tattered clothes. Olive skin. She wondered if perhaps the girl was a slave. "Who do you work for?"

Damascena stiffened and drew in a breath.

"I am not working. I am a student of Shams."

The woman cocked her head, shooed a fly away from her face. "A student?"

Damascena nodded, her cheeks burning from the laughter that erupted from the crowd of children.

"And where is this school of Shams you attend as a *girl*?"

Damascena lowered her voice. "In the field by the white house near the woods."

The woman nodded, smoothed the front of her dress. "I see. You have an active imagination. But everyone knows that the only person who has lived in the white house died there, too, beheaded less than a year ago by a Mongol!" The woman waved the girl away. "Run along then and catch your mother before you catch your death in this stench. And put some shoes on those feet!"

Damascena ran from the woman, rattled by her questions. She stood at the edge of the market, overwhelmed by the whirling activity. Merchants, craftsman, cobblers and hucksters sailed between booths, selling meats, honeys, butter and cheeses, candles, weapons, and beyond the dye stand bedecked with skeins of wool, the soles of cowhide dangled in the still air.

The girl stormed across the street, past the woman she saw outside the butcher's shop and the throng of gossips, and offered the five bronze coins from her pocket to the woman selling the skins. The tanner, a tall, slender woman with light brown eyes, full lips, fair skin and a drape of chestnut colored hair glanced at the coins suspiciously. She reached into Damascena's hands as if to take the payment, but instead closed the girl's fingers, pressing firmly on the coins. "How can I help you, young lady?"

Damascena swallowed. Her eyes could barely stay still and leapt to the smallest piece of cowhide that looked like it would fit her feet. "I need new shoes."

The tanner maneuvered around a bolt of leather and stepped out of the stall to inspect the girl's feet. The girl's heels were cracked and blistered, and her legs bowed where the arches had had no support. She forced a smile.

"That should not be a problem. When do you want your shoes?"

"Today," Damascena said.

"I am a tanner, not a cobbler, but I can help you," she said. "It might take me longer to make you a proper pair of boots. I used to make shoes for my son."

"How long will it take?" Damascena asked, ashamed by her desperation. She would strap a piece of string around the cowhide and shuffle home as long as her feet were covered, and nobody stopped to ask her where her mother was, today or ever.

The tanner reached up and unclipped two strips of cowhide. "No more than a week."

Damascena uncurled her fingers to show the coins. "Do I have enough to pay?"

The tanner met the girl's eyes, seeing the pain of her humiliation. "It is plenty, but I do not want your money," she said and crouched to measure the girl's feet with a small leather lace she pulled from her pocket. Just as she did, in full view of the gossips, she slipped off her shoes and passed them to the girl.

"Try on these so we know your boots will fit."

Damascena's mind raced. "But what will you wear?"

"My house is not far from here. I can wear … my son's shoes," she said and her voice dropped off. She cleared her throat and locked eyes with the girl.

"It is you who walks a great distance to the white house," the tanner said and forced a smile. "Let these shoes make you more comfortable, okay?"

She crouched down and guided the girl's feet into the shoes, ignoring the tear that fell from Damascena's cheek. "Look at that! They almost fit," she said, pulling two leather laces from her pocket and tied them around her ankles.

Damascena gathered the corner of her dress in her fist, feeling her hands sweat. Her words came softly, almost inaudibly. "Thank you for your kindness," she said.

The tanner lowered her voice to make sure no one could hear them. "You're quite welcome. I have been to the white house. I was a friend of the weaver who lived there—may she rest in peace. So I am a friend of whoever lives there now."

Damascena swallowed the rock in her throat. She did not expect to make a friend. "You are a friend of Shams?" she asked.

The tanner looked up, confused.

"Who is Shams?"

"My teacher," Damascena said. "The old man who lives there with me."

The tanner lowered her voice. "What does he teach you?"

"About roses."

The tanner remained crouched by the girl's feet and nodded. She wiped her eyes before she looked up again, but this time she was not smiling.

"Your boots will be ready by next week," she said and stood in bare feet to greet a man who had walked up to her stall. "Now finish your shopping before the storm hits."

Damascena stepped back from the tanner's booth in a daze as lightning flickered overhead. The market flinched under the first crackle of thunder and everyone scattered when a boom shook the cobbles in the streets. She stood in the middle of the stalls watching the chaos of merchants covering their wares, patrons running for cover, relieved to see the market empty. She walked home alone, passing only the rush of water in the streets. She returned with no knife or bread. Only soaked clothes and the shoes.

What a waste of a day and Shams' trust. She felt the humiliation howling inside her. She did not know what time it was when she reached the door. It was dark but not late. Traces of silver threaded the engorged gray sky, matching the weight of her shame. Her mind reeled with the punishment she would suffer when Shams saw the coins in her hands. If this had been his first lesson, she did not intend to stay long in his classroom.

TWO

Damascena took off the tanner's shoes and left them on the stoop, hesitant to open the door. She moved to the front window, seeing the flicker of a small flame burning in the fireplace and the hooded shadow of Shams twirling about the floor with his head tilted up. Her first instinct was to giggle. She did not know the old man could dance. He had complained about his feet aching, but nothing about his movements suggested pain.

Shams wore an odd cone-shaped hat that looked like an upside down flowerpot. He moved in circles, arms outstretched, mouth slightly open as he drew in breath after breath, chanting words that Damascena had never heard and could not understand—a confluence of accents and vowels and rhythms that sounded much like a waterfall. She liked the cleansing, calming effect, even if she had no idea what the old man was saying between the thunder and the rain:

> *There is no salvation for the soul*
> *But to fall in Love*
> *It has to creep and crawl*
> *Among the Lovers first.*
>
> *Only lovers can escape*
> *From these two worlds.*
> *This was written in creation.*

Only from the Heart
Can you reach the Sky,
The rose of Glory
Can only be raised in the Heart.

Shams repeated the verses over and over, faster and faster, gaining speed in his twirling. His left foot was clenched with a nail wedged between his big toe and the one after that, which seemed to keep him in place while he spun in a circle.

He reminded Damascena of a little spinning top, and she was surprised he did not topple over or collapse from dizziness. Watching him spin soothed her in a way she had not felt in a long time, though she found it cruel he could move so easily and still leave her to walk alone. "Your feet don't hurt," she said aloud when he stopped.

Shams turned to the open window, stony-faced.

"Did the monks neglect to teach you not to startle others?"

Damascena's mouth formed a little O and she felt her cheeks burn. She crunched her hand into a fist and entered the house. "I learned from you," she said again, softly. Shams resisted the urge to buckle over laughing.

"I am pleased you speak your mind. At least you have the poise and strength to defend yourself."

Shams straightened, peering through the dim light of the room to the girl's hands. She had no bread. No knife.

"Your journey to Krun was productive?"

"Not really," she said and scratched the back of her head. Her own hair was as wet and matted as Shams and she shivered. Shams motioned to the wool blanket on the bed.

"Come inside and get warm," he said.

She closed the door, keeping the shoes out of his sight, and ambled across the bare floor like an old woman, leaving footprints with her wrinkled soles. Her ankles were red and small circles marked the beginning of blisters. He eyed the shoes under her bed.

"You didn't wear shoes and now you have blisters. Are you so lonely that you had to take on my aching, too?"

Damascena pulled the blanket around her shoulders and lay down on the bed, lifting only her eyes. "You're a horrible teacher," she said.

Shams flicked the lint off his robe; it flickered in the dark room.

"Why do you think that? Because I sent you on an adventure?"

"What friend lets their friend walk alone?"

"But I am always with you."

"You lie."

The words sputtered from her lips and she dropped the blanket onto the mattress, feeling heat surge in her body, waiting for Shams to speak. He said nothing and sat cross-legged on the walnut stump, watching her. She wished that for once he would remove the hood from his head and show his face. Coward, she thought, and crossed the room. She opened the door to leave but stopped, seeing a knife on the stoop where she had left the tanner's shoes. A knife twice the size of her hand, with a decent sheath and a bone handle.

She felt a shiver in her entire body and turned back to Shams.

"Who are you?" she said, feeling afraid. "What do you want with me?"

He paused, studying her face in the firelight, touched by her earnestness.

"You know. I came to help you," he said.

She swallowed, not wanting to believe in his power.

"But how did you do that to the shoes?"

He shook his head. "I did nothing."

"That dance you did. What is that?"

Shams paused, considering what he could tell her now. "It is a way to listen."

"To what?" she asked.

"The rose."

Damascena scowled. She had never heard of a flower—or anything inanimate speaking. Not even the stork spoke to her, though she always felt its presence.

"What does it say?"

Shams lifted his face just enough for her to see the light flickering from his eyes.

"It wants you to know love."

The word love sent shivers up her arms and legs. She held his gaze, suddenly terrified. "What does love have to do with roses?"

"Everything," he said, feeling the pain in her heart. "But you must stay here with this old bird long enough to know."

Shams woke Damascena early, before dawn, to take advantage of the morning, when the stems had not been wilted yet by the sun. She stumbled barefoot out the door, barely awake enough to worry about replacing the tanner's shoes or consider the phenomena of the knife that had taken their place. She rubbed her eyes, yawned.

"Do all your classes begin in the dark?"

Shams smiled and his eyes glowed in the diffused late-August moonlight.

"Many discoveries have been made in darkness."

He motioned for her to join him at the rose bush. Damascena allowed her eyes to adjust to the dark sky and crossed the yard to the rose bush that seemed to have doubled in size overnight.

"It's bigger," she said, astounded, noticing the ring of indentations around the soil, realizing they were footprints twice the size of hers. "How did you do it?"

Damascena had no reason to believe in magic but also no reason not to believe. She had been taught about miracles in the monastery and from what she knew, magic and miracles were no different. Jesus was a miracle. The Immaculate Conception (which she had come to believe meant a very clean one since Ivan always demanded she keep their quarters "immaculate") was as much of a miracle as the rose bush doubling in size. Ivan had told her roses came from hell and it occurred to her, staring at the rose bush in the darkness, that maybe the burning bush Moses stood next to was a rose bush, too.

"It does not matter how. What matters is that you know it happened," Shams said, refusing to indulge her curiosity with any more answers. "The rose is ready to be cut."

He pulled the knife from the rope cinched at his waist and pressed the blade against her hand, already oily with her perspiration.

"I don't understand why we have to cut it," Damascena said, reluctant to take it.

"Separation encourages growth."

Damascena scowled. She caught the dull glint of moonlight in the thin blade, seeing Shams' face in the reflection.

"Then show me how, Old Bird," she said, unsure.

Shams took her hand and guided the knife to the bush. "Most roses form roots on small cuttings with only one or two leaves," he said. "This is the simplest way of propagating roses: by cutting off pieces of the stem and replanting them until they eventually take root. With a little faith, the rose will take root and thrive here."

Then he instructed her to cut a length of stem the size of her foot with at least four five-leaflet leaves. He guided the knife to a forty-five degree angle just above the highest leaf, helped her sever the stem and pluck the two lowest leaves from the cutting as well as any remaining flowers and flower buds. He poked the cutting into the ground in a bed of soil he had dug beside the north side of the house. Then he told her to wait and watch.

Damascena repeated this ritual every day, even when she doubted that the bush could continue to grow after so many cuts. But it only grew more, and the more it grew, the more cuttings Damascena could take.

Each morning, she misted the cuttings and each night, as Shams had instructed, she sat beside them, envisioning the kindly face of the woman in the rose window. In the morning, she checked for roots by tugging gently on the tiny plants.

When she felt the first pull back, she called to Shams, "Bird, look at this! I will do as you say, not as you do!" because he hadn't touched the plants since she had taken the knife to them. She wondered if he had lost interest, but his involvement remained in the darkest hours when Damascena, exhausted, fell into a deep sleep.

In daylight, Damascena and Shams filled the emptiness of the field with the silent rapture of growing roses. When they tired, they fell onto the downy grasses and watched clouds pass, waiting for the sun to set, then moved into the white house to eat wild greens picked from the property. At the table, they talked. She asked about his childhood, if he knew his mother, what she looked like, how she sang. He told her he remembered hiding food in his cuffs and his desire to run away.

Damascena stared at him, stunned.

"Why would you ever want to leave your family?"

Shams lifted his face to hers and for the first time since they met, pulled the hood back to reveal his eyes, milky and opaque, the color of the moon. "God called me away."

Damascena stared at him, and for a moment, felt a pulse coming from the center of her forehead. "For what? Why would God ever call anyone away from their family?"

"For a spiritual ... assignment," he said.

"What is that?" she asked.

"A contract between God and me."

"Oh," she said, feeling a shiver along her arms and neck. "I've never heard of such a thing. This place you come from must be very strange."

"Tabriz is no stranger than any other place."

"Where is Tabriz?" she asked.

He drew a map with his finger, showing her the long valley and volcano.

"There was a garden there, too. Some believe the Garden of Eden," he said.

"I'm glad you come from a land of gardens," she said one night.

"Is that so?" he asked. The intimacy of her small voice surprised him.

She nodded and smiled. "I'm happy you're helping me grow one, too, Old Bird."

She reached across the table and squeezed the old man's hand, too used to the coldness of his fingers to wonder why this was so.

On the first morning of the new moon, Damascena woke in a feverish pitch of worry. She lay in bed and groaned like a wounded animal, wondering how she could ever explain to the tanner that the boots she had given to her had turned into a knife.

"I have to go back to the market and pick up my new shoes."

Shams, who had just then stepped into the house with a bowl of pears, paused.

"What's wrong with those?"

Damascena met his gaze and looked down at the sad strips of worn leather under her bed. Mice had needled the straps with their teeth, leaving little holes that oddly made them look like lace. She was no more likely to wear them than she would the tanner's shoes. They were of no use. She would have to walk barefoot and endure the ridicule of donkeys and the asses who drove them, unless Shams accompanied her to Krun.

"I need you to go with me, Bird."

"I have no need for markets or crowds," he said. "Besides, separation makes a person wise. You must go by the reality of the path."

Shams toed the nose of a squirrel that had scampered up to the threshold, then pulled the door closed and carried the bowl of pears to the table.

"Get up," he said. "You're missing the best light of day."

Damascena tossed the blanket and taciturnly swung her legs over the bed, unnerved by his confidence. The reality was clear. She would suffer.

THREE

When the rose bushes blossomed, Damascena cut off every flower and set off for Krun, determined to earn the tanner's forgiveness and the respect of the gossips in the market. She swung the knife carelessly in the air, severing stem after stem. Her fingers bled from the prick of thorns but she did not stop to wipe them. She let the blood dry in the hot breeze and walked barefoot and high-chinned, aware that the donkey carts and passersby were no longer staring at what her feet lacked, but at what she held in her hands.

"Roses!" they fussed, mesmerized by what had been a fabled flower until then.

Guildsmen and craftsmen, and the whole lot of townspeople paused, stricken with love at first sight. Not one among them had received a formal education like the abbots or monks, but they had listened to stories about roses and had even delighted in making some up. Theirs had been a scattered collection of evidence from learned monks in the village: the myth of Venus, goddess of love, who in her pursuit of Adonis, stepped on a thorn and whose drops of blood sprang up as red roses.

The people of Krun wanted to believe that this flower grew on earth, but seeing a rose was as likely as seeing an angel. They cried and blew kisses to the girl with the roses. "Oh my

Lord, My God," they repeated, needing to be forgiven for doubting the existence of such beauty and perfection.

On the streets and between the stalls, they let her pass in front of them, wafting the air with their hands, hopeful the sweet scent would linger. The news spread quickly. The girl who had stood in feces now smelled as sweet as the rose. Some of them argued they did not know the difference between the scent of the girl or the five-pointed pink flowers. They simply wanted to inhale it, bask in the intoxication of the perfume, and so they followed her to the tanner's stand and stood in the noon sun.

"Good day," Damascena said, trying not to quake in front of the crowd.

The tanner, who had been inspecting the heel on a small boot, paused and smiled seeing the girl's round olive face. Her skin glowed and she could see the kiss of sun, the ruddy cheeks and full lips. The child had not possessed such exuberance a month ago. She held up the boot and tapped the heel with her finger.

"I was just thinking of you. Your boots have been waiting."

Damascena nodded, aware of the onlookers and the whisperings in the market, the butcher's wife among them, mouth gaping, finger pointing straight at her.

Self-conscious, she lifted the bundle of roses to the counter, trying to ignore the butcher's wife and everyone else. "Thank you. These are for you. For the boots," she said.

The tanner gasped and bent over to smell the bouquet. At first, Damascena thought the woman was suddenly ill. Her lips grew white and she lost all color in her cheeks. She covered her mouth—eyes darting, then finally settling on Damascena.

"Where did you find roses?"

"Shams taught me how to grow them," she said, ashamed she did not have more to give. "I hope you can accept them as my payment."

The tanner narrowed her eyes and studied the girl. "You *grew* them? Where?"

"In the field beside the white house."

The tanner lifted her eyes to the sky.

"I shall say it is a place of holy spirits," she said. "Blessed is the ground upon which these roses grow! Blessed is the gardener! You bring us hope from the other side."

"The other side?" the girl asked, unable to understand.

"The weaver died there under the sword of a Mongol. May her soul rest in peace."

More cheers, then a crackling like thunder silenced them all.

"You are heretics!" shrieked a voice and the crowd split, making way for the butcher's wife whose red-skinned, thick arms bulged with veins. Damascena knew she should be afraid but she wanted to laugh. She looked like a boiled boar in a dress, and the whiskers on her chin made the resemblance even more likely.

"Can I help you with something?" the tanner asked.

The butcher's wife pushed up her sleeves, dabbed at the fissure between her breasts now streaked with sweat. She studied the roses, then spit on them.

"These come from the Devil's garden," she hissed.

"Take one with you," the tanner encouraged. "Let it bring love to your house."

As the tanner picked a rose for the butcher's wife, the crowd lurched forward, shoving their hands above Damascena's head, clamoring for *their* rose.

"Give us a rose! We will pay!"

A short, oily-faced man with a dirty tunic brushed the girl's arm with his elbow.

"What is the cost for twelve?"

Damascena cocked her head, calculating. She did not know the value of a rose, let alone a dozen. She had not intended to sell them.

The tanner motioned for the man to keep his distance. "That depends on what the girl needs. Child, what needs have you?" she asked.

Damascena felt dizzy with all the bodies pressing on her. She needed a lot of things. First, to be forgiven for the death of the oblate. She also needed to tell the tanner that the shoes she had loaned her had turned into a knife, and she wasn't sure when or if they would ever turn back. She needed Shams. Mostly, she needed her mother.

"I need air," she said, straining her neck to see the tanner's face beyond all those staring down at her. A pig squealed in the distance. A donkey brayed.

"Give her some space," the tanner ordered.

The crowd backed away, except for the butcher's wife. She stood there, flabbergasted, arms pinned to her hips, neck scorched by the sun. She jabbed a stiff finger into Damascena's shoulder, pushing her against the edge of the booth.

"Remember who provides meat in this town! It is one thing to go without shoes. But I dare you to survive the winter without meat in your bellies!" she said. She lifted her eyes from the girl and looked at the crowd. "Hear me once and hear me loud. I will starve those stupid enough to mistake this flower for love. Whoever buys a rose curses Krun!"

Damascena turned to the tanner, desperate, but the tanner turned to butcher's wife.

"You curse yourself," the tanner snapped back.

It felt as if the air had stopped moving. No one breathed. The only movement was the darting of eyes. Then, slowly, arm after arm shot up. Shouts of *me* and *me* and *me* and *me, too* rang out across the market like bells, punctuated by the mad woman's push across the cobblestones, squashing a mound of cow dung in her haste.

"We'll see what the Guild says about this!" the butcher's wife barked.

The tanner, unfazed, turned to Damascena and her growing line of customers. "Looks like you are the flower girl of Krun. Isn't that exciting?"

Damascena nodded, hardly registering the threat of the butcher's wife. Never before in her life had she been met by such kind, welcoming eyes. She knew that a flower could turn frowns into smiles, and erase the lines of worry and fear among the infirm. Even the ravens, flying over the market, abandoned their squawking for song, as if they, too, could see the effect her roses had on the slumped and defeated people.

They invited her to their homes for food some day, offering to help her in any way. Yes, they wanted more than roses. They needed to believe that such beauty not only existed, but could flourish despite the Mongol brutality all around them under Genghis Khan: the decimation of entire villages, the razing of homes, the rape of women and children, the tens of thousands of men peppered with arrows month after month. It was said the Mongol warriors carried up to sixty arrows each and could keep up a shooting barrage for nearly an hour. They could defeat Teutonic and Templar knights and took over every city and town they came across, leaving only birds to eat the slaughter. They had even managed to smash the strongest cities of stone into pieces. The people of Krun believed it was only a matter time until they were discovered and terminated, before the steppe people rode on to destroy Veliko Turnovo. The girl's roses were a small mercy.

Damascena smiled at admirers as she made her way through the market to the road back to the white house. Just as the word of the rose spread that morning, word of her new business spread again that afternoon. She skipped home in a daze, delighted by the tanner's pronouncement. The flower girl of Krun. Heaven on earth. Love in roses? She felt lightness in her whole being when she walked back to Shams in new shoes.

Rumors circulated quickly. The roses had reunited estranged lovers and acted as a salve for the wounds of husbands and wives whose tongues had lashed each other's hearts over the years. Girls wore roses in their hair to attract suitors, and asked Damascena to make rose crowns for their weddings, believing they brought good luck.

Some spun tales that the simple fragrance of the roses relaxed the fists of the most volatile tempered among them, including a rogue Mongol soldier who had suddenly laid down his sword and sought forgiveness from the villagers he had terrorized. He bought one rose from Damascena, which had since died and dried, yet he offered a single petal to each family he had tortured and robbed. During his last visit to a mountain village between Krun and Veliko Turnovo, he fell in love with the very widow whose husband had died beneath his sword. Seeing the rose in the Mongol's hands, her two children knelt and kissed his feet. The appearance of roses inspired changes in the people who lived near Krun, and no one contested the flower girl's influence.

Over the next few weeks, something awakened in Damascena and burned as bright as fire. She seized every moment to watch the roses grow. Rain or shine, fog or wind, she got up at dawn and sat quietly with the roses, revering the petals and leaves.

Her focus impressed Shams, and he joined her for this daily ritual in silence. Even though she did not see her past as the rich, dark dirt from which her garden grew, Damascena saw her future in the faces of her customers. They were so enamored with her flowers that they no longer waited in the market to buy them, but met her on the road between the white house and Krun. She could have sold them all, but always saved the last rose for the tanner, determined to honor their friendship with this weekly gift.

"Are you sure you want to do this?" the tanner asked one dark afternoon in late October, when Damascena delivered the roses. The valley lay cracked and parched, the cattle dying of thirst, which made the vibrant rose in Damascena's hands an even greater anomaly at the market, fetching six times the girl's asking price. The butcher's wife had just stepped away from the tanner's stall, all beet-faced and sweaty in the heat. She stared down at the girl and spit on the cobblestones, eyeing the rose in Damascena's hand.

"I've never been so sure of anything," she whispered as the woman left. "You gave me your own shoes so that I could walk home. This is the least I can offer you." She looked up at the tanner, shielding her eyes from the bright light in the market.

"Maybe the shoes weren't meant to be returned," the tanner said and smiled.

Damascena straightened, staring at the tanner's feet. The woman had walked barefoot ever since they had met, and calluses and corns encrusted her heals and toes. She had been walking the same distance to the white house to deliver food without complaint.

"But you've done so much for me," she said handing a rose to the tanner.

The tanner tucked the rose behind her left ear and the pink petals complimented her ruddy cheeks. Her eyes were large and the color of a light tea and her lips were full as figs. She possessed a long slender smooth neck with no bumps or wrinkles. Damascena wondered what happened to her son. She seemed like she would be a gentle, loving mother the way she cupped Damascena's chin in her hands.

"Please receive *my* gratitude," the tanner said.

Damascena smiled and held onto the tanner's hand, feeling her fingers soften. She did not know what it felt like to save a life, or that her life might have needed saving, but she knew this woman had changed her life—and had asked nothing of her in return, not even the whereabouts of her mother, as if she knew to avoid the subject.

"As long as I know you, I will bring you roses," Damascena promised her.

"All I want is to know you are safe. Bring me that and your debt is cleared."

As the days grew shorter and the nights longer, when the leaves on the trees had turned to gold, the girl stopped waking in fits from seeing Ivan in her dreams. She dreamed instead about growing roses for her mother. Though she had not seen her in the roses yet, she wondered if they would help to reveal who she was.

Then one morning in late October, when the full moon filled the sky and frost laced the ground at the white house, she reached into a bush to pick a flower but drew blood instead. It was not the first prick she had felt. It was the first time she understood the nature of the pain. She withdrew her arm and pulled out the long, thick thorn that had pierced the vein inside her elbow and thought, *So this is you, mother. Hello.*

Her mother had left her but she hadn't lied. She was in the roses, after all. She decided to remove the thorns, unwittingly soliciting more concerns and questions.

"Why did you do that?" her customers asked at the market that week.

"Because they hurt," she said, thinking she had done them a favor.

"But you'll hurt yourself trying to take them off."

She was not concerned about the pricks and puncture marks. The pain was bearable compared to the questions they asked about her mother. They assumed her mother was her teacher. They wanted to know where she learned to grow roses and how it was possible to make them thrive despite the cold rains and the early frosts of autumn. How the girl managed to grow the roses through winter took on an even greater mystery.

Inland Bulgaria was no greenhouse in January and February, and the vernal equinox in March promised only more snow, at least for a few more weeks. Everyone from Krun knew that flowers didn't grow in the snow, but oddly, the roses continued to thrive. Each week, despite the inclement weather, the girl showed up with her bundle of flowers as if they'd been plucked on a fair day in June, astounding the town again.

One night in mid-February, Damascena feigned sleeping and followed Shams out of the white house to see where he went each night. She hid at the base of the hill, feeling cold air lift the bottom of her nightgown, but she was not cold. Oddly, she felt heat and could not make out the source until she followed a small path in the snow and glimpsed a woodless bonfire, streaking the winter sky with bands of silver and gold.

Spirals of smoke formed familiar figures in the darkness, and for the first time, Damascena understood the winged creatures to be angels. She gasped seeing Shams fly through the air above the hill, twirling in circles, flames trailing from his ankles and wrists. She heard a plucking noise, like that of harp strings, and the slow haunting notes of a flute, though she saw no musicians. She pressed her ear against the chilly night sky and listened, hearing Shams' joyous laughter from above.

At one point, he paused and engaged in conversation with thin air. Fully animated, he demonstrated more, then kicked the earth as if frustrated by his steps until he took flight again and levitated in his dance with fire. He moved slowly at first with outstretched arms, right hand turned up toward heaven and the left turned down to the earth, gaining speed as he circled the roses.

Damascena stood there staring, mouth agape at the phenomenon before her—the more Shams danced and twirled, the more the roses grew. She heard the cracking and bursting of rose hips, the stretching and popping of the stalks shooting out of the earth and the tearing open of the tender buds revealing the roses within. Then a shriek from the property boundary. She turned seeing the butcher's wife clutch her heart and run.

"I've seen the Devil!" the butcher's wife announced to the Guild. "And the rose girl is the Devil's daughter!" She demanded they strip Damascena of her merchant status, before the roses brought misfortune to Krun, but there were only signs of robust health. Color had returned to the cheeks of the most ashen among them in the dead of winter.

If anything, concerns abounded about Damascena's health. She looked thin, her cheekbones hollowed by hunger. Did she need more food? Warmer clothes? Did she and her teacher need help at the white house?

Damascena, more wary than ever, avoided their questions, ducking beneath them as if they were swords. She feigned distraction, shifting her eyes from the inquiring souls to the swarms of new customers that continued to find her. They came from local villages and when the snow had melted and spring had returned to the vast plain of Thracian royalty, they came from remote mountain hamlets, traveling for days to buy a single rose.

She was flattered. Nobody had ever traveled this far on her behalf. They regaled her with tales of their journey to meet her. She listened well, remembering the facts and faces of the storytellers, asking about their families, their children, their mothers, their health, tuning out the lingering concerns of her most loyal customers: the neighbors who considered themselves friends. They concluded that Damascena shouldn't be left alone.

The tanner objected, defending the girl's independence at such a young age. Couldn't they see? Damascena was grounded, well rested, alert, of bright mind and determined spirit, even ethereal to those who knew how to read her eyes. Still, her neighbors expressed concerns about her health and well being, carrying their secret desires like fleas. They vied to supervise her business and share the profits equally, and by the spring, they were fighting each other—not for a rose, but for custody of the girl.

Custody. The word felt like a spike in Damascena's heart, and she grew more suspicious with each advancing offer. First a pot of honey to last a year, then a chicken, a blanket, a new dress, two sheep and a goat. She could not be persuaded that anyone from Krun knew how to tend to the roses better than Shams.

"It is not the roses we are concerned about," they said. "We want to tend to you."

"I do not need tending to," she said, politely declining their offers at the market. When they refused to stop, she spoke to them in riddles, in the manner of Shams, hearing the whispers of the voice that had begun to speak to her in her sleep lately.

Could you ever find another market like this? Where with your one rose you can buy thousands of rose gardens and with one final breath, the Divine Wind?

The words drew curious looks and nervous laughter from her inquisitors and they scuttled away, embarrassed they had even thought to manipulate Damascena. They did not need to see her teacher to know he had contributed to the intelligence of this girl.

Damascena finally held up her hands, dewy and dirty from the fields, and asked them to stop. Then she spoke the whispered words again, exactly as she had heard them.

Breathe in the secret. No more words. Hear only the voice within.

"What?" they asked, owl-eyed, failing to comprehend her words, then tottered to the taverns to get drunk at mid-day. Soon, they placed wagers on who could outsmart the girl; and the butcher's wife placed the highest bet.

Room and board, meat for her teacher to last through the next winter, a new wool blanket, a winter coat and shoes for her growing feet. Damascena would appear foolish to refuse such abundance, but living with the butcher's wife was the last thing she wanted.

"I have my teacher, Shams," she said, surprised the butcher's wife had walked all the way from town to the white house to make her offer in the darkness of morning.

"Ah. Yes. Shams. A funny name. If this is true, then why is he never here?"

Damascena looked up from the table where she worked under the moonlight, weaving stems of roses into a crown for the daughter of the butcher's wife. She wished Shams would appear. Just then, the whispered words floated in as gently as the breeze.

If you could see the ugliest leper with the eyes of love, his beauty would out-dazzle the starlit sea. If one drop of love's vision could rinse your eyes, wherever you looked, you would weep with wonder.

Hearing this, Damascena clenched her jaw and swallowed. It was no time to speak of love in front of the butcher's wife, who would tell everyone she lost her mind.

"Somebody will take custody of you sooner or later," the butcher's wife said, and her hand came down hard on Damascena's shoulder.

"Do you have protection, child?"

Damascena's jaw tightened and her heart raced. "Why would I need protection?"

The butcher's wife saw the terror on the girl's face. She continued, savoring each syllable of her words. "You are alone."

"I'm not alone," Damascena said and shuddered, knowing she was.

"Look around you! You have no mother."

Damascena straightened and cast her eyes across the table, surrendering a tear.

"Do not cry for her," the butcher's wife said. "She left you."

"I have a teacher," Damascena said, but did not look up from the table.

"Then where is he? Nobody from Krun has ever seen him," she said and poked her head into the house for signs of a man. No shoes. No footprints, just bare wood. "There is no one else who lives here but you."

"He's hunting," Damascena said, feeling the intensity of the lie. In truth, she had no idea where Shams went. Sometimes he left for days between lessons.

"And what is he teaching you in his absence?"

Damascena swallowed. "About roses. About love."

"You cannot be serious."

"Yes," she said and stood from the table, handing her the crown of roses.

"What do you know of love? You are just an orphan!"

Damascena lifted her eyes to the woman and spoke the whispered words flooding her just then. "*My heart is like a vast rose garden of light. An ocean of agony drowned it again and again but it became a warrior after being slaughtered a hundred times.*"

The butcher's wife covered her mouth with a hand. "Your teacher is a poet, too?"

The girl shook her head. Shams was many things, a silly old man who danced in circles and made roses grow, but he was not a poet. It was not his voice whispering to her. Perhaps the words that came of late were the threads of poetry, but Damascena did not intend to discuss poetry or anything more with the butcher's wife. Except this.

"Your offer is late," she said, trembling. "I have given my custody to the tanner."

The butcher's wife shrieked and dropped the rose crown on the ground between herself and Damascena. An eerie silence followed, and just as the sun rose above the horizon, a rush of cold air swirled around the woman's ankles. She lifted her skirt and shrieked again, seeing a ring of blood on the dirt where there had been roses.

FOUR

Overnight, rumors of witchcraft spread through the valley and up the mountains like whiffs of plague. Fires soon followed, suspected witches burned. Throngs of inquisitors lurked through the villages. The butcher's wife told everyone that the girl's teacher was the tanner and that the tanner was the Devil. The tanner remained calm, tethered to the tasks of her trade, skinning the hides of cows slaughtered by the butcher's wife. They exchanged pleasantries at market, two skirted and civilized women doing business, but no sooner would the butcher's wife withdraw from the crowd than she would mutter curses.

The next day, the butcher's sons met up with Damascena on her way to town, with rocks in their hands and bows and arrows on their backs. She was startled to see them on the wooded trail to the white house, but believed them when they said they were hunting.

"*Svinia*," they said.

"There are swine around here?" Damascena asked, eyes cast on the dappled light that fell across the trunks of alders and pines. The boys nodded slowly, then rattled off the rest of the wild things they'd like to kill there. *Sheebanyak, Kopele. Putka.*

Damascena stiffened when she heard *Putka*. One of Ivan's words for her mother. It meant pie, but it was not a nice word. "How do you hunt for ... pies?" she asked the oldest son. He smirked and smiled. "You follow the scent of bruised fruit." Damascena glanced up at the white blossoms on the forest canopy. "But it's too early for bruises. The fruit has yet to come."

"Not all fruit falls from trees," he said, letting Damascena pass him on the path, only after his arm grazed the back of her neck.

When she reached the tanner's house that afternoon, perspired and thirsty from running, she paused, seeing a one-eyed black cat dangling from its tail nailed to the door and a rose in place of its missing eye. Smeared along the doorknob was a blood so dark it appeared black. She did not have to knock. The tanner expected her arrival and opened the door. Without a word, she took Damascena by the hand and ushered her through the tidy, thatched roof house into the back garden and wiped the girl's cheek.

"Do not cry for the cat, child. It had nine lives."

Damascena looked up and rubbed her eyes. "I cry for you."

"Then you waste precious resources. Here," she said, reaching behind her to pick a sprig of wild lavender. "Rub this between your fingers and breathe."

But Damascena couldn't breathe with such a lie lodged between her lungs. She coughed, and the sticky ball of words spewed forth into the hot afternoon air.

"I told the butcher's wife you have taken custody of me," she said, her cheeks burning. "I shouldn't have brought trouble into your home. But I will continue to bring you roses, even if I risk my own life. I owe you at least that."

The tanner took a deep breath. "Slow down, child. When did you see her?"

"Yesterday. She came by to pick up her daughter's rose crown."

"The butcher's wife wanted roses?" the tanner asked, suspicious, eyes steady on the girl who paced the garden. She had never seen Damascena so frantic and exhausted. Dark rings circled her eyes, the tips of her fingers pricked by thorns and thick with scabs.

"Her daughter is getting married tomorrow," Damascena said, gritting her teeth, regretting that the rose crown she had worked so hard to make had turned to blood.

The tanner crossed her arm, lifted her chin. "She was married last week."

Damascena stared at her. "But she sent her sons to the white house last night to tell me to rush. I woke before dawn to pick."

"Why rise so early for the butcher's wife when she doesn't even like roses?"

"I rise early for the roses. It is best to pick them with dew. They retain their smell and I wanted the perfume more than anything to linger for the wedding," Damascena said and paused, disappointed. "But you say the wedding was last week?"

"The butcher's daughter moved to a village by Shipka Pass," she said, never lifting her eyes off the girl. "What else did she want?"

"Answers. She kept poking around the house, asking all sorts of questions."

"Where was Shams?"

"I don't know. He's always gone," Damascena said and shifted her eyes to the sun.

The tanner drew in a deep breath and paced the garden. She paused and turned back to Damascena. "You will stay with me," she said. "This is your home now."

For three days and two nights, Damascena lived in the comfort of the tanner's home as spring bloomed throughout Krun. The tanner offered her late son's bed and the quilt she had made from his clothes, then she immediately altered one of her own dresses so that Damascena would have more to wear than threads woven with twigs and leaves. She bathed her the first night and washed her hair, then after she fed her a stew of roasted root vegetables, she sang folk songs until the girl fell asleep.

In the morning, they woke to the sound of birds and the smell of fruit trees in bloom, the air fragrant with new grass. They sat in the tanner's garden in the early light and ate fresh *mekitsi*, stacks of circular fried breads that they spread with jam and soft cheese. They drank tea and talked like old friends who had not seen each other in years.

Damascena enjoyed being in the tanner's tidy kitchen, admiring the small glass jars of herbs and spices, and the colorful weavings that decorated the walls and floors. Though simple, the décor was a stark contrast to the white house. It struck her that she had lived her entire life in the company of men, and she welcomed the colors and smells of the tanner's house. Not even the meals cooked in the rectory could compare to how the tanner's food made her feel so nourished and loved. She relished every meal the tanner prepared and was happy to contribute two quails she shot and plucked for the fire. She loved learning how to cook new dishes, especially *patatnik*, a thick potato pancake that filled her belly and made her sleep long and hard, and *Gabena chorba*, soup made from fresh mushrooms. She wondered why Shams had never insisted they make soup from his foraging, and she wished he had been half the cook that the tanner was. She had not realized how bland the food in the monastery was until she had eaten at the tanner's table.

"How did you learn how to cook like this?"

The tanner lifted her eyes and dabbed her mouth with a cloth. "My mother," she said.

Damascena broke off a piece of *Tutmanik*, a bread made with cheese that they had just pulled from the oven. Steam rose between them. "That must be nice," she said.

The tanner paused, then reached out for her own piece. "Learning to cook?" she asked.

Damascena shook her head. "Having a mother to teach you."

The tanner offered her butter. "Would you like more?"

Damascena plunged her knife into the butter. "No. I want to know why you're the only one who doesn't ask me about her. Don't you want to know?"

The tanner put the bread on her plate and sat up straighter.

"I figured you would have told me by now. I thought you ran away."

Damascena let out a sad laugh. "I did run away, but not from her."

"From who?"

She told the tanner the story of her birth, the monastery, Ivan and Shams.

"Maybe it was all meant to be," the tanner said after a long pause.

"What?"

"All of this. I believe there are no coincidences, Damascena. I lost my family. I prayed every day that I would get another chance to share my life with a child and a man I love. I did not get the man yet," she said and laughed, "But I got you."

They did not speak much that second night, enjoying the simple ritual of washing and drying dishes, mending clothes by the fire, singing songs. When they got dressed for bed, the tanner walked over to Damascena and pulled her son's quilt under the girl's chin.

"Sleep well," she said.

"I've never slept better," Damascena insisted. "I like it here."

The tanner nodded then blew out the lantern. She climbed into her own bed and called out to Damascena. "Maybe your mother is teaching you … even in her absence."

The third knock woke Damascena from a deep sleep. She bolted up from the bed in a sweat, hearing the low murmuring of the voices below. She could see the flicker of the tanner's lantern between the floorboards and the shine of black boots.

She could not make out the faces. The men stood at the door in dark hoods.

"Can I help you?" the tanner asked, masking the terror in her voice.

"We are looking for the rose girl. The butcher's wife said you have taken custody of her. Is this true?"

"No. I know nothing of the arrangement."

"We've been looking for her for days. We understand you might be helping her."

"Yes. Of course. I have helped her," the tanner said, her words slow and even. "I have given her a pair of shoes. That certainly does not make me her custodian."

"We understand she engages in witchcraft."

Damascena flinched, overhearing the accusation against the crushing pitch of cicadas outside the window—both splintering her ears.

"Of what kind?"

"The Devil's work. Strange things are happening because of the roses."

"Do you mean because people are happier?"

The men grunted.

"If you know where she is, we will spare you any more questions."

Without hesitation, the tanner offered up her answer. "She went home."

"Home?" they asked.

"Yes. To the monastery at Rila."

When the tanner closed and bolted the door, she let out a small cry then climbed the stairs in the dark to Damascena's bed, sensing the girl was awake by now.

She spoke in a whisper, her voice quaking.

"You have to go back now," she implored.

"To the monastery?"

"To the white house. They will be on their way to Rila tonight, I am sure."

Damascena trembled in the bed. "No! I don't want to leave you."

"You must! I do not have the power to protect you."

"But Shams does?" the girl asked, fighting the tears of her terror.

"No. I do not believe Shams has any more power than I do in your safekeeping."

"Then who? Who can help me? I have no one in this world to trust."

The tanner held up a finger in the dark.

"The roses," she said, and laid her hand on Damascena's heart. "As long as you return to the roses, your safekeeping is guaranteed. You must trust what I say."

Damascena stared up at the woman with the milky skin in the moonlight. She wanted to stay with the tanner, not return to the flowers that had come to bring such mystery and misery to her life.

"What if something happens to the roses?" she asked, "Then what will I do?"

"Ask God to protect them and you."

Damascena looked up. "I am not sure I trust God," she said. "I'm scared."

"I know, child. We are all scared, but do not run. Turn toward yourself. That is where God lives."

The tanner pulled Damascena toward her, wrapping the girl's thin arms around her hips, remembering the last time her husband and son had done so before the fever took them. Her tear fell onto Damascena's head, and they held each other in the dark for one blessed moment, becoming for the other what they had lost.

FIVE

Damascena was scared to leave the roses. As much as she missed her trips to the market, she did not miss the terror she felt there. She fixed one eye on the roses, the other on the woods. Every now and then, she heard the snap of a twig branch and flinched, straining to see the dark forms running through the forest in the blackest hours of night, wanting to believe that the footprints she found in the garden the next day were those of a wild boar.

Not even Shams could reassure her she was safe, but she was living among the roses and they were thriving. He told her that deep digging of the soil encouraged better cultivation, instructing her to dig trenches around the plants and pour warm water into the ditch once the rosebuds had formed to force their growth. He pointed out the comparison to Damascena, but she had stopped seeking his advice. She knew nothing of his whereabouts.

When the nights turned warm in early May, Damascena slept among the roses on a mat of woven grass and did not leave the white house. She took the tanner's words literally about the protection offered by the roses. Not saints. Her faith had become as threadbare as the rags she wore, and nothing but roses shared any meaning with her now.

She built a small structure in the middle of the garden, a lean-to constructed of a fallen walnut tree and extra hides the tanner had given her to protect her from storms.

"I don't mind the rain," she told Shams when he finally returned a week later, her voice tinged with bitterness. "As much as I mind your absence."

He handed her the wool blanket from the house.

"But you must not get sick. Your health is that of the roses."

"Why would you care about my well being? You are never here. Where have you been? Where do you go when you leave?"

"Nowhere. I am always with you."

"That is impossible!" she sputtered.

He turned away to dowse the property with his stick.

"What are you looking for now?" she demanded.

"Your faith," he said and tapped the ground.

Damascena laughed, "Do not look too far! My only faith is in the roses now."

"Then my teachings are working."

Shams danced in the garden, warming the soil, while the roses continued to solicit Damascena's curiosity. She took note of the shifting colors, the deepening pink in the rose petals, the hum among the bushes that kept the deer at bay, a hum so low that any normal human being would not have been able to detect it. But the girl was listening. She pressed her ear to the valley floor and communicated with the roots. In Shams' absence, she had trouble tolerating the solitude, but sought it now.

The roses had taken to the soil so well by mid-May that the white house appeared as it did in her dream: a small white square floating in the midst of a wide pink lake, so expansive she was drawn to sit with the roses for hours, as if meditation had been her rightful posture from birth. She no longer saw pure air, but a yellow-green oily haze coating everything, which is why she did not believe Shams when he said the sunset was a reflection of the garden. She hadn't seen the sun for days, not that she expected him to notice. He was never around long enough to notice much of anything.

"Something's burning in Krun," she said, catching him before he set off again.

He stared at her. "Damascena, something is always burning."

Sleep did not come easily. She worried about the tanner. She tossed and turned, seeing flames, and awakened to the smell of wood smoke and some acrid stench she could not identify, burning hair perhaps or just refuse. She noticed a fine grey ash that coated the dew on the rose petals and accumulated on the horizon each day as if the whole town lay smoldering. When she asked Shams about the fires on the rare morning that he showed up and sat with her for breakfast, he seemed indifferent.

"I hope they are okay."

"Who?"

She stared at him.

"All the people who live in Krun. You act as if fire is nothing to worry about."

He lifted his face to hers, letting her see his moon-colored eyes again.

"There *is* nothing to worry about."

"What if the wind carries the flames here?"

"Then we shall welcome them. Like a guest."

She glared at him and stabbed at the porridge, a mixture of wheat berries and oats that he brought back with him from one of his trips.

"If the fire destroys the people and the roses, how can we welcome that?"

Shams turned his eyes back to the small bird he was whittling from a hunk of cherry wood. "*This being human is a guest house. Every morning a new arrival. A joy, a depression, a meanness, some momentary awareness comes as an unexpected visitor. Welcome and entertain them all! Even if they're a crowd of sorrows who unexpectedly empty your house of its furniture, still, treat each guest honorably—*"

Damascena grabbed the knife from Shams' hand, having already heard these same words whispered to her in her mind. "*He may be clearing you out for some new delight.*"

"Yes. Precisely."

"Tell me whose words are these!" she demanded, batting his hand away when he reached for his carving knife, infuriated by his calm.

"Do you not yet know?"

"No," Damascena said, frustrated. "Tell me, Bird! Is it you who whispers to me?"

Shams reached across the table and took the knife back and cut into the bird, forming a wing. "No. You know it is not me."

"Then tell me!" she demanded.

"What do you want to know? Who whispers, or how to welcome the fire?"

She stood, furious, feeling the tears well up. "You are cruel. You make Ivan seem almost kind! At least his words didn't make my head pound … or my heart break."

"The words make your heart break *open*."

"What?" she cried. She pointed her finger, stiff with accusation. "If you don't help me do something about the fires and they destroy the roses, you will have ended my life. Without the roses, my heart won't be anything but broken."

The woman with the olive skin and long dark hair startled the merchants of Krun. She emerged from the rising smoke of the market, like an apparition, drawing curious looks from everyone in her path. Her beauty immediately struck them as familiar and tragic; one glimpse of the woman's eyes revealed they were related to Damascena, but her daughter did not carry the long scar that divided her left cheek and stopped at her throat.

The tanner had hoped to speak with her first, but the woman had unwittingly attracted the attention of the town gossips when she inquired about the girl who sold roses. They had directed the woman with the exotic face to the butcher, but the tanner raced across the square and stopped her before she got to the shop door.

"May I help you?" the tanner asked, catching her breath, feeling the eyes of the gossips. It was hot and she felt the heat rising from the cobblestones under her feet.

The woman eyed the tanner, trying to detect if she could trust her.

"I am looking for a girl," she said and lowered her voice, "Who is said to sell roses here."

The tanner nodded but did not speak, gesturing for the woman to follow her into the nearest alley, dark at twilight. She untied the thin scarf around her neck and gave it to the woman, leaving her eyes uncovered, then quickly led her through the narrow passage, passing a group of ragged children playing with wooden balls where the air was laced with the smell of their mother's cooking and the walls dripped with freshly washed clothing hung out to dry. They turned again at the end of the alley, passing a well, then strode into the safety of her home, where the tanner locked the front gate and the door.

"I know the girl you wish to find," the tanner said and drew the curtains shut.

The woman stood at the door, shifting, uncertain of her safety. "How do you know her?" she asked.

"She is a friend of mine," the tanner said. "I check on her from time to time."

The woman peered out from the headscarf, taking in the tanner's house, scanning for any evidence of this relationship. "Thank you for that, kind woman. May God bless you," she said, her voice breaking. "Can you tell me where she is?"

The woman lifted the headscarf and gave it back to the tanner.

"Yes, but I hesitate to encourage you to seek her without endangering you both," the tanner admonished. She hung the scarf on a nail in the wall and struck a match to light the fire, setting a kettle to boil. It was dark in the house, the moon curled in the upper corner of the window in the kitchen. "Not after everything you survived to find her," she said, examining the woman's scar.

The women adjusted their eyes to the light of an oil lamp that burned on the floor, where a small round table, laden with fruit, sat low to the ground. The tanner had nothing but black cherries to offer, wishing she had something more to comfort the woman whose hands trembled with the tea cup. She had wanted to ask Damascena many questions about her mother, but never dared to do so. Now, in the woman's presence, all the accusations and judgments fell away and she asked only one.

"Who did that to you?" she asked, feeling the anger rising, seeing the woman's left cheek again, the mottled scar in the lamplight. The skin was slightly raised, tight and shiny along the bone, as if it had taken on the properties of its assailant's weapon.

The woman set her teacup on the table and lifted her eyes to the tanner.

"What matters is that he kept my daughter alive," she said, staring into the flames, recalling the knife that ripped her face and Ivan's words. *You do not deserve her love!* "He threatened to kill me and Damascena if I ever came back again."

"Did you try?" the tanner asked.

"Of course! She is my only child. I did everything I could. And I wrote letters begging to get her back. Not a single letter was answered. But I kept writing and every year on Damascena's birthday, I made the journey back for her when the snow had cleared from the mountains. It is a month-long journey. Ivan refused to let her go."

"Ivan?" the tanner asked.

The woman turned her face. "Ivan Balev. A monk near Rila."

The tanner clasped her hand over her mouth, horrified by the injustice and irony.

"Why didn't you seek help? What about the girl's father?"

The woman lifted her eyes, swollen with tears. "She has no ... no father."

The tanner offered her a cup of tea. "I am sorry for your loss."

"Do not be," she said and coolness swept over her voice. "I never saw his face."

The tanner paused with the kettle, registering the events, realizing the severity of the violation—and her dilemma. She had risked her life so that her child could live.

"I trusted only that the child was God's," the woman said and straightened. "When I found out I was with child, my mother had a vision."

"A vision?"

The woman nodded. "Yes. Do you mind me speaking of such things?"

The tanner gestured for her to go on.

"She saw a monastery on a mountain and knew this was the place I was supposed to give birth. That it was a place of healing and miracles. But only sorrow has come."

"Why did you ever leave? Why didn't you stay with the monks and raise her?"

"We were indentured to the king at Veliko Turnovo," the woman said, fighting her tears. "I tried to tell her all about this in the letters."

"How is it that you are now free to claim her?"

"The indenture ended on my mother's deathbed. She wanted to meet Damascena before she passed on. I want to take Damascena to her grave. Will you help me find her?"

"No. I cannot," the tanner said, unwilling to jeopardize the girl. The woman looked stricken.

"I have waited twelve years to be with my child! I cannot wait another day."

"You must. You are her rightful mother but do you know how much that threatens the people of Krun? There has been talk of inquisitors lurking here. You must leave at once until it is safe to return for your daughter. She is not leaving the white house. She knows that where there are roses, she is safe. You will find her there when God wills it, but you must be on your way if you have any hope of living to see Damascena again."

While the fires raged in Krun, Damascena remained in meditation by the roses—keeping her promise to the tanner, though nothing had restored her sense of safety. She longed to see the tanner and talk, but when Shams left again, she found companionship with the roses instead. She wanted to tell the tanner that she had not turned toward herself. The whispered words had broken her heart in half, and she wanted to tell Shams that he was wrong about the fires.

She sensed it was not the hand of God who had cast the dark plume of smoke over Krun. The fires were the work of many, and their frequency alluded to a ritual she could not see through the forest. Every now and then, she'd hear a cacophony of laughter and the crackling followed by a succession of shrieks then silence. It sounded more like a sacrificial offering than any lightning storm.

Despite this threat, Damascena worked as if commanded by unseen forces. She woke each day one hour before dawn, not to pick the roses, but to collect the petals. She worked in a trance-like state, pausing only on occasion to pick a thorn from her finger and wipe the blood so that the petals stayed clean. She did not complain, and preferred the silence of her work to the cacophony of shrieking that accompanied the fires. They had turned the skies so black that she could no longer distinguish night from day in Krun.

She was frightened even though Shams had told her not to despair.

"When the darkness becomes long, after that the brightness will be long," he said one night, visiting her with a pot of warm tea. He'd roused her from her trance and parted her lips for the liquid. He could see her ribs through her dress and watched the rise and fall of her collarbone that appeared like a small branch caught beneath her skin. When she slept, he told her: *whatever your debt, whatever your affliction, both will be proportional in time. You just have to make it through the demands of the bloom.*

Damascena had never worked as hard or as fast to harvest the roses. She used both hands, pulling the entire blossom between her fingers, leaving nothing but the bare stem. Each bush had produced clusters of thirteen to eighteen buds. A few carried up to twenty-one. She deposited the blossoms into the burlap sack that she wore folded in half and tied with a rope around her waist. She cleared half an acre in two hours, sometimes one in four hours, less depending on the rain, which made her fingers cold and cramped.

To the boys who wandered the woods, Damascena had virtually destroyed the rose fields. "Of her own volition, too! She's gone mad," they reported to their friends and families in Krun. Neighbors wore the devastation in their faces, black with the soot that hung over the town for days. The butcher's wife expressed the most shock. She marched out to see for herself one morning, but wild boars chased her from the woods, while a confederacy of ravens cawed in mock applause as she fled.

Damascena felt the heat of the fires threaten the rose fields when the winds shifted. She figured it was only a matter of days until the flames chased down the roses. She worked compulsively to harvest the petals, filling sack after sack to capacity until her back ached, then dragged them, as instructed by Shams, to an enclosed shed he had built over a spring. "The bank," he said the day he finished it. "For your fortune."

He had opened the springhouse door and Damascena followed him to the huge, bell-shaped copper pot sitting inside, straddling a pile of cut logs.

"What is it?" she asked.

"A still."

It looked like a giant coffee kettle she had seen the cook use in the rectory, except this one had a turban-shaped cap on top of its round belly. Though it was shoulder height, she was surprised by how light it was when Shams asked her to lift it and reposition it on a more level surface so that it could connect with another small copper pot he called a condenser. Inside the condenser were a series of wire coils that connected to the long, thin gooseneck flowing elegantly out of the head of the still.

"What does it do?"

"It makes the invisible visible."

She yawned and scratched her head, no longer infuriated by his frequent absences. She was actually relieved to see him again.

"What has that got to do with roses?"

"Hidden inside the cells of the rose is a secret. Distill them to reveal it."

The girl did not ask more questions. She felt heavy and fuzzy. "I need to rest," she said.

He led her back to the house and wrapped her with his own robe and a wool blanket to warm her feet. Despite Damascena's desperation to give in to her body, he had urged her back to the fields. Time was running out.

"Focus on the secret," he said.

She surrendered to the mental numbness of physical exhaustion, relieved to keep her mind off the flames. She worked quickly, filling a dozen or more bags each day, puzzled by the copper still and the distillation of secrets. She did not know what she would do with the petals once they had been picked and stored in the springhouse. They would not be sold. Shams had said that selling rose petals was not the point of her labor, but he refused to say what was. Exhausted, on her knees, Damascena cursed him and the heavenly-scent that drowned her every time she opened the springhouse door.

SIX

The first time Damascena experienced moving across the earth without moving her body, she thought it was a dream. She remembered walking through the rose fields the eve of her thirteenth birthday, then suddenly stepping into a dark chamber illuminated by the flicker of a glass lamp burning from a table, where a book lay open beside a pot of ink and a quill so white it glowed in the darkness.

She ran her fingers over the feather, recognizing the plume of a stork. She pressed it against her heart as she had done as a child on the days she felt most alone, searching the sky for a glimpse of the majestic white wings in flight. With luck, she would see its full form, sleek, strong, soaring through the mountain air above the monastery.

Damascena ran the feather under her nose, delighted by the tickle, then set it down beside the lamp, realizing upon closer inspection that it was not a lamp at all but a small, thin bottle containing a greenish-yellow oil.

She inched closer to get a better look. The oil emitted a fragrance so subtle and sweet that she felt slightly intoxicated when she touched the bottle. The glass was slippery, coated lightly with a viscous substance she assumed was the greenish-yellow liquid inside. She was overcome by a sense of calm and well being. Though she could not see roses inside the bottle, she smelled them as if they had filled the room.

She fixed her eyes on the bottle, seeing the greenish-yellow colors separate, then come together, as she had seen of the skies lately that burned over Krun.

Do you believe love comes from the heart?

This time, a woman's voice whispered in the silence and she felt herself stiffen, seeing the faint form of a tall woman in the darkness. She could not make out her body and when the woman turned to face her, she saw only flames in her face.

"Who are you?" Damascena asked, feeling afraid.

The girl's question echoed in the chamber and was followed by a long silence. Damascena covered her arms, feeling chilled despite the fire that burned inside the woman. The woman turned toward the table, illuminating the pages of the opened book that showed a series of formulas, numbers and letters connected by a series of lines that formed honeycombs and other geometric shapes.

"What is it?" Damascena whispered.

The woman of fire said nothing but reached down and handed the opened book to Damascena. It was a large book, bigger than any she had ever seen in the monastery. She expected it to be heavy, but as soon as she touched it, the weight of the book lifted and she noticed the pages were suddenly blank.

She looked at her arms, down her chest, at her legs, feet and hands, seeing numbers floating off the pages and transferring themselves to her body like falling snow. When the numbers had settled, the book dissolved and the woman of fire disappeared, leaving Damascena alone in the rose field, arms outstretched, right palm skyward, left hand pointing down to the earth, her body moving in circles, dancing like Shams.

Damascena traveled a second time that night, moving in circles in the rose field. When she opened her eyes, she expected to see the woman of fire, but instead looked at another woman entirely, a girl a few years older than herself, with huge luminous jade-colored eyes and shiny black hair that fell past her shoulders to her waist. She was only slightly taller than Damascena, with olive skin. She wore a simple dress made of linen. The sleeves were torn and bloodstained, as if the young woman had been attacked, though her posture defied any trauma. She stood poised, eyes lifted to the sky, hands clasped in prayer, lips muttering words Damascena could not understand.

She stood in the middle of a dusty road in an unknown city filled with frantic people running toward the gates, leading camels packed with rugs and candle sticks, oil lamps and salt bags. The city was built of clay with ramparts and many gates. Though she had never seen a castle, she sensed the massive structure in the background near the domed building covered with bright green tiles was the home of a queen or king.

She smelled the tang of horses and men. A group of dark bearded soldiers wearing black turbans on their heads, encircled the praying girl on horses. Damascena did not understand the language that the girl or the soldiers were speaking. It sounded like two distinct tongues, but she could read their faces and understood the soldiers' words conveyed rage and vengeance. They were frothing at the mouth, spitting at the praying girl, some whistling, some clapping, others hissing like cats.

The girl remained still, eyes heavenward, hands clasped. She seemed fearless in the face of these mounted men, though Damascena glimpsed the sweat running down the girl's neck. Damascena heard the girl's heart pounding, but realized it was her own.

She wanted the praying girl to lower her eyes and see these men, burst through the circle and run, but she stood silent, relentless in her faith, as if to protest the terror they wished to evoke in her and everyone else fleeing the city.

Damascena stood inches from one of the horses, a huge black and dusty stallion whose coat lay matted beneath the saddle. The stallion lifted its hoof and stamped the ground, landing on Damascena's foot, but she felt no pain. She looked down and noticed her foot had disappeared inside the horse's hoof as if she had become part of it.

She reached out slowly with her hand and touched the horse's leg, seeing she could plunge herself into the horse just as easily. She reached out with her other hand and did the same to the soldier's leg, touching him lightly on the calf, feeling the knife blade tucked inside his boot. He remained in his saddle, paying no attention to Damascena.

"Leave her!" she shouted, but he did not look at her and instead seemed even more intensely focused on the praying girl.

Damascena called out to the praying girl, "Run!" but she did not turn.

She called out to the woman of fire. "I want to go home!"

"You have just returned," the woman of fire called back, but Damascena could not trace the voice to any face in the crowd. Everything moved so quickly outside the circle of mounted soldiers. Dust kicked up by stampeding horses blurred her vision and made her cough. She didn't know why she was there or how. She didn't know what was worse: staring at the fires blazing over Krun or the drama playing out before her.

The longer the praying girl stayed still, the more the soldiers inched closer to her, impatient, wielding knives and swords and threatening words. She clasped her hands so tightly now they trembled and slid apart momentarily, revealing a small mound of what appeared to be dark red beads. One fell by the praying girl's feet, but she did not shift her eyes to look or move to pick it up.

The bead looked oddly familiar to Damascena. She crouched down and palmed it, realizing that what she held was no bead at all, but a rosehip. She glanced at the praying girl, wondering what she was doing with roses and what she knew of the flowers or of Shams. The girl prayed louder, faster, swaying on her feet, tears streaming down her cheeks leaving streaks of dirt where there had been dried blood.

Damascena noticed a boy her age watching from across the street. He stood with a tall, distinguished looking man, presumably his father, and his mother and siblings who moved quickly, carrying small sacks over their shoulders. The father continued to glance over his shoulder, hearing his name called over and over by the fleeing crowd, *Bahauddin! Bahauddin!*

The voices grew louder and shriller with the advancing Mongol soldiers churning up terror in the dusty city. The man kept turning his head, as if he did not trust anyone at his back, even those desperate for his attention. He seemed to attract as much attention as the Mongol soldiers. Hordes of young men ran after him, pleading, "Professor, if you leave, who will guide us?" Baha ud-Din did not answer them. He glanced at his youngest son who was running toward the praying girl.

The boy rushed toward her, ignoring the stampeding horses and throngs of mounted men churning up dust. More soldiers galloped across the road and plunged swords into a family that had just then fled their home, dodging flames crawling up the door. People screamed and cried. The men ripped babies out of their mother's arms.

They hissed, spat, and unfastened waist belts. One lowered a knife to the praying girl's throat. She trembled when the blade grazed her neck, but she continued to pray.

Damascena stood between the boy and the praying girl, and watched, bewildered. She wanted to reach out and touch whatever had emboldened the girl. She smelled the boy's sweat, the fetid odor of his fear, and she coughed, hoping he might notice her, but his eyes did not move from the praying girl. Just then, Damascena felt an invisible force lift her arms and open her hands, making contact with the boy and the girl.

Damascena held the rosehip in her left hand and laid her palm upright on the boy's shoulder. With her right hand, she reached out and held the praying girl's hands and immediately felt a surge of heat in her body, radiating through her fingers. Her hands tingled, and she felt oddly at peace. She was not sure how long she would stand between the boy and girl, why she was there, or how long the feeling would last. She simply followed her instinct to stand quietly and connect them in the midst of the chaos.

Her heart had consented to open like the smallest rose bud. She felt related to these two people, and strangely to the soldiers. It was as if they were part of a larger family whose blood was made of darkness and of light; and for reasons she could not comprehend just then, the soldiers turned away from the praying girl and left her alone.

Damascena stood dumbfounded in the dust. When the circle of men dispersed, the praying girl opened her eyes—two luminous jade discs, blinking at the daylight. She looked directly into Damascena eyes and smiled.

"Do not make your mother wait," she said to the boy. She parted her hands and showed him the rosehips, and he swooped to the ground to collect one that had fallen.

"Know it is God's," the praying girl said.

The boy kissed it and dropped it in his pocket, than ran back to meet his mother, who had crossed to the middle of the road. She took him by the arm and led him through the city gates. He offered up his apology with an open hand, showing her the rosehip.

SEVEN

Damascena woke feverish. Her cheeks burned and her back ached from sleeping on her side all night. Her hands were clasped in prayer. She held them up to the sun as if they were the wings of ravens that needed warmth to spread and fly. After a moment, she pushed herself off the wet ground. She breathed in the sweetness of the roses, petals sparkling with morning dew. Her head felt heavy, filled with the weight of dreams.

Damascena knew what she needed to do. She focused on the rose field to regain her balance then walked toward the springhouse where Shams was waiting. He sat on a small stool by the door and held out a cup of tea and a bowl of steamed mushrooms.

"Happy birthday," he said and smiled.

It was the sixth day of the sixth month. She took the tea and drank it without stopping as if to swallow the bitter truth that she had turned thirteen and had still not met her mother. "I feel ancient," she said. "But I am only thirteen."

"Maybe you have lived a thousand lives," Shams said and smiled.

"Perhaps that is required to turn roses into oil," she said and opened the doors of the springhouse. She knelt at the threshold, facing the floor to ceiling pile of rose petals, fully understanding the point of her labor.

"Oil?" Shams asked. "Oil is meant for lamps."

Damascena scratched her head. The notion still sounded strange to her. The instructions involved a process using steam distillation to extract the oil from the rose petals by placing them in water, heating the water to create steam, and collecting and condensing the steam. It was not complicated but it did require faith. Her hands trembled and her chest tightened seeing the flames rise up around the still.

"This oil is not for lamps," she said. "But it will bring light."

Shams stood and pulled Damascena to her feet. He clutched the girl's shoulders. Her face glowed, radiating joy and new determination.

"Of what light do you speak?" he asked, trying his best to act ignorant.

Damascena gripped the old man's papery wrist and whispered. "The light that shows God's face."

Damascena had never intended to lay waste to the rose fields she had come to love; and she felt the lump growing in her throat every time she set more logs on the fire. She had known no greater pleasure than watching the first blossoms unfurl, but now she felt the agony of loss in the wake of their destruction. Daunted, she sat with her knees to her chest, breathing in the sweet rose steam, eyes cast on the flames, listening to the whispered words in vapors.

> *Only from the Heart*
> *Can you reach the Sky,*
> *The rose of Glory*
> *Can only be raised in the Heart*

She cried out in the darkness.

"Who speaks such words? Show me your face!"

She knew not to look for Shams. It had never been his voice

whispering to her. She waited for a response, hearing nothing but the crackling of the fire, the hiss of steam, the pulsing of blood in her ears. She tried reverence and bowed her head like the praying girl, hoping God would hear her words.

"Why have you chosen me? I did not choose to learn this!" she cried, though the woman of fire had made it clear that the book had been opened for her alone. She wished she had been like other girls, illiterate and safe without her visions.

There was nothing glorious about the death of roses. She crouched and faced the flames, stoking the fire with a stick. She curled her hands into fists and buried her face, hoping Shams would not hear her cry.

"Forgive me!" she wailed. "I do not know why you must suffer."

The whispered words plagued her again. *Garden of miracles, what kind of garden are you? A garden neither autumn nor winter makes afraid.* But she was very afraid.

The fire that burned in the springhouse did not coat the skies with soot. Instead, the most delicate scent filled the valley and was thought to herald holy spirits. The people who had emerged from the taverns that day spoke of the angels they saw in the sky. Dark angels, light angels, angels without wings, angels whirling in circles and whipping themselves into frothy clouds. They took it as an omen that the inquisitors had stopped burning suspected witches; and their hearts fluttered with the hope that Damascena would return to the market.

They mashed barley and made porridge with a giddiness they had not known since the girl first brought her roses to Krun. In bed, with their spouses, they reminisced about their honeymoons with longing, and revived the union that the roses had inspired. For a few hours on the sixth day of the sixth month, the skies looked lighter and brighter.

June sixth. The Day of Roses. To most everyone other than Damascena, the sixth day of the sixth month was indeed a day to celebrate, and so they set out to gather in the taverns for bread and beer and home-made cheese, raising their mugs to Damascena, the girl who had once walked in feces but with roses could clear the smoke from their skies.

Damascena would have liked to join them. Not to celebrate, but to remind them that she was no miracle worker. A day after the still had cooled and the last roses had been drowned with water, she tried to make sense of the result: a greenish-yellow oil that had floated to the surface of the distilled rose water and filled a glass tube no longer than her thumb. She stared dumbfounded at the oil, trying to find the logic. *Four tons* of rose petals had produced no more than one kilo of rose oil.

Surely there had been a mistake. Perhaps she had misinterpreted the instructions, but what could she do now? The roses were gone. And she was still without a mother.

"Shams!" she cried out, again and again. She waited, but he did not come.

She felt like a fool and did not hide her disappointment. She sulked. She cried. She raged. She kicked the door. Broke furniture. Hacked the wooden table into splinters, then her bed, and when there was nothing left to destroy in the white house, she took the bottle of rose oil and walked to Krun, craving the company of a friend she could trust.

Damascena entered an empty town. Only chickens wandered the streets, casting small shadows over the cobbles, now blackened with soot. The great Krun fire had burned for seven days and left patches in the thatched roofs like little windows where the sun burned through, revealing hearths left unattended, tables unoccupied, chairs bare.

If it weren't for the baby swinging alone in a hammock spanning two mature oak trees, Damascena would have believed the town had been deserted. The baby pawed the netting as if to greet the girl and she waved back, wondering where everyone was.

She heard distant clapping, the crescendo of laughter in the direction of the market, but it was not market day. She wondered if she had missed some holiday, seeing the black wreathes of an unfamiliar ritual on doors and large flocks of dark birds gathered on the rooftops in silence.

She turned down the lane to the tanner's house, following a low stone wall to the front gate. Boot prints of various sizes had stamped the muddy path, riddled with weeds and small rocks. Damascena had never seen the tanner's garden in such disarray, and she navigated past shards of glass in the footpath. She paused midway, seeing what appeared to be a broken bird's nest, but when she crouched to pick it up, her fingers froze, feeling not brittle grass, but the softness of chestnut hair that had once draped the tanner's back.

She felt a chill and looked up, hearing the flap of a raven's wings swooshing low across the yard. She could see light coming through the hole in the door where there had been a knob and a handle. She saw movement inside the house, then the eye of a face pressed against the hole staring out at her. A familiar voice spoke to her from the other side of the door. A voice both harsh and serrated, a voice that had struggled to soothe her with lullabies and lies.

"Happy belated birthday, Damascena. You didn't think I'd forget, did you?"

She had almost convinced herself that she would never hear Ivan's voice again, would never cower in its presence. But there he was in the tanner's house. Her gasp scattered the flock of ravens from the roof when Ivan opened the door.

"You didn't invite me to the celebration," he said, feigning disappointment.

"There was no celebration," she said and stared at him. His thick arms crossed his chest, fingers tapping the mounds of flesh. He had grown fat and wore a beard. She hardly recognized him.

"You look well," he said. "Tell me, is it true the roses have made you a fortune?"

She shifted awkwardly on the path. "I haven't sold any in a long time."

"Quite a pity, don't you think?"

"They were not meant to be sold," she said, fingering the rose oil in her pocket.

"Says who? You have disappointed many good people in Krun, you know."

Beads of sweat fringed her forehead and she felt the flush of blood in her cheeks.

"What are you doing here?" Her throat was dry, and her words were hard and flat.

"I've come to take you home. You are mine."

The words sent shivers down her legs. She wanted to tell him she had a home among the roses, now that she had learned to sleep on the ground and wander different worlds by leaving her body at night. She had learned to hunt morels and make a rabbit stew hearty enough to keep her belly full for a week. She would not go back to the monastery. That life had faded with the blooming of the roses, but now that they were gone, she was without a home again.

"I'm staying here," she said.

Ivan laughed. "But you are my family."

He opened his arms to her, but nothing about his posture suggested warmth or sanctity. She craned her neck to see beyond the bulk of him and into the house. She glimpsed a large rat scurrying across the floor of the front room. No sign of the tanner.

"Where is she? What did you do to her?" she asked, eyes narrowing to slits.

He scratched the tuft of rusted beard on his chin and leaned against the house.

"Trust me. I did nothing to your friend."

Damascena heard footsteps behind her and turned, seeing a small boy with dirty cheeks peering at them through the open gate. He shifted awkwardly under her gaze, holding one of the black wreathes from the doors. He looked lost and confused.

"Did anyone hurt her?" Damascena asked him, hopeful he'd know more about the tanner's whereabouts. The boy pointed to the house and wiped his eyes.

"The men with the rocks took her away."

Damascena whispered, unable to digest the gravity of his words.

"Where did they take her?"

The boy choked back a tear and ran off. Ivan fixed a smug smile on his lips. He descended the steps to the front garden, walking toward Damascena, unconcerned about the glass he crushed under his heels.

"Come with me."

He reached out to touch her shoulder but she swatted him away. He was surprised to feel the mound of muscle on her arms, the thickness of her back, the way the veins bulged in her neck just then. Damascena had grown up. He could see the woman she was to become. He studied her hands, followed the ticking of the thorn marks across her arms as if they held the clues he needed to know about the roses. The dried blood gave her an edge that he had never seen in the girl, but her wild green eyes had given way to a depth that confounded him, threatening to call his bluff at any moment.

"I will not go with you. I will stay with the tanner forever!"

He licked the spittle off his lips and looked into her eyes.

"That is not possible, my child."

She refused to capitulate. At thirteen, she was no longer a child.

"Why, because you say so? You are not my master."

He stiffened but smiled, half-amused by the girl's defiance. If he had had half the strength of will at her age, he would have never set foot in the monastery; however, he was certain that he would win the battle with Damascena today. He walked past her to open the gate and delivered the words with force, savoring their intensity.

"No," he said. "Because the tanner is dead."

EIGHT

Nothing about the market looked familiar other than the crowd pressed into the square. There were no stalls aside from a few wooden carts on the fringes selling beer. Small children stood hidden behind their mothers' legs, grasping the corners of aprons and skirts with clenched fists as if to squelch their own cries. They shrank at the crescendo of the crowd, the crack of a whip from some distant quadrant in the square.

At first, Damascena thought it might have been a sporting event involving horses. She had never been to a joust but had heard an oblate speak of seeing one in the castle grounds of Veliko Turnovo where his uncle had worked as a falconer. The boy spoke of swords and knights in armor so shiny he could see his reflection in the metal.

And now, walking toward the crowd in the market square, Damascena was overwhelmed by the attention. Almost instantly, the crowd parted and an eerie silence thickened the air as Ivan led her past the onlookers. The alternating footfall of their feet on the cobblestones was the only sound. She recognized the dazed faces of her customers. Gone were the smiles and adoration. Their faces wore the shadows of the haunted now.

She caught the profile of the butcher's sons who turned away from her approach. The butcher's wife stood stiffly beside them, mouth and hands clenched. She refused to meet Damascena's eyes and lifted her chin when the girl passed, then covered her mouth with a small scarf. Damascena noticed that she and Ivan were the only ones without something to cover their mouths. She detected something foul in the air—a mix of wood smoke and rancid meat, and she doubted it had come from any tavern merriment. She turned back to Ivan who nudged her through the crush of people. Her voice broke the silence.

"What's going on?"

"I did not see the whole thing, thank God. It was enough to turn my stomach."

"Tell me what's happening here!"

A woman's voice cried out. "Run, Damascena!"

She did not run. She stood in the market square transfixed, as if the roots of the earth had conspired to pin her to the stones forever. The scene was like some crude ink painting she had seen in the tablets of bored oblates, only this one was far more obscene and surreal. Krun had never struck her as a barbaric town. Its thatched roofs and tidy wooden houses had become the stuff of nightmares.

She did not want to understand the configuration before her. Braided into the wheels of the very cart from which she had sold roses were the bruised and broken legs and arms of the tanner. Her head had been severed and sat on a platform hovering above the crowd, where men in dark hoods had gathered behind a table. One waved a gloved hand in the air, directing Damascena's gaze to the charred torso that lay on the table.

"NO!" she cried, sending her plea skywards.

Could you ever find another market like this? Where with your one rose you can buy thousands of rose gardens and with one final breath, the Divine Wind?

The whispered words swirled around her and blurred her vision. She felt dizzy and nauseous. She felt a constriction in her lungs, imagining the flames whipping around the tanner's severed torso, devouring her body and her dignity. It did not take a monk to explain the shame of dying without a proper burial, as if that was the final punishment for the tanner's transgressions, whatever they were.

Ivan rested a hand on her shoulder. It felt heavy and cold, and Damascena lifted it and flung it away. Her jaw stiffened and she fought the tears. The words felt like splinters in her throat. "Tell me they burned her after they broke her body."

Ivan pinned his shoulders back and straightened.

"The fire didn't kill her, so they decided to use the wheel."

"Only a monster could do such a thing," an old man whispered.

Damascena stood dumbstruck, absorbing Ivan's words.

"What did she do to deserve this?" she asked, fearing she knew the answer: the tanner had helped her.

No one spoke.

"Did she hurt you?" she asked the young man on her left. "Or you?" she said and spun around to the woman behind her, "Or you?" she asked the children.

"We did nothing to her! We swear, Damascena. It was the inquisitors!"

"But you did nothing to stop this?"

She pushed herself through the crowd, the surge of anger rising inside her. Hands reached out to pull her back, but she slapped them away. Sickened, she called above the crowd. "Tell me what crime she committed other than helping me!"

Nobody dared utter a word. Damascena's kirtle ripped as she pushed harder through the crowd to the stage. She looked up at the executioners, smelling the pungent iron of blood that had soaked the planks on which they stood. They shifted in her presence, whispering among themselves, exchanging words behind their hoods.

The tall one in the middle spoke. "Have you come to denounce yourself?"

"Denounce myself?" Damascena laughed, her voice edged with hysteria. She stared at the cracked leather boots on the executioners' feet and wondered which among them belonged to the tracks they'd left around the white house.

"We can offer you an easy punishment for your confession."

"Of what?"

"Anything you might have done with the tanner."

She lifted the tattered cape around her shoulders and hiked up the kirtle, revealing her legs and feet. The crowd gasped again. "I have walked in her shoes. Is that such a crime? We drank tea and talked in her garden. I received her kindness and her love."

The inquisitor pointed his finger at the girl. "You engaged with the Devil's work!"

"The Devil's work?"

"Your roses turned to blood! The butcher's wife saw it with her own eyes!"

Damascena spun around, scanning the crowd for the ham-armed woman.

"The tanner had nothing to do with that."

"Perhaps," the inquisitor said and cleared his throat.

Damascena locked eyes with the butcher's wife, feeling the rage surge.

"She sees what she wants to see. She wanted custody of me!"

"Only God is your rightful custodian. We will see to that now that the tanner is gone," he said. "It's the only consensus we've reached. We just need your admission."

"I have nothing to admit," Damascena said, eyes fixed on the butcher's wife. "And I would rather hang than give *you* my respect. You will burn in hell."

Damascena grabbed the edge of the platform and hoisted herself to the planks to stand among the executioners, drawing gasps from the growing crowd. She dug into a pocket sewn inside her skirt and pulled out the bottle of rose oil.

"I will admit to this."

The executioner beside her, a short, round man with a pointy beard, leaned forward. "What is it?" he asked.

"The oil of a rose."

"You lie," the inquisitor bellowed. "There is no such thing as rose oil! Who do you take us to be? Did you hear that citizens of Krun? The girl has not only associated herself with the accused, she lies about God's creations."

Damascena drew in a breath then covered her mouth, smelling the tanner's rotting torso. She covered her nose with her hand. "It is no lie," she said. "I destroyed my roses to make that oil."

The inquisitor sniffed the air, smelling nothing but the stench of slow death.

"And why did you destroy your roses?" he asked.

"I have boiled them down to their essence."

"Essence? What do you mean?"

"The roses let me see God," she whispered; it was the first time she had acknowledged it herself.

The crowd roared, delighted. "Let her go!"

The inquisitor shouted above the din, raising Damascena's hands and the bottle of rose oil. "The Devil's workshop still lives!"

Hisses, cries and shrieks rose to the platform. "Do not kill her!"

"You give too much credit to the Devil," Damascena said and snatched the bottle from his hand. "This is the work of God."

"Leave her alone. Please! She is a child of God! I raised her myself in the monastery on Lozen Mountain," Ivan pleaded, then looked at Damascena and whispered, "Do not say another word."

She felt Ivan's hand around her ankles and looked down. He extended a shaking finger and pointed to the small gallows behind the table, gallows that had been built for a small person, gallows whose height matched her own. The inquisitors had blocked her view. The wood was fresh and the smell of pine drifted over her when the wind blew. She dropped her head like the girl in the besieged city and mumbled prayers over the rose oil. Hearing the whispered words once again, she spoke them aloud this time, projecting her voice so the wind could carry it across the market square.

"My Face is everywhere—and all you are gazing at are roses."

She paused, waiting for the wind to shift, understanding for the first time the meaning of the whispered words. She pulled the cork stopper from the bottle of rose oil, releasing the sweet odor into the air and stood dazed with the rest of the crowd as the smell of roses wafted over the market, above the roofs, through the open windows of homes and shops, cleansing the air so distinctly of rotting flesh and smoke that not even the executioners or the inquisitors could deny its purity. Even Ivan stood there transfixed, nose tipped toward the sweet scent.

The executioner held out his hand and led the girl away from the gallows and down the wooden stairs of the platform, where the crowd parted. Damascena stood before them, eyes closed, inhaling the sweet scent thickening the air, then walked back through the crowd, sadly realizing that the tanner was right; the roses had saved her life.

A woman's cry filled the square and her words penetrated Damascena's heart.

"You are loved, Damascena! No matter what they tell you. You are loved!"

PART III

*All around the bramble field of hell
the road is roses and sweet herbs.*
—Shams of Tabriz

ONE

The beauty Ivan Balev had witnessed with the rest of Krun had not only devastated its inquisitors, it had awakened their hearts. A new myth had been decreed from the heavens: the girl had created rose oil so that others could see God's face. People believed the girl was a saint. Even the butcher's wife painfully pleaded forgiveness.

Ivan could not have been more thrilled. Living saints, no matter how contested, were a boon to an ailing monastery. Ivan intended that no one in the country would be denied a visit with the rose girl of Krun. He planned tours as soon as he could return Damascena to the mountain where, he promised, she "could be that much closer to God."

Damascena stood outside the white house, detesting her dilemma. She did not trust the rose oil's lasting power on the inquisitors and was not going to risk her life waiting around Krun to find out. Returning to the monastery was the last thing she ever wanted, but living high in the mountains, above the fires and the gallows, seemed far safer. Her mind reeled, and she spat on the threshold and cursed Ivan's name, wishing that Shams would be there when she needed him.

She crossed the abandoned room to the Old Bird's walnut stump, thinking that the vision of Shams sitting there after his dance had been an illusion. She had not seen him since she left for Krun that morning. He gave no indication of his whereabouts. For all she knew, the Old Bird could have poisoned himself on the mushrooms he claimed to be hunting in the forest.

"Where are you?" she cried out in the dark. "I need your help!"

Shams had run away from home when he was a child, not much older than herself. He had left his parents forever. The cruelty struck her only in retrospect. Now, he had left *her*, and she considered the possibility that she might never see him again.

She crossed the room they had shared and closed the door behind her. She held fast to the doorknob, unable to let go, feeling a weight upon her, suddenly aware of a presence lifting her hand even though she was alone. She then heard a voice mutter, "Let go," and she believed at first Shams had come back, but when she turned, she saw Ivan standing by the peach tree, waiting for her with two mangy horses. They nudged their necks against the trunk, nosing the rotten fruit that had fallen and permeated the air with a sweet, moldy musk. Ivan mounted the larger horse, patting its matted gray mane. He pointed to the sky. Thick bands of clouds hung over the fields.

"We need to leave now if we want to make it to the Seven Lakes tonight."

"What if my teacher returns?" she asked, not believing he would.

"I have returned for you. That's all that matters now," Ivan said and pointed to his heart, though the girl did not feel any love. He beckoned to the horses. "Let's go."

She froze, unable to move toward the austerity of the monastery. She refused to believe the Heavenly Father who lived there was any more compassionate and caring than the one she knew in the song birds and the fruit trees surrounding the white house, or the deer that visited each morning. She liked the warmer weather in the valley. She had grown used to sleeping on the ground, preferring it to a bed, and did not wish to readjust to cold wooden beds or the rigidity of the monks and their constant philosophizing. They would be no match for everything she had learned from Shams, and she would miss him, too. If she left now, she would be leaving a part of herself in the rose fields, the part that had once trusted she would find her mother there one day.

She did not object to leaving the white house after all; she objected to living with Ivan again. She narrowed her eyes, hating him, and met his cold stare.

"I will go with you," she said. "On two conditions."

"And what might those conditions be?"

"I want to live alone and I want a lock on my door."

"For what? Thieves? Should I remind you that you're returning to God's house?"

She straightened.

"Should I remind you that you violated God's house?"

"And I have paid my repentance. I've changed since you have left."

"So have I."

Ivan drew in a sharp breath, fighting the urge to strike her. Getting her back to the monastery would be no simple task. She had taught him patience in her infancy; now she was teaching him compromise. He was sure God had chosen him to bring her back to the church, and for the first time in his life, he had not resisted the duty. He was already thirty-one and could not afford to destroy this last chance to redeem himself.

"Agreed. I can arrange for a lock."

"And I want a garden."

"We have a garden. That's three conditions."
She pointed to the rose fields.
"You will transport every rose bush to the mountain."
"But you cannot grow a rose in those conditions."
"I can grow roses anywhere."
"But they will die in the snow."
"They *will* die. Of that, I am certain. They will die when they meet the fire," she said, pointing into the stills beyond the springhouse door.
"You plan to make rose oil at the monastery?"
"Yes," she said, "God has willed it."

Ivan named June sixth, Saint Damascena Day, and delegated a team of scribes to invite anyone needing a miracle to visit the girl throughout the year. The abbot appointed Ivan as his assistant, rescinding any judgment of his prior behavior, believing this was Ivan's unique way of seeking redemption. Half the monks had left after the oblate's death and the artisans and craftsman refused to return, believing the monastery was haunted. It had fallen into disrepair. Damascena's return promised to revitalize the decrepit place.

Soon, appointments and meetings filled Ivan's days. At night, rather than attend vespers, he deliberated over his plan to capitalize on the roses. Even if he didn't believe the girl and her roses were God's gift, others did, and that, he believed, would restore the monastery's reputation and make him a very rich man.

The monks took notice, too, and responded to the power he now possessed being the girl's "rightful" custodian, inviting him into their card games and chess tournaments. He declined; he had other games to consider. What Ivan Balev lacked in piety, he possessed in politics, and for the first time, he flourished under the abbot's tutelage.

Despite rumors of divine intervention, Damascena did not feel like a saint. She felt like a weary, exhausted girl. She searched everywhere for the stork but found no evidence it had ever lived at the monastery, not even a fallen feather to comfort her.

The bird of her childhood, the bird that sat perched on the edge of the window looking in at her while she lay in her crib, had only been a figment of her imagination. It's not as if she could have asked Ivan or anyone else to look after it when she left. The bird was not hers to possess, only roses were and she needed them now.

She was sad to have left the white house. She was sad that the roses were gone. Most of all, she was sad that the tanner was gone. Even months after she had stepped away from the gallows, the vision of the charred torso haunted her. She could not look at a wheel without thinking of the tanner. On windy days, she swore she heard the tanner's anguished howl echo off the mountains and she'd slip into a depression for days.

She slept with the curtains drawn, waking in fits of sweat, hearing strains of the monks' chanting. The clanging of the bell in the chapel made her shudder and the acrid smells of fried liver from the rectory churned her stomach. She missed the peach trees and pears and the walnuts that had sustained her. Grief, she thought, was the great thief that stole appetites and spirits. She had never felt more alone.

Returning to the monastery was not what Damascena had in mind for doing God's work, even if her life had been spared.

Ivan encouraged her to cast off her worries, telling her to relax and enjoy her new role.

"But I'm not performing any miracles," she said, looking into the floor length mirror that the abbot had installed in her room as a welcome home gift. Ivan crouched before her on the stone floor, stitching up the holes in her dress. He promised the abbot he would keep her presentable, though she refused to cut the matted locks from her hair. They smelled of roses and dirt, and they were the only things that comforted her now.

"That's the point," Ivan said, speaking with a needle in his mouth. He held the hem of her kirtle between his fingers and let it out. The girl was growing in every way.

"What point?"

"Everyone believes you will. *Anticipation* is what keeps them coming."

"Then they are fools."

"Those fools are keeping a roof over your head."

"Then I want to sleep outside."

"Then you are the fool." Ivan looked up from the floor and yanked on her skirt. "If I were you, I would be happy to have so many people like me, lest you forget the gallows others once made for you. Do not disappoint these people. Embrace the pilgrims as if they are your family."

She caught his gaze. "What family is that?"

Damascena had never met a pilgrim before, and had a hard time believing the droves of people visiting the monastery each week had risked life and limb to see her. One night, after sitting in the chapel and staring at the woman in the stained glass, she found a bowl of apples outside her door with a note.

Keep up the great work, Your Friend, Ivan.

She did not recognize the handwriting. She had never seen Ivan hold a pen or a pot of ink. She asked him the next morning in the rectory what he meant by work.

He was in the middle of a cup of tea and put it down, perturbed. "Work? I never said you're working."

She held out the note, pointed to the word.

"Right here. W-O-R-K," she said, her finger following the dips and curves of the Cyrillic. It would have been easier to write in Latin. Ivan turned toward the young oblates sitting at the next table, his face deepening into a jam red, fully abashed. He kicked the table leg hard, loosening the joint, eliciting terror in the boys.

Damascena looked at them, but they stared into their bowls. She turned to Ivan, waiting for an answer.

Ivan shifted uncomfortably and wiped the corners of his mouth with his napkin. "I meant you're being saintly," he said and patted the top of her shoulder twice as if she was a dog. She flinched.

"But I just sit there. I do nothing."

"Because you choose to do nothing. You are the first reluctant saint," he told her.

"Is there such a thing as a reluctant saint?"

Ivan looked up and smiled. "Yes. I wanted nothing to do with you the day you were born, but I managed to get over it, and look where we are now! At least God's granted me this one clemency. We've come a long way, haven't we?"

"I guess God *is* merciful," she said, sarcastically, forcing herself to believe that the distance two people traveled in tolerating each other was something to be celebrated.

Ivan motioned for the girl to eat. "You'll need strength today. Two tours are coming before lunch. One before vespers," he said, offering her the rest of his porridge and half an apple.

"You see? It all works out in the end. This is God's plan."

Damascena could not understand Ivan's jubilance. His sudden interest in her felt forced and awkward. She felt no comfort in the ways he had accommodated her since they had met again, and she waited patiently, day after day, for the team of laborers Ivan had hired to dig up what was left of the roses and transport them to the monastery on the backs of donkeys. He reminded her then of the extra effort he had put into the task.

"We have wrapped the roots with silk at your request."

She watched his face, searching for any twitch of a lie. He was serious. She was stunned he had been so thorough. The words crawled slowly up her throat.

"Thank you, Ivan," she said, but her breath felt cold and heavy.

He nodded, satisfied. "Do not forget what I do for you."

TWO

And now he gave her an audience. Damascena wondered what the pilgrims saw, if they could feel the struggle in her heart, if they knew that the 'girl saint' was cursing God while they filled Ivan's pockets with coins. She could overhear Ivan, his voice carrying through the transept with a chilling wind, telling the latest arrivals that the girl had been born on the chapel floor. He embellished his role in her birth each time he told the story.

She asked him about it at dinner the next week.

"Why have you waited my whole life to tell the story of my birth to strangers?"

"Because they are paying for intimate details."

"Did you tell them you destroyed my mother's letters?"

He turned to her, indignant, his face measuring disgust.

"You have your story wrong. I know the right story."

With each iteration, he remembered more details and fully exploited them, careful to omit the part about the newborn flying around with what he believed to be the Devil. He could not afford to lose any wages by sharing the complete truth of what happened.

One day, when Damascena had had enough of feeling like a caged animal on display in the chapel, she snapped in Ivan's presence.

"Did you tell them you lied about my mother?"

A few pilgrims gasped, hearing her speak for the first time.

Ivan lowered his chin and glared, stepping toward Damascena.

"One more word out of you and you will *never* see your precious roses."

She stiffened, then whispered, sensing her voice had made the pilgrims uneasy.

"I will leave and end this charade if the roses don't come soon!" she said, glaring at Ivan. "Don't you know I am not performing miracles? I never have. Give them their money back."

"Enough!" Ivan hissed.

Her words had condemned the merry band of pilgrims to self-conscious stillness, and they scattered to the latrines, to the rectory for a cup of tea, feigning interest in the architecture of the monastery, though the girl had been the whole point of their journey.

Ivan ran into the rectory after his guests. "Please, forgive her. She is tired."

He did not pay notice to the pilgrim who had stepped away from the group into the chapel and approached Damascena. He was tall with a square jaw and sleek nose, and the girl felt her neck burn when he smiled at her. He was a few years older than Ivan, mid-thirties, but his eyes shone with a boyish glint.

"Do you know about your mother?" he whispered, sliding into the pew beside her. Damascena stiffened. He smelled of pine and she could see the resin encrusted on his knuckles that shone like gold, wondering about his line of work. She did not feel comfortable discussing her mother with anyone, let alone a stranger.

"I know I had a mother," she said, feeling conflicted.

"You still do. She saw you recently," he said, alarmed by her terseness.

"When? Where?"

"In Krun. In the market. It was her voice that called out to you when you left."

You are loved, Damascena. The words had filled her with hope, but she had never once imagined they were from her own flesh and blood. For a split second, she was bewitched by the memory, pinioned between the desire for it to be true and the dismay at realizing it *was* true. Her mother had seen her, heard her, spoke to her—but she had still not seen her mother's face.

"How do you know this?"

"I was standing beside her."

Her mind raced with questions, overwhelmed by her mother's proximity.

"What was she doing there?"

"She came to get you."

"How do you know this?" Damascena asked again.

"She visited my cousin," he said, and his voice fell away. "The tanner."

"I am sorry," she said and cast her eyes on the back of the pews.

The pilgrim reached out to take her hand, but she pulled away and wiped her eyes.

"We are all sorry about her passing but she lived her life with purpose. I am here to do what she would have done for you," he said and peeled back layers of oilcloth to reach into his vest and pull out a scroll sealed with reddish-black wax as dark as blood.

"Your mother asked for this to be delivered to you. She has news."

"Of what?" the girl whispered, body trembling. "Why didn't she deliver it herself? Where is she now?"

"Somewhere outside Krun. After she saw what happened to my cousin, she did not want to identify herself and risk having you both killed."

Damascena stared at the scroll, terrified.

"I do not want it," she said and turned away from the pilgrim, craning her head to see if Ivan was watching, remembering the calamity of the last time someone held a letter from her mother. "Take it back."

"No. I promised not to leave until you took the letter in your own hands."

"You promised her?" she said, hearing the hitch in her voice, then cleared her throat. "What does my mother know of keeping promises?"

The pilgrim looked away from her and wiped the corner of his eyes.

"Please, just go. Just leave me alone."

The pilgrim laid the scroll in her lap, closed his vest and stood, readjusting the collar of his oilcloth coat. "Please, do as she says. She is not expecting you to respond now. She just wants you to know—" He caught himself and stopped the flood of words.

"Know *what*?" she cried. "What does she want me to know?"

The pilgrim turned one last time before leaving, but said nothing.

Damascena did not sleep. She did not eat. She feigned croup, coughing so hard and so loud that the muscles in her stomach spasmed involuntarily whenever Ivan came knocking to check on her, trying to rouse her to cure the hordes of pilgrims who arrived with suffering in their hearts and heads. She could not help them. She wanted silence and to sit in her room and read under the light of a half moon.

2 June, 1269 Ano Domini ...

She paused, wondering why it had taken so long for the letter to arrive.

My dear Damascena,

You probably expected this to be from your mother, but it is I, your grandmother, who must communicate with you now as I fear we will not meet in this lifetime. When I was your age, the Mongols came to destroy my city and I prayed for a better future. I refused to let them terrorize me, and I trusted God to deliver me, and he did, but I sense my days are limited now. Before I pass into the next life, I wanted you to know who I am so that you can know whom your mother is, and who you are.

One day you will learn my story and know it was not your mother's choice to give birth and leave you at the monastery. It is I who had the vision; I am certain you already know this. She has been writing to you, and weeping, every day since you have been born. Nothing I could have said or done consoled her, other than the fact that you were alive.

Your mother is a kindly woman, bright, of healthy disposition and yet what she passed to you through her body has been the source of darkness for many generations of women in our family. We share the bloodline of the rose, which is why your mother wore rose hips around her neck when she carried you and when she gave birth. She did what she was told and instructed Ivan to plant them on the first full moon after your birth. The roses were meant to protect you, as they are to protect each of us who know the secret.

I trust you will understand all of this, or perhaps you already do. May you know the way of the rose by staying rooted deep in the earth and showered in bright light. May you faithfully guard the secret of the rose and its fortune. Share it only with those who fully understand, honor and respect the powers given to you. And no matter what pain you still carry, I pray that you may honor me by finding a way back to your mother.

With love and blessings,
Your Grandmother

Damascena's fingers trembled and she wiped her eyes, aware of the pilgrims gathered outside her window watching, faces pressed against the small pane of glass. She drew in a breath and got up from the bed, then crossed the room and opened the door, blinded by darkness. She was ready to hear *their* prayers and cries, for it was her grandmother's request that she feared she would never be able to fulfill.

THREE

Now more than ever, Damascena longed for Shams. She missed his dancing. She missed his companionship. She even missed his riddles. Now that she had neither his protection nor the roses, she found herself unable to sleep and sought comfort in the chapel late at night, making small circles with her steps that resembled the old man's whirling, hoping to summon him in some way.

She had read the letter over and over, pausing to consider the date, June 2. She wondered if her grandmother had passed yet, and if she had done so before or after her birthday. She traced the handwriting with her finger, trying to feel the presence of her grandmother's blood and flesh, as if its detection would prove her mother to be true.

Damascena was no more ready to find her mother than she was ready to perform the miracles Ivan expected of her. Pilgrims from as far as Greece had traveled through the Rhodope and Rila Mountains to meet the girl saint. They spread tales that she cured their fevers and blisters, wounds and coughs, rheumatism and goiters, which the only other living saints Thomas Aquinas, Bonaventure, and Assisi had not done for them.

Damascena doubted she did anything to aid the ailing men and women. She simply listened to their stories and recounted their symptoms to the cook, who had offered the monks treatments for as long as she could remember. He had always known about curing basic annoyances like common headaches and sore throats. Once he fixed her toothache by mixing vinegar, olive oil, and sulfur, then rubbing it over her diseased gum and tooth. He said he had wished someone had taught him the recipe when he was her age and rolled back his cracked lips to reveal black and rotted teeth.

When she complained of the taste, he laughed.

"You don't want the alternative treatment," he said.

"What's that?"

The cook grimaced and wiped his hand across his mouth as if he had tasted a putrid and fetid thing. He went on to describe a procedure involving a mixture of mutton fat, the seed of sea holly, and fire. "You simply coat the bad tooth then hold the flame up, like this." He demonstrated by pulling the candle toward his mouth.

Damascena flinched, wide-eyed.

"Won't you burn yourself?"

"There's always a risk, yes. That's the point. The worms living inside the tooth don't like the heat and they'll come out. You have to catch them in a bowl of water."

Damascena refrained from the most offensive substances commonly used to treat ailments, preferring herbal remedies over any combination of urine, animal feces, and powdered earthworms believed to cure simple illnesses.

"This mixture is no miracle," she said, mixing up the vinegar and oil for a group of young men who hadn't slept in weeks, complaining of severe mouth pains that drove them to drink so much that one died of liver failure on his way to meet the girl saint.

"But it is! Call it what you want. We will call it what it is," they proclaimed.

They found instant relief and implored her to do more, pointing out their sore backs, strained necks, and sprained ankles. "You've climbed a mountain to be with me," she reminded them. "All you need is a good night's rest. And sleep is *God's* gift."

She did not want to be associated with the miraculous cures of the Virgin Mother, already fearing the stories spewing from the pilgrims' lips. Apparently, more than a century earlier, a man in France had his foot amputated to spare him from a certain cancer ravaging the country. He had hobbled into a cathedral to pray to the Virgin and fell asleep, only to wake up and see that his foot had been restored and he could walk.

"I can't part seas," she emphasized. "And I can't bring the dead back to life."

But one night, she woke to the murmuring of more pilgrims and Ivan's voice at her door. "Get dressed. They've come all the way from Constantinople!"

She sat up, alarmed. "Where?"

"The city of magic carpets. Sultans and fig trees! It is a splendid place."

"Why have they come so far?"

"Most people will do anything to meet you," he assured her, unsympathetic to her lack of sleep and the sorrow dampening her eyes. She had shrunken to almost nothing and the monks had begun to call her Bird Legs behind closed doors. Ivan didn't mind the hair she was losing. He loathed the matted locks of hair, wanting to hack them off.

"Get dressed and meet your guests with a smile."

"I'm tired," she said, her voice groggy and stiff from the cold air coming down from the mountain. "Can't I meet them in the morning?"

Ivan stood at the door and turned on his heels.

"This is not a role of convenience. Saints serve when they are needed. Get up!"

She swung her legs over the edge of the bed and rubbed her eyes, wondering what time it was. She could hardly see her feet to put on socks and shoes. She blew on her hand, smelling the metallic odor of sleep in her mouth, tasting blood from the cough. It perplexed her that nobody had questioned her legitimacy when she hadn't even cured herself. She wondered how much longer she could go on playing this role before it actually killed her. She knew her spirit was dying without the roses, and nothing about the coming summer and the promise of the sun made her any more hopeful.

She pulled her wool cloak tight around her and stumbled to the door, opening it slowly. When her eyes adjusted, she saw a stork that lay twitching outside her door.

She looked at the pilgrims for an explanation.

"It fell from the sky like a star!" they said and told her they'd been waiting for her to awaken and do something to assist the poor creature.

Damascena recognized the stork instantly. Its eyes appeared strangely opaque in the moonlight. They were familiar eyes, moon-like and haunting, and when she got on her knees to look closer, she shuddered, seeing the eyes of Shams.

"Old Bird," she cried and stroked the bird's head, hardly believing this could be true. *You've come back to me,* she thought. *You never left.* The stork lay on its side twitching, breast blood-soaked and matted, tail feathers missing, left wing broken and dangling as if from a hinge. She felt the eyes of the pilgrims, waiting for her to heal it.

She was freezing and stuffed her hand into her pocket, feeling the smooth glass of the bottle of rose oil, the only thing she had brought with her from Krun. She didn't put much more thought into pulling it out and opening it than clearing the air of the putrid stench of travel-weary pilgrims and whatever sickness had ravaged the bird. She simply waved the bottle over the bird's head, waiting for a response. It stopped twitching and lifted its head, astonishing the crowd when Damascena spilled a few drops of the golden liquid onto the bird's broken wing. The scent of roses had transfixed the pilgrims so much that only a few saw the bird's wing flutter; and by the time they stopped talking, the bird had already stood and flew into the darkness as fast as it had fallen.

Damascena told herself the miracle was luck. Surely a fool could see her healing powers were as potent as the next charlatan. She had no more ability to fix a broken wing than she did to repair the scars in her heart. She wanted to tell the pilgrims their story was wrong, that everything they had seen was purely an accident, chance at best, but they had already retreated to the woods.

They returned to their villages, invigorated, boasting of the miracle they had witnessed, comparing the girl's power with the famed monk of St. Gall who used urine analysis to detect disease in the ninth century. Around knife-carved tables of darkened taverns, they swapped half-informed tales of historic healers, listening with mouths agape and frothy with beer to stories of restored health. They wagered the girl saint would be just as famous and transform the world with her rose oil. Some went as far as to speculate that Damascena could cure leprosy and bubonic plague.

Even the most skeptical avowed Damascena's powers, encouraging others to trek to the mountain monastery and see for themselves, offering to pay should they return uninspired. They would have liked to return themselves to keep living the story. And for days after the stork had fallen from the sky, they smelled roses upon waking and roused their loved ones, children included, recounting the story of the ailing stork once again.

Damascena prayed to God to cure her of this arduous role, feeling powerless over the turn of events, especially the death of the oblate and the tanner. She walked for miles to clear her head, vowing to walk until she froze and could not feel a thing.

During one such hike in late January, Damascena saw blood-covered tracks in the snow. She followed the dribbled trail, seeing the footprints converge with a jumble of boot prints leading to a small open-aired shepherds' hut, overtaken by Mongol troops. They filled their mouths with flasks of drink and foul words. They stuttered, drunken and stared at her, lifting limp fingers to point at the girl as if she had been late. She wanted to run and hide but there was no way to avoid them sitting out in the open.

"What took you so long?" they moaned. There were three of them, and they sat huddled shoulder to shoulder under the thatched roof of the open-air hut.

The soldier in the middle, the injured man holding his hand over his right eye, swatted his comrades away as if to gain some kind of respect from the girl.

"You heard my prayer," he said, struggling to stand. "That is enough."

Damascena squinted in the light. "Prayer?" she said and coughed. "I have heard nothing but my own voice."

The injured man staggered toward her, then slumped in the snow at her feet.

"Then you missed the voices of many. I've been calling for you since morning."

He lifted his hand off his eye, exposing a hole. Blood oozed from the socket and tiny rivulets ran down his fingers. Beside him lay a bloodied arrow. He folded his hands in prayer and nudged the girl's knees. "Please help me see."

She stiffened and shifted, sinking deeper in the snow as heat flushed her body.

"I cannot do that."

"Why not? Are you not the girl saint?"

"I am only a girl," she said, suddenly aware she wished to be more when the soldier on the left pushed himself off the third man's shoulder and stood. He lunged at Damascena, jabbing a finger into the air near her face. He reeked of alcohol and sweat. A putrid, fetid odor of infection sprayed from his mouth.

"You lie! We have seen sketches of you," he said, lifting a matted lock. He sniffed it and flung it over her shoulder. "She certainly does not smell like a rose."

The sodden man covered his mouth and coughed.

"No, she does not. But neither do you," the injured man said.

"Shut up, you filthy beast. Let me speak to her."

The injured man turned back to Damascena, arm extended, palm up, unrolling his finger toward the girl. She flinched.

"You're afraid of us?" he asked.

She met his gaze, felt her chin quiver.

"Do not be afraid, girl," the sodden man said, interrupting. "We simply want to admire you. Forgive us, but we have never seen a saint before and you are more beautiful than they say. Everyone speaks of your miracle, but no one mentions the miracle of your face. Or your body," he said, working his way into her cloak with his hand, grazing the branches of her collarbone, winding his way around her slender neck, down her throat, cupping the small mound of flesh at her breasts. He leaned in to smell her again.

"So fresh. Like a spring lamb."

"Please, stop," Damascena whispered, surprised her voice had grown so hoarse. A raven swooped off the boughs of a pine tree and dusted them all with snow. She felt the chill on her skin but did not move to adjust her cloak. She shivered instead, feeling the man's finger pressing on the back of her neck.

"What's that?" he asked, distracted, brushing snow off her shoulders.

Damascena's voice grew even smaller. "I … said … stop."

The drunken man lifted his other hand to his ear and leaned into the wind.

"I'm sorry. But I cannot hear you. I guess you now know the disappointment of my friend when he called to you this morning after his mishap. What a shame you did not come earlier. At this point, we can assume he has lost his eye for good and any hope for his vision, since you are not the saint we thought you to be. What a pity," he said and stretched, then leaned against her hip and steadied himself on her shoulder.

Damascena closed her eyes, feeling the drunken man's fingers grip her thighs. She wanted to scream but no words came out.

"Let her go," the injured man pleaded, locking eyes with her. "She has come all this way. Let her help! Tell him you will help me. Say it is so. Be the saint you are, girl!"

She wanted him to stop hurting. She wanted to know she had the power to heal him, but she stood numb. It was one thing to heal a bird. Another to heal a man.

Suddenly, she heard the whispered words as if they had drifted in on the wind to greet her just then. *The dawn of joy has arisen and this is the moment of vision.*

The words echoed off the snowdrifts and rang in her ears.
... this is the moment of vision.

She flung the drunken man's hands off her leg and pulled the vial of rose oil out of the pocket she had sewn into her cloak, her movements jerky, reflexive. She opened the bottle and poured a single drop of rose oil into the injured man's eye socket. She repeated the whispered words, her voice oddly calm as the scent of roses overcame them.

The injured man fell silent and cowered.

"Tell me what it is you wish to see and I will try to help you," she said.

The injured man cast his good eye at the blood-streaked snow. "I do not know," he said and wept.

"That is because your head speaks. Let your heart be heard now."

The other two soldiers recoiled, cowering in the corner of the hut.

Damascena wondered who spoke through her. She sounded deep throated, recalling the demeanor of the woman of fire. Perhaps it was she who had whispered the words. The rose-sweetened air filled her with might, and she inhaled deeply and spoke again. "Tell me what you have seen that makes you want to see again?"

The injured man pounded the snow with his fists then looked up.

"I have seen nothing! Nothing of life!" he shouted, turning to his comrades. "Only darkness and blood. What more can a Mongol soldier see? If what we have seen in the killing fields is vision, then leave me to be half-blind. Forgive us the imposition we have put upon you and for the respect we did not show to a holy girl such as yourself."

He wiped the tears with the sleeve of his elbow and fisted the snow again. Damascena knelt beside him and placed a hand on his shoulder. She took his head in her hands and tilted it back once again, rubbing a few drops of rose oil in the middle of his forehead. "I cannot bring back your eye, but your vision is something else."

"Then take the other!" he cried, reaching for the bloodied arrow, but Damascena caught it.

"Is that what you want?" she asked, brandishing the arrow over her head.

The injured man stared at the girl with his good eye, suddenly ashamed.

"What kind of man will I be without eyes?"

"You do not need eyes to see God!" she cried and thrust the arrow back at him, hearing the final whispered words. "*Even a blind man can see holiness.*"

He sat kneeling, staring at her, paralyzed by the truth of her words—for in that moment, with only one eye, the man was no longer looking at the girl's face, but at God's.

FOUR

The story continued unabated for weeks. A one-eyed Mongol who saw God? No one knew which part of the story to emphasize. The soldier's one eye, his seeing God, or seeing God in the girl's face did not seem to matter to the storytellers, most of whom were monks sent by Ivan to spread the tale as far as possible. He called it a Crusade.

Even villagers who had no interest in making a pilgrimage to the monastery indulged in the rumor that Damascena would be the first girl to attend the school of medicine in Salerno. Never mind the fortune it would cost to send her there from Bulgaria, or the fact that she did not speak Italian or Greek, and would not be able to read the medical manuscripts penned there some three hundred years ago.

Ivan Balev had no intention of letting this miracle worker out of his sight. He refused to send Damascena to train as a physician at the most important university in Europe. He doubted she could tolerate the coursework: three years of study in liberal arts followed by four years of medical study with a fifth year in practical work under the supervision of a qualified physician. He did not intend to share her with anyone else.

"Please, Ivan. We beg you to reconsider. It might do her good."

The incident with the Mongols had left her dazed and withdrawn. She was withering away, refusing to eat. Concerned, the abbot called Ivan into his office and counted the proceeds from the most recent flood of pilgrims, fingering sacks of coins. The girl had earned more than enough to fund her own trip and tuition, especially after the pilgrims had paid double for seeing the stork fly.

"Maybe she will get better there," the abbot suggested.

"Do you honestly believe that is the best idea? Especially now?"

"A sheltered bay along the coast sounds more appealing than a cold mountain top to restore her health."

Ivan sniggered. "I recall you were the one who sought to help this monastery by targeting our 'saint' as the primary means of our subsidy," he said.

The abbot met his cold stare.

"Perhaps you have a better idea for helping the girl?" he said.

Ivan shrugged. "None at all. A girl like her can help herself."

"If she dies—" the abbot said, pointing a finger.

"Then she'll make this place famous. And as long as this monastery stands, every abbot and monk who lives here shall benefit by the grace of God. Amen."

Ivan smiled, exchanging a knowing look with the abbot. Infuriated, the abbot cleared his throat and stood, smoothing his robe to keep his hands from trembling.

"Damascena is not a student anymore," Ivan continued. "She is a saint and her rightful place is among God and His word here on the mountain, not among medical manuscripts scattered by," he said and spat, "Some sheltered bay by the sea."

The abbot nodded, feeling the chill in the air. "She is sick. She needs help."

Ivan wiped the spittle from his lips and beamed.

"I know. And I have the perfect cure."

Ivan stood outside Damascena's door, shifting in the cold night air. No matter how many times he had rehearsed for this moment, his heart still pounded. She was more resilient than he had thought, but he worried that the Mongols had pushed her to the edge. She had always been quiet among the monks, but her sudden despondency flustered them all, including himself. Not even the cook could engage her smile with his jokes. She left honeycombs untouched outside her door. Boiled eggs to freeze. Apples to rot.

She had grown humorless and homely, her eyes dull and void of depth. Gone was the luminosity in her gaze. She hid behind the thick coils of her hair, moving her eyes over the monks as if they had never met. Though she had tolerated Ivan in the past, she recoiled in his sight. Gone were the barbed sentences she had carried with her from Krun. Her silence unnerved him, and for once he wished to hear her voice. She seemed lost in her own thoughts, and he feared her suspicion of him.

Ivan had done his best to cover his tracks but wondered if the slingshot he had fashioned from the gut of a goat should have been burned. He had been lucky with the stork. He stood on the chapel roof and launched a piece of broken bottle from a slingshot made from entrails. He never intended to injure the creature, just render it unconscious; but he was pleased that its bloody, broken wing had enhanced the theatrics of the week. He believed the Mongol soldier incident had been divine intervention, and he'd thanked God for such a beautiful turn of events. For once, everything was aligning in his favor.

Damascena sat crossed legged in the twilight, covering her hands with her mouth, trying to stay warm, flinching when she heard the knock at her door. For days, she feared the Mongols would find her here, begging for new legs, new arms, stronger hands, cleaner spleens, ruddier cheeks and everything else they would inevitably ask her to cure. She cursed the snow and the cold for driving her indoors. Had it been spring, she would have fled the monastery forever. She heard another knock on the door.

"Go away," she said. "I'm not feeling well."

"Then open the door and you will feel better."

The sound of Ivan's voice only rattled her more.

Her head throbbed as if someone had wedged it inside a vice. It even hurt to look at the moonlight. She realized she had been holding her breath and when she exhaled, she felt a sharp pain in her lungs as if they had been filled with shards of glass.

"Time to wake up, Damascena. There's something you need to see."

She glanced up at the door, shifting her eyes to the window, seeing a raven fly by. She did not know what time it was or how long she'd stayed in her room. She simply felt exhausted and suffocated beneath the tapestry of lies he had spun around her. Her neck was stiff from the cold and her cloak was soaked from the fever that had broken.

"Do not be rude, Damascena. People are waiting for you."

She gathered her heavy cloak and carried herself to the door, and when she opened it, she felt a surge of strength in the middle of her body. She squinted not at the sun, but at the sight of the rose bushes lined up behind Ivan. Not just one, but hundreds, wrapped in silk and emitting a faint glow in the early evening sky. She staggered over the threshold, astonished to see every monk standing along the footpath, holding a rose bush in each arm; and her heart broke open again. She knelt and wept and did not stand until Ivan lifted her off the flagstones and carried her to the field that he had cleared for her.

Small mounds of dirt dotted the entire landscape. Damascena would have mistaken the depressions for graves if it weren't for the monks hovering over them, hands blackened with soil. Ivan whistled and clapped, orchestrating their work. Together they knelt by the holes they had dug and replanted each rose bush into the ground, the soil silver in the gathering light. The night air vibrated with their chanting.

Damascena had never seen anything so beautiful. She felt filled with a life force she had not known was missing and breathed in the air, invigorated by the work that lay ahead of her. She turned to Ivan, her lips trembling with the words.

"Thank you," she said.

Ivan beamed.

"You doubted you would see the roses again, didn't you?"

She lowered her head and nodded, seeking forgiveness for all the ways she had damned Ivan for failing to deliver on his promise. How could she be so cruel, she thought, and at the same time love the roses? Perhaps she ought to love Ivan, too, even if he had withheld her mother's letters. Even if he had killed a man. If a man didn't need two eyes to see God, she thought, maybe a man didn't need to be good to be loved.

"I'm sorry for doubting you," she said, feeling even smaller beside him.

"Never mind," he said and turned from her, beckoning the monks to follow him back to the monastery.

"We must leave for vespers," he said. "You stay here awhile. Keep the roses company. I know they have missed you as much as you have missed them."

Damascena felt her throat tighten and her eyes well up. She was embarrassed and quickly wiped her cheeks with the edge of her thumb. "I want to create the most beautiful garden this monastery has ever seen," she said with a determination she'd never known.

"You will do that and more," he said, finger pointed in the direction of the distillery he had built to house the copper still. "You will turn every rose into oil."

Spring had returned to the monastery grounds. Sunlight had melted the last snow and everywhere buds bejeweled the trees like pearls. The streams were full. The coffers were filling. Everything seemed to stretch into a smile. Even Ivan's mouth. Damascena, too, appeared taller and walked to her garden with such purpose each morning that the monks stopped to bow. She had developed such an appetite tending to the roses that the cook joked about a pregnancy.

"Pregnant with miracles," Ivan quipped, dancing through the kitchen, waving the latest list of reservations from those wishing to see the girl's rose garden.

"She is eating for two," the cook reported, showing the latest stack of bowls he'd collected outside her door. "Could it be another immaculate conception?"

Ivan turned to him and laughed. "Yes. And the almighty Father is a rose."

The cook handed him a flask of mead. "How old is she now?"

Ivan paused, wiping the tang of fermented honey from his lips. "She'll be fourteen in three weeks."

"Has she started bleeding?"

Ivan frowned. "No. God, no," Ivan said, having never taken into account the impending disaster.

"Don't act like it won't happen. And once it does, we ought to take precautions with the younger oblates."

"There's a lock on her door," Ivan offered, feeling displaced by the dialogue.

The cook chuckled and directed his gaze out the window, toward the garden.

"Maybe so, Ivan Balev. You know her better than any of us. I doubt Damascena will ever turn her attention away from the roses."

None of the monks could hear exactly what the girl murmured when she worked in the garden. She spent her mornings reciting words that sounded like incantations. They began to wonder if the girl was not a saint after all, but a sorcerer or mystic. She repeated the list: *tawba, mujahida, khalwa, 'uzla, taqwa, ward' zuhd, samt, khawf, raja' hizn. Hizn.*

They thought she was talking to the stork that had fallen from the sky—the stork who owed its healing to the girl and her rose oil, but they didn't see a bird or evidence of any creature that lived in the garden. Not even rabbits could penetrate the sacred space; Ivan made sure they ate plenty of stew that spring. They stared confounded by the girl's wild gesticulation and concluded she was not talking to herself. Who, they could not say, and speculated among themselves that perhaps she was losing her mind.

They argued that she worked too hard and wasn't getting enough sleep and should rest in a proper bed, indoors, at night, not on the ground beside the roses. They worried that too much exposure to the stars had caused her mind to explode. They fretted about her stability, wondering how the pilgrims might interpret her behavior. Ivan did not worry; he was pleased that the rumors of the girl saint were layered with more mystique.

No one had the audacity to interrupt Damascena while she made her garden grow. The monks could not land on the right word to describe her passion. Driven? Compelled? Obsessed? Only the most candid concluded the girl was possessed.

Ivan scheduled shifts among the monks to observe her. They stood intrigued and dumbfounded by the chapel windows where they waited for something to change and prove their theories wrong. At night, during their breaks, they talked.

Indeed, this was the Holy Spirit at work. A form of prayer. A ritual for the roses.

"Looks like she is raising the dead," they'd say.

"She did. She gave a Mongol the chance to see God."

They swapped shifts to observe her during the darkest hours of the night when she demonstrated the most peculiar behavior of all. She embraced something they could not see. She wrapped her arms around it—no wider than her own slim hips—then began to dance in circles. Not a drunken dance they would share in the village taverns. It was a dance far more sober and somber than they had ever seen. The most erudite attributed it to the Greek Dionysian mysteries, animal representation, spirit possession, or worse, purification. They worried, fearing something dark and mighty had entered Damascena.

One night in late May, Damascena noticed small halos forming around the roses when she danced in the garden. The more she twirled in circles, the brighter the light grew. Even villagers from as far as Krun claimed they could see the monastery on the mountain in the dark like a star.

"Old Bird!" she cried, seeing only fragments in the dark, half-man, half-bird, soaring over the roses. She paused, rubbed her eyes, wondering if she was tired.

She resumed her dancing but as soon as she lifted her hands to the sky, she smelled the sweet, musky scent.

"Shams," she said, incredulous, when he appeared in the garden.

He stood in the moonlight and bowed to her, slowly, reverently.

"Damascena," he whispered and withdrew his hood, staring at her with the eyes of the fallen stork. My God, she thought. The monks are right. I *am* losing my mind, but she wondered why his long absence had only made him appear more real now.

She stared at the papery skin on his arms and wrists. He looked older than ever. His robe had become threadbare and the hollows of his cheeks looked like the scooped out halves of a winter squash. She reached out and ran her finger down his arms and took his fingers into hers. She did not mind that they were cold. She curled them into hers and pressed them against her lips, seeing just then a flash of light from inside his robe.

"It is you, isn't it?"

He nodded and wiped the tear from her cheek.

"I missed you."

"And I, you. But I had important matters to tend to."

"Another assignment?"

Shams smiled and laughed. "Yes. You remember."

"Where did you go?"

"To visit my friend."

She met his gaze, seeing the reflection of stars in his eyes.

"You went to see Rumi."

"Yes," he said, sparing her the details of his visit.

"Where is he?"

"In Konya. Far from here."

"Is that why you took so long?" she asked, then reconsidered. "Is he sick?"

"He suffers a broken heart and is old," Shams said and sighed, gazing at the sky.

"Is he going to die soon?" she asked.

Shams stiffened.

"Soon enough. I'm sure even death is not fast enough for him at times."

"He wants to die?"

Shams shook his head. "Yes. The part of him that is sad."

Damascena wanted to tell him about her latest doubts about God, and her dream with the praying girl. She only said, "Maybe I am already friends with Rumi."

"Why do you say that?"

"Because I'd like the sad parts in me to die, too."

Shams studied the girl in the half-light of the stars.

"Then I am certain they will."

Damascena could not believe no one else could see Shams. She wondered if the monks chose to ignore the old man because he was the only person she talked to. They were jealous of her companionship. How sad, she thought.

She wondered if perhaps Shams had offered even one dull coin for his lodging, they would share the same hospitality they offered to strangers, but he required nothing of them. He did not eat their food. He slept outside. He had no need other than to keep the girl company and manage the fire burning within her. Shams was her teacher, she had told them. He deserved to be respected. She had grown increasingly frustrated when his greetings fell on deaf ears and his arm remained extended, unmet by the monks.

"Monks do not admire those who call themselves teacher," Shams had told her the first night he'd arrived, unmet by a single brother. "Please do not be upset with them."

But she was. She wanted to spit on the stones they walked on. And she told him.

"What good will that do? You will only have wet stones."

"Yes. Better for them to slip."

"But it is you who might end up slipping and falling. A mystic would be wiser."

It was the first time she had smiled since he met her in the field.

"So I am a mystic now?" she asked and laughed. "First, I am a witch. Then a saint. Then a saint who performs miracles. Did you know that's what they say? In every village, the story is the same."

Shams scratched the stubble on his chin.

"Appearances can be deceiving. You of all people know this."

She nodded, silencing her anger, when a few young oblates passed in the field, literally grazing the old man's arm. For a moment, it looked like they had walked through him, but Damascena attributed it to the glare from the sun.

"Why don't they see you?" she asked.

"They see what they want to see. Just like you."

She stared at his robe, the flash of lightning in the threads.

FIVE

Damascena tolerated the pilgrims who traipsed through the garden, relieved to no longer be the focus of their attention. Yes, they still considered her saintly, but the garden itself was the miracle they had come to see, even before her roses had bloomed that year. They asked her how she had come to make roses grow in such challenging conditions.

"I have a great teacher. A master gardener," she'd say, pointing her finger in the direction of Shams, who would inevitably be dancing on the perimeter or dozing under the shade of sprawling oak trees.

They stared blankly then redirected their gaze to the garden.

"Yes. The sun is a powerful force," they would say.

Damascena corrected them. "My teacher is more powerful than the sun."

"The real power is your love," Shams said one night. He lay on the ground beside Damascena, sharing a wool blanket and looked up into the moonless sky. The air was damp from a recent rain and laced with the delicate scent of roses in bloom. She would begin harvesting tomorrow, and he sensed the bittersweet end of the growing season.

"What is the point in all of this?"

"The point is to turn your grief into love. The roses are helping you find grace."

"But I can't."

"You can't or you won't? It is your choice."

She pulled the blanket around her closer, missing the tanner's embrace; and no matter how much time she spent in the garden, she could no longer bring herself to look at the woman in the rose window without feeling a sharpness in her chest.

Damascena stood beside Shams in the field the next morning, watching the assembly of monks who had risen before dawn to pick rose petals, laden with dew and full of oils. "Is this what you meant by grace?" she asked.

Shams turned to her and smiled.

The monks staggered among the bushes, waists tied with large burlap sacks that hung past their knees. Ivan distributed protective sheathes made of cracked cowhide, to protect their arms from thorns. They worked quickly, filling sacks with as many rose petals as they could before the sun rose and dried the dew. Their chanting charged the cool morning air and echoed off the mountain.

The roses needed to be picked quickly and distilled immediately if there was any oil to be extracted—and sold. If the oil had allowed a man to see God's face, what else could it do? As far as Ivan was concerned, they were sitting on a gold mine. *His* gold mine, and for once, he was grateful that Rasa had squatted on the chapel floor to give birth to his future. He would never tell anyone that he had tossed the rose hips into the snow when he was young and reckless. At least God had given him a second chance.

He prodded the monks to pick faster. Between chants, they mumbled curse words for the duty Ivan had assigned them. Then they cursed the Abbot for putting Ivan in charge, wishing just one of them had even half the skills that Ivan did with bows and arrows; even with his palsied hands, he shot enough game to keep them alive each winter. No amount of prayer could keep their storehouse full of cured meats. This, they trusted, but they doubted the gold Ivan had promised in return for their labor harvesting roses.

Damascena wanted to believe that this sudden collaboration with Ivan was indeed a gift from God. The roses had been picked; it was her responsibility to turn them into oil now. Stacks of wood had been chopped and lay ready to burn in the fire beneath the still.

Ivan appeared to be preparing for a storm, the way he had been digging trenches, designed, she believed, for the runoff from the distillery. It would take many rose petals, and much water, to turn them all into oil. With each distillation, the oil would become even purer. She recognized this from her first attempt at the white house and had impressed upon Ivan the importance of multiple distillations to obtain the highest quality rose oil. He simply shrugged.

"No one would know if it weren't the highest quality. Miracles are miracles."

"But I would know," Damascena said. "And so would God."

No use arguing with a saint, Ivan thought.

He agreed to upgrade the distillery and had overseen the construction of one far more sophisticated than what Shams had built at the white house. It had taken less than a week. Damascena had never seen Ivan so focused or organized. He waltzed around the grounds with a leather bound book, checking off lists, creating a small laboratory of sorts, complete with the original copper still and something new: an athanor that rivaled a large hearth. She wasn't sure what need she would have for such a great furnace and asked him.

"I only need to heat water," she said. "For the vapors."

Ivan nodded. "You never know what else you might need to burn."

"Maybe," Damascena said, perplexed by the complexity of it all. The springhouse was so much simpler. She simply burned wood under a still full of roses and spring water, collected the vapors, condensed them back into water, then repeated the process until she had only the green-yellow liquid of the rose oil floating on the top. She worried that people might start believing she was an alchemist, too.

When she told him, he smiled.

"Turning roses into oil is a sort of," he circled the air with his finger searching for the right word, "Botanical alchemy. There's no denying that."

She was touched by Ivan's unflagging insistence on meeting every condition she had proposed. He had even built her a small bedroom at the back of the distillery.

"I already have a bedroom," she said, curious. "And it suits me just fine."

"But this one is closer to the fire," he said. "So you can watch over it." He had handed her a key and pointed to the door.

"There's a lock."

Damascena smiled. Ivan encouraged her to try it. She opened the door and was taken by the simple elegance of the room. It had the air of a castle. Small, oil-painted icons hung on the walls; in the middle was a painting of the woman in the rose window. The bed was lined with a soft rose-colored silk duvet.

"From China," he said. "A gift from us all."

She approached the bed and ran her hand over the silky cover, feeling her throat tighten and her eyes cloud with tears. It was simply the most beautiful bed she had ever seen. "It's almost too beautiful to sleep in," she said.

Ivan flushed. "Maybe. But you will be exhausted when all of this is done."

"Yes. It's a lot of work. Thanks to you, the hardest part is over."

He met her eyes, but said nothing, then left her in the privacy of her new room, where she invited Shams to sit with her. A voice of warning sounded in her head, but she wondered if she had been too quick and harsh to judge Ivan. Perhaps Ivan's kindness was a miracle she had performed unawares. Clearly, he was devoted to the roses now and she told herself a saint would not stop that.

When the distillation started, the scent of roses filled the air above the monastery and blew down over the valley, intensifying the prophecy ascribed to Damascena. Even the oldest monks, who had been burdened by sleep and breathing troubles, were shocked to feel the current of energy running through them, as if the scent of roses had restored their vitality. They spent their days walking in the forests, absorbing its forgotten beauties, having neglected the hiking trails for years in their hermitage. Young and old spoke of seeing God between the trees, within the trees, in the clouds and in the face of the sun. The abbot, too, noticed the life force that had awakened among them.

Only Ivan Balev suffered from debilitating headaches and could not leave his room for a week. He stumbled into the rectory at night, claiming he could only see in the darkness now and that his head felt like it had been struck by an anvil.

He grumbled and swore at the cheerful oblates who looked barrel-chested beneath their robes.

"She will never have you, dogs, if that's what you're thinking."

They stopped eating and stared at him, then erupted into thunderous laughter. But the storm didn't pass and only raged within him. Each time Ivan smelled roses, his headaches turned into a constant nausea that no amount of vomiting could relieve. He sought an elixir from the cook who gave him broth and salted bread.

"Perhaps it is you who are with child," he had said, meeting Ivan's bloodshot eyes.

Ivan dry-heaved. "If I am with anything, it is the Devil!"

The scent of roses sickened him and the more it penetrated the air, the more restless he became, unable to sleep at all. Sleep deprivation gave way to hallucinations, and he started to lose his hair. He considered it a small calamity that his hands smelled of roses wherever he went, and a catastrophe that he saw Damascena's face in every monk.

He drank wine to stop the visions, but they only intensified. After emptying his flagon one night, he saw Damascena engaged in her odd dance, twirling, orbiting the transept in one perfectly calculated circle. While she danced, the stork swooped down over his head, grazing the bald patch with its claws, drawing blood.

Ivan cried, feeling the warm trickle down his forehead. The girl had stopped twirling immediately and extended her arms, reaching for the stork that glowed in the darkness. She set the stork on her shoulder and moved with it, turning slowly at first, then gaining speed until they appeared as one inside Ivan's blurry vision. He rubbed his eyes into swollen slits as the ghostly image of the girl and the stork dissolved into the mottled moonlight.

Then one night, while he walked alone on the trails, the stork flew out of a tree and startled him again, blocking his path.

"Go on, get away from me!" Ivan barked and swatted it away with his foot.

The stork jabbed the tip of its long beak into his ankle, pinning him to the ground. He cried out in pain, then thrust his arms outward, reaching for the stork's neck, and squeezed, releasing the frustration and jealousy the bird had built up in him. His head ached too much to think about the consequences of harming a stork, and while he squeezed its neck, he saw the most terrifying hallucination: the bird turned into an old man wearing a hooded robe made of lightning. Ivan let go of its neck and the old man spun, faster and faster, until he turned so fast that his feet no longer touched the ground.

There was nothing to prevent Damascena from completing her duties by the end of the distillation process, only the nagging feeling that something wasn't right.

She sat on the bed and faced Shams, feeling defeated.

"I don't trust myself," she confessed.

"Why not?"

"What if there is no oil this time? What if it was all just a fluke?"

Shams laid his hand on her shoulder. "Do you want that to be true?"

She shook her head, wiping the tears streaming down her cheek. "No," she said and looked into the Old Bird's eyes. "I am not sure my mother told the truth."

"Are these the sad parts that you wish to die?"

She nodded and leaned her head against his chest, grabbing at the light in the threads of his sleeves. "I don't want to meet her."

He reached out and stroked her cheek. "You already have," he said. "You can no more renounce your mother than I can renounce the light of the sun. I would not exist without it. Trust what gives life and ecstasy, Damascena. Do not mourn what does not exist. Embrace what does! There is power in the oil. And that power is yours to share."

"What power is that?"

"Love," he said, then left her to sleep in her new bed under the rose silk cover.

❀

Damascena awoke with chest pains and a cough. She swore she smelled something burning and when she ran to open the door, she realized the key was gone from the lock. She searched the floor in the dark, running her fingers along the bottom of the door, seeing smoke rising in the sliver of moonlight coming through the stained glass, realizing she had no way to break the leading in the window.

She pounded on the door, trying to wake the monks, but Ivan had built the distillery far from the dormitory, on the windward side of the property. Nobody would hear her no matter how hard she screamed. Her voice had grown hoarse and her throat burned with the smoke.

Her lungs heaved, gasping for air. It would be better not to breathe at all, she told herself. She would have liked to believe she was all those things everyone wanted her to be, but there was no miracle she could perform that would stop the fire in the room beside her, the room where, after seven days of tending to the cask, she had distilled all six acres of roses petals —16,000 kilos to make only four kilos of rose oil. The light in her room appeared yellow and greasy and she thought it was the oil being released into the air but she smelled no roses, only burning wood.

An explosion in the distillery startled her, and she dropped to her knees hearing the spray of shattering glass. She crawled along the floor to the wall on the other side of the furnace, feeling the heat of the flames. She felt dizzy, realizing everything that mattered now was being destroyed—strangely in her favor.

God had finally answered her prayers. She did not feel sad. She did not feel afraid. Death would be the ultimate gift of sovereignty. For a moment, she felt a sudden and unexpected relief roll through her entire body. It was her fourteenth birthday, and she was certain now that she would never meet her mother or ever have to forgive her.

Ivan stood in the rose fields with a large shovel, watching smoke pour from the chapel windows. He had doused the pews with kerosene then closed and locked the door behind him, saying goodbye to the memory of Damascena's mother, of her Devil baby and everything that had led him to this point. He could no longer take the hallucinations. The rose oil was wicked. Had he seen Satan or God in the bird? He was losing his mind and he was terrified. If his actions were despicable, God would be the judge.

He had poisoned the porridge that everyone ate for breakfast. The bodies were heavier than he thought, and he perspired so much his robe was soaked and sticking to his back. The ground was soft where the monks had dug their own graves months earlier, believing them to be trenches for the roses. He overturned the soil, wondering how he should arrange the bodies. Head to toe? Or curled around each other to give them comfort? He considered burning them in the chapel; it would have been much easier but he feared they would have sensed his corralling strategy and fled. He did not have the strength to carry the dead bodies now. Besides, he believed they deserved a proper burial.

Only when he covered the abbot with dirt did he feel sorrow, realizing he would never have a right to complain about anything after this. He had destroyed everything that had ever held him back. He was not ashamed to admit he would have wished his mother had been in the chapel. Misery loves company, he thought, and patted the soil around the abbot's head. Let this community of believers revel in their fellowship forever.

He watched the roof give way on the chapel, seeing the plume of smoke and flames bursting from the eaves. He stood and massaged his lower back, wiping the sweat off his top lip, feeling the heat at this dark hour. There was something exhilarating about watching a building as huge as the chapel burn, flames rising in the clear night, illuminating the mountains behind it. He felt a surge of relief watching the great flames devour everything he had come to hate.

Except riches. And thank God, or the Devil, he still didn't know to whom he owed his gratitude, he would never have to worry about money for the rest of his life. It was almost comic the way it had turned in his favor. First the girl, then her gift. He considered the rose oil payment for everything he had sacrificed, all the years he had looked after her, keeping her fed, clothed, schooled, and safe, most of all from her mother, that wretched woman who had started all of this.

He would start again in Konya, where the Mongols had guaranteed his safekeeping for their share of the riches. He was eager to be someone there, and happy he would be rich. When he rolled the abbot and cook into the shallow grave, it struck him that he *had* become someone—a businessman. He was creating a better future for himself and everyone who would benefit from the rose oil. He considered selling the copper still, but it was too much of a risk now that he had the rose oil in his possession. He carried the bottles to the edge of the field farthest from the fire, and buried them deep in the earth.

Ivan stopped digging to admire the color of the rose oil. He held a bottle up to the firelight. The yellow-green liquid reminded him of the color of a cat's eye, and he had to look away when he saw what appeared to be a cat staring at him through the bottle. He had seen the cat before—nailed to the tanner's front door; and he dropped it, and the cork loosened enough for some oil to spill on the ground. He coughed, feeling nauseous.

He re-corked the bottle and buried it as fast as he could, too afraid to look at the other bottles for fear of seeing something he did not want to see. Like God's face. What he saw though was more terrifying—the gleam of a small hunting knife. Startled, he turned, seeing not one, but three Mongol soldiers approach him, mouths screwed tight.

"You took us for fools!"

Ivan felt his legs go limp. "No! I saved the rose oil for all of us!"

"Traitor!" they roared and threw him on the ground while one of them forced his mouth open with a small stick, then proceeded to slice out his tongue.

It happened so fast that Ivan was not certain he had felt anything at all, wondering if this, too, had been one of his hallucinations. Only when the blood trickled down his lips and throat, when the pain of the separation struck him and he called out to God for mercy did he realize this was no hallucination. He believed he would surely bleed to death. He gasped, struggling to speak, but no words came, only a sputtering of hideous, unintelligible sound. For a moment, he floated above his body, seeing one of the Mongols running not away from the fire, but toward it. He thrust a knife into the flames, turning the blade in the heat. Then just as quickly as Ivan had left his body, he felt the searing hot blade of the knife in his mouth, cauterizing the wound. He could not make out the face of the Mongol warrior who spoke, but heard, in no uncertain terms, the fate of his plan.

"You work for us now," he said and spat into the blood pooled on the floor of Ivan's mouth. Then he joined the other Mongols to dig up every bottle of rose oil and run into the woods, leaving Ivan alone and dazed.

Ivan could not recount the time that had passed between when he had lost his tongue and the rose oil. His whole life, at least any prospect of hope, was gone. It would not be long before the Mongols returned to indenture him and he wished he had died instead. Anything would be better than the twisted fate that befell him now. He turned his gaze to the distillery, startled, hearing the door heave and crack. He thought at first the girl had survived and was pushing her way outside. If he was meant to die just then, he would have liked to see proof that the girl was indeed a saint to survive *this* fire.

But the miracle he saw was not of her doing. The stork, who had turned into an old man, appeared to be coming through the locked door—carrying Damascena's body toward him. He froze, seeing that her face, miraculously, had not been touched. Only the left side of her body had been burned, though he did not know the extent of her injuries. He trembled when the man in the hooded cloak handed him the limp body.

"Take her to Rumi. He is the only person who can heal her now."

PART IV

Come, come, whoever you are!
Wanderer, Worshipper,
Lover of Leaving,
This is not a caravan of despair.

—Jalal al-din Mevlana Rumi

ONE
Konya, Turkey 1270

For weeks, Rumi sat with the girl in silence while the smell of roses filled Konya. Rumors wound themselves through the dusty alleys and climbed over walls into gardens and storerooms, slipping into the space between tea and talk. Their master had slid into a meditation as deep as any since the day he had met Shams, the disheveled stranger with knotty, long hair who appeared on the eastern side of Alaeddin Hill on a donkey one day. People had called it the meeting point of two seas ever since; and now with Damascena suddenly in his life, he felt as if all the waters of the universe had converged in Konya.

He cancelled every obligation after the 'funeral' to tend to Damascena, worrying the ruling Seljuks, and the rest of the city's residents, that he might not be available to defend them pending a Mongol attack. Rumi had disengaged from the dervish lodge, and to many who feared the worst, he had gone mad again.

Rumi's disciples were the first to notice his absence at the lodge. Hosam, Rumi's favorite student and head scribe, told them that their master had fallen ill, yet many doubted the validity of such an excuse. Rumi's wife, Kerra, told her friends and neighbors that she had never seen her husband looking more robust. She joked Rumi had taken up meditating even in the bathhouse, now that he had offered Damascena a room in their house. Kerra had married his light and his shadows. She tried to convey this to Hosam, but he could not find the grace to accept Rumi's capricious nature. Despite what he'd promised, the girl had become a liability; Rumi was no longer engrossed in his poetry.

Rumi heard the agitated breaths of Hosam, who waited anxiously outside the girl's bedroom with pen and paper, ready to record his words in the event that he launched into spontaneous poetry. Rumi wanted him to leave. He figured if God wanted him to remember the words, he would send them again. Besides, he believed his purpose was to help the girl remember why she had come to him—a duty he thought Hosam should celebrate, not lament with his petulant sighs. A spoiled school boy, he thought.

Rumi heard Hosam kick the floor just then as if he had read his mind.

"Has he spoken to you?" Hosam asked Kerra on her way down the hall.

"Not yet," she said. "I don't suspect he will say a word until the girl wakes up."

"Do you think he is in conversation with her spirit?"

"Your guess is as good as mine."

Rumi smiled overhearing their small quarrel in the hallway. Kerra was used to Hosam in their house, though they did not typically talk to each other. Kerra went on with her daily business—leaving the deceptively modest house so that Rumi could work on his final collection of spiritual couplets, *Maṭnawīye Ma'nawī*. He had completed the quatrains and odes of the

Divan, the six books comprising the *Masnavi*, and had published various discourses, letters and sermons. He had hoped Hosam would see this as an opportunity to take a break. They'd been at it for years and lately, the intensity of their work had been so palapable that he felt the air thicken when Hosam entered the house each morning. Didn't Hosam see the girl's presence as an opportunity for a short repose?

"You'll die trying to change him," Kerra said. "I gave up long ago."

"Doesn't the girl's presence make you angry?" Hosam asked.

A strong cross-breeze blew open the door to the girl's room and Rumi could see Kerra leaning against the wall, morning light through the hall window casting a slim, yet curved shadow of her body on the bright red carpet running the length of the hallway floor. She shook her head and bent down to pick up a feather on the carpet.

"Why should I be angry about the girl? What point does anger serve?" Hosam stared at her, perturbed. "You are his wife. You know devotion."

Kerra nodded. She rarely spoke to Hosam like this. She had come to accept him as she had come to accept all the guests who wandered in their home. It was not uncommon to see groups of strangers, always men, gathered around the elaborate fountain in their garden courtyard on hot days, then falling asleep under the intoxicating canopy of jasmine trees in bloom and staying the night. She had once joked to Rumi, "Why do we have a door when it is always open and you welcome everyone who enters?" It was the only time Rumi kissed her after their children were born, though she always longed to have more affection. She asked Rumi why he had kissed her then.

He told her, "You see me, Kerra. Thank you." And now Kerra offered Hosam the same opportunity. "Try to see him. That is true devotion."

"That is all I have ever tried to do," Hosam said.

"Give it time. Just when you think you know what you see, he will change."

"Like the wind."

"Yes. This is true. I married the wind and the ocean," Kerra said.

Rumi parted his lips, about to smile, remembering Hosam sitting like a child on the floor, waiting for him. It reminded him of his own children who had so desperately wanted his affection and time, vying for the chance to play with puppets or throw dice for one round of backgammon. Kerra had also grown frustrated about his inaccessibility when she only wanted a few hours of the day with him. She was fine if he stayed up all night to study, just as long as they could share dinner, but even that was asking too much.

"I wish it was easier to get his attention," Hosam admitted.

"God comes first," Kerra reminded him and handed him the feather.

"But I am his disciple and his top scribe."

"And I am his wife. We are one of many for *Mevlana*."

Hosam seethed. "I cannot share Our Master with that girl."

"You do not get to choose. God has already decided."

TWO

Damascena fought the spoon in her mouth, refusing food. In the first few days, she had regained enough strength in her arms to bat away the hand feeding her. Who could be so cruel as to keep her alive? She did not have the courage to look into the eyes of the face hovering over her. She closed her eyes, feeling the brush of his beard whenever he leaned across her body to change the sheets or pull the covers up to her chin. He said nothing, and yet, she felt as if they were communicating when she heard the whispered words.

Welcome difficulty as a familiar comrade.
Joke with torment brought by the Friend.

Damascena did not see the joke in her torment. If this was supposed to be funny, she wanted never to laugh. There was no friend in this, aside from the man trying to feed her, the same man who wept when she parted her lips and allowed him to give her a few drops of water. The man who refused to leave her side, who she knew was not Shams.

❦

On the fortieth day of the girl's convalescence, Rumi finally spoke. "Water, please."

The walls vibrated with his voice and a cool air came in through the windows, filling the second-floor hallway like a fresh breath. The walls looked pink in the light of an April dawn, matching the faint color that had returned to the girl's parched lips.

His voice boomed again. "Water, please!"

The urgency roused Hosam from the floor where he had been waiting, and he entered the room where the girl, still draped by the black wool cloak, lay sitting up in a bed—an indication of the girl's status. Not even Rumi's children slept in beds. He made sure they slept on mattresses on the floor like the rest of society, though as he got older, he accepted the special bed crafted for him by his disciples. He refused to have benches built into his home that would elevate him above his guests. For years, people marveled that the pillows on his floor welcomed sultans and their servants. Everyone sat equally in his presence, yet he had given special priority to the girl's comfort. The windows were lined with blue ceramic pitchers full of red tulips and roses. Kerra's touch. She was the only being, aside from the cat, that Rumi had permitted past the door. She brought poultices and herbal teas to help the girl's burns, even though Hosam had tried many times to offer herbs from his own garden. He would have liked to see Rumi holding his own daughter's hand then, not Damascena's. Rumi leaned forward and kissed her wrist.

Seeing this, Hosam felt light-headed crossing the threshold. He moved slowly toward the girl who moved only her eyes. The deep green color reminded him of the lakes depicted in Persian poetry—alpine lakes, water reflecting the cerulean of minerals. Her hair had been singed and lay in clumps on her head. She reminded him of a doll, wide-eyed, still, watching—waiting, it seemed, to be held.

"*Merhaba,*" he said, greeting her in Turkish. He refused to speak to her in high Turkish, with its many Persian and Arabic words. Instead, he spoke to her in the barely intelligible rough Turkish, used by the poor and uneducated—nomads like her.

Her lips parted into a smile but she did not speak. When she placed her fingers around her throat, Hosam realized that she *could not* speak and he quickly moved to refill the empty glass on the nightstand. She reached out and drank it so quickly it made her swallowing look violent. He could see the skin on her throat was still mottled and raw from the burns, but it had improved dramatically. She was flushed and her skin shone as if she had perspired, or just broken a fever.

Hosam stood awkwardly before her, unsure of what he was suppose to do. Hug her? Kiss her hand? He dropped to the floor on his knees and pressed his face into the floorboards. He coughed, breathing in the dust. The room had not been cleaned in a month. He thought he might be sick and gagged.

Seeing the strange man prostrate to her, Damascena flinched. Rumi gently patted her shoulder. "This is my disciple, Hosam," he said.

"Your spiritual successor," Hosam corrected him, proud he had been chosen.

Rumi looked up and smiled. "You can trust him. He is like a son to me."

Damascena turned to Rumi, wide-eyed and nodded. Hosam got off the floor. "What is her name?" he asked, wondering why he should ever trust *her*.

Rumi turned to him. "You can call her Sister."

Hosam felt his lips tighten. "But I do not know her."

Rumi held his gaze. "I did not know you either when you first came to me."

"Why has she come to you?"

"She knows the secrets."

Hosam looked stricken and reached out to find the wall with his hand. He felt hot and queasy. A girl could hardly know anything about Divine Truth.

Rumi inhaled and smiled, stroking Damascena's forehead with his finger. She had fallen back into a deep sleep and did not move again. Such were her waking moments. They lasted a few minutes at most. He doubted she would remember any of them. Rumi did not meet Hosam's gaze, but detected the anger and struggle in his disciple's voice.

"She has come for all of us to love. As God's daughter," Rumi said.

Hosam coughed, feeling as if he might choke on the dust motes in the air.

"Drink from her glass," Rumi said, "As if you are entering God's mouth."

Hosam nodded slowly. After forty days of silence—a directive? He missed the spontaneous poetry that flowed from Rumi's lips and wished for another flood of words, hoping their meaning might have the power to wash away the effects of the girl, but the words only made her more real. He listened with rapt attention as Rumi spoke.

> *Spring is here.*
> *The rose is dancing with its thorn*
> *Beauties have come from the invisible*
> *To call you home.*

When Rumi finished, he looked up and smiled, relief on his face as Hosam drank.

"You see, Hosam, I will help the girl live because she has come to help me die."

Nothing on the surface suggested Rumi was going to die anytime soon. After Hosam had shared the news, Kerra refused to believe that her husband was a dying man. She doubted he would die before he completed his latest manuscript. He seemed full of vigor, insisting on meditating and praying in the girl's room each morning, but Kerra had other reasons to worry about her husband. Rumi had no explanation for his insistence on nursing Damascena when there were plenty of doctors in Konya.

"Don't you think she should get proper care?" Kerra asked.

"What is wrong with my care?"

"You are many things to many people, but you are not a nurse."

"God has made me that," Rumi said, but did not look up to meet her eyes.

Kerra set a basket of fresh linens on the floor, having come to change the sheets once each week, despite herself. She was no longer being magnanimous. A sudden jealousy drove her to the room where Rumi had once sat with Shams and passed far too many hours, in her opinion, to consider him a guest. She thought Damascena would be gone by now. She lowered her voice, hoping Hosam would not overhear her. "Everyone is asking when you will teach again."

"Tell them I am teaching right now. And that I am being taught."

Kerra stood, arms akimbo, hands hooked on her slender hips.

"No paper. No books. What could you possibly be learning by a sick bed?"

Rumi looked up like a child caught in the middle of a daydream. "Faith."

"In what?" she said, barely able to look at the girl. "The cruelty of men?"

Rumi reached out to touch Kerra's hand but she withdrew and walked around him to peel the dirty sheets from Damascena. They were sticky from the poultice of honey and lavender oil and covered with a yellow-brown crust from oozing blisters. She worked quickly, holding her breath, trying hard not to vomit. It was hard to look at the girl. Her hands were so disfigured by burns that Kerra doubted that Rumi knew anything about helping her heal. It didn't take a doctor to see the infection. She lifted the girl's head off the pillow and removed the case. She had never seen hair knotted as badly. It felt scratchy like un-carded wool. She paused, seeing black bugs.

"You will need to shave her head."

Rumi looked up. "Why?"

"She has lice. Haven't you noticed?"

Rumi shifted his soft gaze to her. His eyes were bloodshot. "I have."

"How long has she had lice?"

"I don't know. A few weeks, maybe. I saw the eggs when she arrived."

Kerra took in a deep breath.

"You let the eggs stay on her head for almost a month?"

Rumi nodded bashfully. It infuriated her when all she could see of him was a boy, because as much as she wanted to be angry with him, she could not. She simply felt sorry that his complexity had to complicate everything, even the most simple.

"Are you angry?" he asked.

Kerra stared at him. "You should have told me. Lice in our house?"

"We must welcome all who show up at our door, even vermin."

"Yes, until you kill us with your hospitality."

Rumi smiled. He was used to Kerra's serrated tongue. The lice didn't bother him, and they certainly weren't doing any harm to the girl.

"They found a home in her hair," he said. "They are happy there." Kerra replaced the coverlet and smoothed out the wrinkles.

"I will be happy when she's out of *my* hair."

Rumi glanced at her. She stiffened, reading the disappointment in his eyes.

"You want her to leave?"

"I want her to go where she can get proper care. You are trained in the law. You are a professor. You know nothing of medicine," she said, her face reddening. "You know that this house is already haunted. What if she dies here? That makes two ghosts."

Rumi reached out and took Kerra's arm. He held her firmly, refusing to believe that Shams had been killed outside his own door.

"I will call a doctor if we need one. But for now, I trust the medicine of the heart."

Kerra jerked her arm away.

"Why do you care so much about her?"

Rumi shook his head, unsure of how much he could share with Kerra.

"God asked me to care," he said.

Kerra stared at him, her mind already made up. "Why didn't God ask you to care about me?" She squeezed back the tears and turned to the window. She could not take the intensity of Rumi's gaze now, even when his attention was all she ever wanted from him.

"You stare as if she is the rising sun and you are soaking in her rays. I asked your disciples. They said you didn't even look at Shams that way. They are worried about you, too. There are rumors, Jalala-din," she said, whispering his birth name as if he was her child and needed to be reminded of his origins.

"Rumors?"

Kerra turned back from the window and wiped her cheek with her wrist.

"She is not safe here. You ought to know that by now. Do not threaten her life with your ... philosophies and *agendas*."

"And what agenda is that?"

"She is a girl. *A girl.* If you invite her into *sema*, they will kill her. Or you."

Rumi shook his head and felt the wave of sorrow wash over him. He could never understand why only men were permitted to do the sacred dance; the invitation to connect with the Divine was the birthright of all people. Sadly, most of them forgot this.

"I will protect her," he said. "From my disciples and anyone else." Kerra smoothed out the wrinkles in her dress and sobbed.

"But what about your love?" she asked and turned, outraged, her jealousy lashing her breast like a belt. She clutched her chest. "I think you are in love with her?"

At last. The truth spreading like water from a broken blister. Rumi appreciated Kerra's vulnerability. He only wished she had shown more of it with him. She got up and crossed the room, but just as she reached the door, the girl suddenly spoke.

"Shams!" Damascena cried in her sleep. It was all Kerra needed to hear to know that Rumi did not love the girl. He still loved the man the girl spoke of in her dreams.

THREE

Damascena sat up many nights in Rumi's house, praying that Shams would visit. Once, she drifted off to sleep and woke up drowsy, seeing him standing at the foot of her bed. *Old Bird*, she thought, feeling the rush of excitement. *You came back!*

She reached out to touch him but he was gone. He came to her three more times the same way, always standing at the end of her bed, looking down on her with a smile.

She did not speak, fearing she would drive him away before she got a good look. He appeared fragmented, with streaks and splotches of light. His frailty worried her. She wished that she could take care of *him* now—wrap him in wool and feed him peaches.

She dreamed of fire and roses and woke screaming. The recurring nightmares and the smell of rotting flesh often made her sick. She was horrified to realize one day, when someone was changing the bandages on her hands, that the odor was coming from her. Her hair still carried the smell of smoke, and whenever she cried, she tasted salt and ash. She remembered the tanner and cried again.

She felt a new bandage being applied, lifting the skin around her leg. She reached out and clawed the air feeling the vinegar hit the exposed wound. The smell woke her momentarily—like a sobering punch, and she gasped in pain.

"Breathe," said the voice.

She turned her head toward the sound. "Everything hurts," she whispered.

"Keep breathing."

She did not want to breathe. The last thing she breathed was fire, and she felt the lick of flames rise up in her throat with the words. She told herself not to speak again. Days passed. Great clouds blotted out the sky that seemed to go on forever from the window where she lay and looked up. She felt many unpleasant things, mostly memories.

She remembered seeing the rose window for the last time before it exploded and shattered glass rained down on her face. She had the sense to shield her eyes and held her hands over her head, but now felt the prick of glass shards when she moved her fingers.

She felt a warm hand on hers, pressing lightly.

"Be still. Let the splinters work themselves out like thorns."

Then she heard the whispered words and they offered her comfort.

Almost everyone must be bound and dragged here.
Only a few come on their own.

She remembered the camel drivers, the bumps and ruts of the wagon bed where she had lain for weeks. Their songs seemed to play for days until one day, they stopped singing. She heard excited murmurings. Then the landing of feet on the ground as the drivers dismounted from their camels and horses. She thought there might have been an accident, a wagon wheel ruptured or a camel fallen ill. She was still too weak to sit up, but opened her eyes and managed to move her head and peer over the edge of the wagon.

Hundreds of storks had perched across the road and in the fields. The storks' white robes of feathers looked like snow. The camel drivers and every traveler on the road had paused to prostrate to the pious birds, believed to have gone to Mecca on a pilgrimage, they said. That the birds should greet this band of merchants and travelers bode well for everyone, a sign that God was watching them and blessing their passage.

Damascena woke again, feeling the sharp blade of a razor running over her scalp. She raised her hands to her head, sobered by the stubble. Her drowsy stupor vanished when she sat up and felt patches of short tufts that the blade had missed. She felt something warm and wet and pulled her hands away, seeing blood. Her eyes darted around the room. The walls were painted a light lemon yellow. Small colorful rugs covered the floor. This was not the room that Ivan Balev had built. A thin white curtain blew back from the window and bars of light fell between her and the old man sitting beside her with a tray and two small cups of tea.

"Shams?" she asked, feeling the soreness in her throat when she spoke. She adjusted her eyes to the light. Everything was blurry. The last thing she remembered seeing was the storks. It felt like a lifetime ago just like her life at the monastery. She could hear the bray of donkeys, the clop of horses, and a sound not unlike a dying cow.

At the sound, the old man got up from the chair by the bed and crossed the room to the window where a small rug lay perpendicular on the floor. He pulled back the curtain and the scent of mulberry trees in bloom drifted in with a warm breeze. The old man removed his shoes and stood at the back of the rug, raised his arms to his ears and recited the Shahada.

"*Allahu akbar,*" he began, then crossed his hands over his chest for Fatiyah, bowed and touched his knees. Then he got on his knees, leaned forward and touched his forehead to the ground, kissing the floor with his lips—repeating the whole process twice. When he finished, he looked over his right and left shoulder, as if to greet someone he could not see.

"Shams?" she asked again, straining her eyes to see in the bright light.

The man turned to her and smiled, then got up and returned to the chair by her bed. He looked unlike any man she had ever met with his long white beard and turban. He smiled at her kindly, but not with pity, eyes brimming with joy and relief as he spoke, and his words sounded soft and melodic like a song.

"Shams of Tabriz," he said.

She recognized the name and smiled.

"Shams of Tabriz!" he repeated, his voice bursting with excitement.

The man offered her a plate of pomegranate seeds and fresh figs, a sea of red and green on white. The colors were so vibrant. She remembered the peaches that Shams had given her at the white house so long ago, but the old man feeding her was not Shams. He had not complained about his feet hurting when he prostrated, and he could touch his toes. She would have liked him to be Shams because nothing about the room looked familiar. The woodwork possessed a variegated and other worldly quality, and she marveled at the calligraphy carved into the door, even though she could not read it.

The old man followed her gaze and uttered something unintelligible. She watched his lips move and heard him speak, but again, she could not understand a word of his language or any of the words drifting up from the street.

She thought at first it was the effect of the fire, as if a part of her mind had melted. Her memory certainly had. She could not remember the details about that last day at the monastery, only the shock of seeing Shams appear at her bed, removing the black wool cloak off himself for the first time since they had met. He covered her with it, but she did not remember seeing his old body, only light, when he lifted her in the air.

"Go to Rumi," he had said. "Make the rose oil again—for him and on the morning of his death, and only then, give it to him and tell him it is a gift from The Friend."

She murmured. "Rumi?"

The man beside her bed smiled and nodded.

"*Evet. Evet.* Rumi," he said and pointed to his heart, beaming at her.

Damascena awoke from the memory and glanced down at her feet. Two bloodied and blistered limbs protruded from the dark wool cloak still covering her. She recognized the cloak immediately as Shams', but nothing about her own body looked familiar. She had seen plenty of ailing pilgrims at the monastery exposing their maladies. She had treated frost-bitten hands and fingers, clubbed feet and ankles swollen with fluids and infested by maggots, but she had never seen anything so unsightly as herself.

Her hands were still wrapped in white gauze, dried black with blood. A putrid and fetid odor drifted up from the sheets and she turned and vomited on the side of the bed. She moaned then cried out, suddenly hearing the whispered words rise up again as if to absorb everything that tasted foul in her mouth, the bile, the bitterness, the betrayals she had suffered and survived. She heard the voice again.

My heart is like a vast rose garden of light ...

She batted the air with her hand, "Who speaks?" she demanded of the old man, though he had not moved his mouth. He had only moved toward her with water. When he continued, however, she finally recognized him. It was *his* voice that had whispered.

"*An ocean of agony drowned it again and again,*" he said aloud. "*But it became a warrior after being slaughtered a hundred times.*"

From the bed, Damascena could hear Rumi waiting outside her room for hours. He often paced, and the rhythm of his footfall induced deep and dramatic dreams. Every so often she could see a blue light envelop her, the color of cobalt tiles, and the heat in her burns would diminish and allow her to sleep longer and travel. Rumi followed her.

Each time the dream took her deeper, she searched frantically for the woman of fire, desperate to orient herself to what she believed was death, but she found nothing in the darkness, not even God's face in the midst of her struggle.

She was furious that God hadn't rewarded her with death. She left her body in the bed while she slept, and as a spirit, passed unfamiliar faces on the streets of Konya, searching not for the woman of fire, but for Shams. She wanted to know why he had sent her here. She wanted to know why he hadn't come with her. If Rumi had been the friend he had claimed, why hadn't Shams gone to Konya himself? What good could bringing him rose oil do? Clearly, the rose oil had only led to destruction. She had hoped she would never have use of it again, though she missed the garden.

"Shams," she called out. "Show me your face. Don't make me believe that you are as much of a coward as Ivan Balev!"

Her spirit body asked everyone she passed if they had seen an old man wearing a robe woven of light who danced in circles. She was met with ridicule and disapproving looks. She suspected the men wearing robes who called themselves dervishes wanted something the way they cast their eyes on her in the streets. They gathered with merchants around small wooden tables playing backgammon in the shade of mulberry trees. She could not understand their language or read the calligraphy on the signs in the shop windows. At one point, her spirit walked through the goldsmith's bazaar and Rumi appeared standing in the doorway.

"Welcome," he said. "I've been waiting for you my whole life."

She looked back across the dusty street, seeing another group of men playing backgammon and small boys carrying rolled up rugs slung across their shoulders.

"Where am I? What am I doing here?"

"You have come to Konya," he said and pulled her up to the threshold while the goldsmith pounded his precious metal. "You have come to learn the ways of the dervish."

She looked up, unsure. This was news. She had been called a saint, a witch, a miracle worker and a flower girl. She had never heard of dervishes.

"What is a dervish?"

"One who stands on the threshold of something, like me. One who is ready to move on and transform themselves, like you."

She scratched her head. "Transform myself? I am just a girl."

"You will go through the most significant change of your life here."

She sighed and looked away. "Does it involve performing miracles?"

Rumi exchanged a knowing look with the goldsmith and smiled at the girl. "The transformation itself is the miracle."

Outside the dream, Rumi wanted to leech everything that had poisoned Damascena, but he could not interfere with her learning.

He wanted to tell her that one day, she would find a remedy for her pain. He had never felt more compelled to help anyone as much as her. Despite what Hosam thought of the contract between them, Rumi believed this act of service for Damascena was holier than his poetry.

"I have writer's block," he said when Hosam demanded he start writing again. They met in the garden courtyard, under the open window of Damascena's room. Kerra had left a plate of figs and cherries on the small tiled table, the pits of which Rumi spat on the ground in a continuous barrage, only aggravating Hosam more.

Hosam seethed. "We cannot wait for the block to lift. You must write through it."

Rumi reclined on the huge pillows strewn about the tiled patio. His relaxed posture was reminiscent of his four-year hiatus after the completion of his first major work, *Divan-e Kabir* or *Shams-e Tabrizi,* comprised of 35,000 Persian couplets and 2,000 quatrains. Hosam suspected his current work to be a masterpiece, possibly multiple volumes, maybe six books, and more than 27,000 verses of mystical poetry. Yes, Rumi would need to rest, but Hosam refused to let that much time lapse again, especially if he was facing the end—though he hated to admit that and give Damascena's presence any more power. Hosam stiffened and pointed to her window.

"The only block you have is lying in that bed!"

Rumi tilted his head and pressed a finger to his lips.

"Listen. Do you hear it?"

Hosam relaxed, anticipating a rush of poetry. He readied himself with the quill and tablet he carried at all times in the presence of *Mevlana*. "What is it you hear?"

"The chipping of stone. I believe there is something beautiful in the block."

Hosam pressed the quill and tablet into Rumi's chest and fumed.

"When the words do come, record them yourself," he said and stood.

"Where are you going?" Rumi asked, when Hosam strode toward the gate.

"To my home and garden, where I will stay until this nonsense passes."

"Where will you go when the wind and rain visit?"

Hosam gritted his teeth, reminded of the 90th Path. The Gift of Resistance.

Rumi fixed his gaze on him. "I am the wind and the rain that have come to test you. Without resistance, how strong would the plants in your garden be?" he asked, meeting Hosam at the gate. "You could join her," Rumi continued. "After all, you stand here like *you* are bound to that bed, but please go. Remove the block yourself. Purge everything that's holding you back. Whatever it is you feel you are being deprived of, trust the limitation serves to bring you *more* of what you want. I assure you, it is not my poetry."

Hosam felt his jaw tremble but he could not move his lips to speak, hearing the girl's anguished cries, leading half the town to wonder if she would live another day.

"Why do you choose to ignore her?" Rumi asked.

Hosam lowered his head. "She is not worthy of being your student, or friend."

Rumi cleared his throat. He rarely got angry with Hosam, but wanted him to hear the truth. "Is that so? Remember what I have always told you and everyone else; anyone looking for friends without faults shall remain friendless. The choice is yours."

FOUR

Rumi stood outside the door for three more days, leaving a crack wide enough to watch over Damascena. She clutched the edge of the bed and heaved again and again. On the second day, her sobs gave way to gasps, then to panting and prayers, until her faith collapsed under the burdens plaguing her heart. On the third day, she sat on the floor and hummed, rocking back and forth. A silence swelled up around her by midnight. When only her breath filled the room, and Rumi was sure she had emptied herself completely, he would enter again as her servant.

Rumi insisted on cooking for Damascena. He woke Kerra in the middle of the night to tell her and asked her to go to the market first thing in the morning. Kerra rolled over, staring at her husband. The sight of him, wild-eyed and wild-haired in bed, startled her. "What are you doing?" she asked.

"Cooking her first meal."

Kerra bolted upright and sniffed the air. The last time Rumi had tried to cook, he almost burned down the house making almond helva to satisfy a sweet tooth. "I don't smell anything. Nothing's caught fire," Kerra said, relieved.

"I want to make the girl chickpeas."

"Chickpeas? Why not *tandir borek*?" she asked, wondering why her husband was going to the trouble of cooking for Damascena—a miracle in itself, he wouldn't attempt to make Konya's most superb borek, considered to be the food of the Gods. Even she had not mastered this dish with its legendary aroma, cooked in the glowing tandir, then spread with butter and apricot preserves made from trees growing around Konya. At the least, she assumed, he'd offer to sprinkle gold dust in her sherbet, like they did for the Sultan. After all, he treated the girl as if she was royalty. A dish like this was appropriate.

"Chickpeas are simple. They are all her body needs right now."

Kerra studied his face. He was so earnest it was hard to doubt him.

"You've been thinking about this all night, haven't you?"

"Four nights and forty days," he said, eyes beaming in the moonlight.

"Your love isn't enough to quell her hunger?"

Rumi lifted Kerra's hand and kissed her wrist. "Maybe not. But your love for me might help." Kerra sighed and rolled over on her pillow, relishing her husband's touch.

"And Ates-baz Veli is on strike? Why don't you go to his kitchen?" she inquired of Rumi's personal cook at the dervish school and the most famous chef in Anatolia.

"Because the girl needs to recover from the first fire before she endures his."

Kerra stared at him, digesting the news. Her lips flattened.

"You're going to train her as a dervish, aren't you?"

Rumi nodded, hearing a neighbor's dog barking outside the window.

"And you think she will survive? They will tear her to shreds in there."

"Her heart has already been torn, Kerra. She is ready for it to be *torn open* here."

"Don't you think she's too young to go through so many years of denial and training? She is too frail for the rigors of becoming a dervish."

Rumi shook his head. "She has spent her entire childhood paying penance. I know that she has the discipline and dedication to follow this path."

"For what? How do you know that? She talks to no one."

"She talks to me in her sleep. I meet her in a field."

Kerra tilted her head. She had heard Rumi speak of many supernatural things. This was no more bizarre than the other instances of Rumi's wanderings in the spirit world, but it spooked her to hear him speak like this.

"What field?" she asked.

"A rose field. We meet there each night and she talks."

"Has she told you she wants to become a dervish?"

"She needs to heal. I know that much."

"And dancing *sema* will relieve her pain?"

"It will help move it through her so that she can move toward her source."

Kerra frowned. "Seems like a long journey to end up where she started."

Rumi laughed with appreciation.

"The road to love is long. We all know that."

Kerra reached out and took her husband's hand. Her fingers trembled, imagining how their lives could become undone if Rumi taught the girl how to spin—just as Shams had taught him once. She wasn't sure she had the strength to endure another death.

When Damascena was well enough to walk, Rumi led her slowly up the hills overlooking Konya, so lush and green in May, insisting the air was good for her wounds. When she had gained more strength and could walk longer distances, he led her five miles from the city center to Silla, the village outside town populated by Christians. He often came to meditate there and hoped the girl might find comfort and familiarity.

They would sit for hours listening to the creeks, gushing with snowmelt from the mountains. Rumi soaked up the scene and burst into spontaneous song, encouraging the girl to join him. She refused, cheeks flushed, too embarrassed to speak his language for fear of macerating such beautiful sounds in her mouth. He would slow down, offering one word, then the other, as if he were teaching her how to walk. She felt awkward, like an infant, but repeated after him, day after day, the names of words that meant something. *Bird, trout, brook, stream, creek, sky, sun. Spin, whirl, leap, sing. Laugh. Be. Love.*

Later, he labeled household items in Turkish, for her edification, too: bed, chair, door, window, cup, bowl, spoon. Sheet, towel, pillow, bath. Rest. Wake. Eat. Pray. She quickly developed a practical tongue, yet she struggled to express herself completely.

One day in Silla, he asked her if she would like to stay.

"Why?"

"I thought you might want to be among your people."

It took her a moment to find the words. "I do not know who my people are."

"What about your parents?"

Damascena turned away. "My mother left when I was born," she said and pushed the words into her gut. Rumi said nothing but met her eyes with a smile.

"Then you are more like me than I thought. Everyone is your people."

At twilight, after the final call to prayer when the streets were empty, Rumi led Damascena through the city, pointing out the buildings he admired, where he worked, mostly holy places: the honey-colored stonework of Alaeddin Camii on the citadel hill framed by distant mountains, settled during the Copper Age; the ornate prayer niche of the city's hospital and its enormous marble slabs; Keluk Ibn Abdullah's slender minaret and its gorgeous Baroque style tiles, and the square-shaped and massively domed Iplikci Mosque with its twelve massive columns, each designed to be an elephant's foot. He told her it was this mosque, known as the yarn-makers mosque, where his family had come to pray when they first arrived in Konya. He took a deep breath, relishing the memories of these beloved places. He told her that he felt at home in the presence of them all.

"You have many homes," Damascena said, impressed.

Rumi turned to her and nodded. "Yes, I am blessed that way."

"I would like to have just one."

"Ah-ha. I see. Let me tell you how it is possible to feel at home in many places. I go to the synagogue, I go to the church, I go to the mosque, and I see the same altar, and I feel the same spirit. Do you understand? It is all one."

"What spirit is that?" she asked, wondering if there was more than the Holy Spirit.

Rumi simply smiled but did not answer her while they continued to walk, resisting the urge to share anecdotes of wandering the same streets with Shams. Instead, he taught her how to read the Persian calligraphy in the turquoise and blue tiles, then he instructed her by the light of an oil lamp how to write. He hoped that if she did not find her home in any of these buildings, or in his own house, she might feel at home using a new language where her heart was safe to speak.

Damascena appreciated Rumi's patience and slow instruction, but the script in the tiles continued to mystify her. It was as if between the letters was a larger mystery. One night, standing in front of a fountain, she mustered the courage to see herself, all baldness and burns, in the watery reflection of these magnificent tiles.

"Does everything beautiful burn?" she asked, her chest tightening when she remembered everyone and the roses that had perished in the fire.

"Everything that has ever become beautiful has been burned. Like you."

She considered his words, no longer having to pause to translate them. She had simply learned to absorb their energy to understand the meaning.

"You remind me of Shams."

Rumi smiled. It was the first time the girl had mentioned him outside her dreams.

"I miss him," she continued. "I wish he had come with me."

Rumi smiled and led her to the Kartay Madrasa, the city's newest school, a small square building with an innovative spherical dome made of limestone—a work commissioned by the ruling Seljuks to disseminate knowledge and educate Konya's elite.

"When did you meet Shams?"

Rumi glanced up at the dome and sighed. "Here. In Konya. On Alaeddin Hill. I was thirty seven years old. It feels like a lifetime ago. Shams was almost as old as I am now," he said and laughed at the irony. He lifted his turban to scratch the top of his head, feeling the bald spot as familiar as the moon.

Damascena turned to him. "How old are you?"

"Sixty," he said. "Ancient."

Damascena paused to calculate. "Shams must be very old now."

"He is an old soul. I recognized him the first time I saw him on the hill. Everyone believed him to be a beggar, but I saw the light in his eyes and knew he held a lot of ... let's say, information, that I needed to learn."

"What kind of information?"

"The kind no book can ever give you. Do you know Shams burned my books?"

Damascena looked at him with concern, remembering what Shams had told her at the white house. "Yes. He said so. Why would he ever do such a thing?"

"He claimed the knowledge I needed was beyond books and my mind."

Damascena laughed. "That sounds like Shams. I thought I was losing my mind many times with him. He always speaks in riddles and I do not always understand him."

Rumi reached out and touched her gently once in the middle of her forehead.

"I think that is the point, Damascena."

"I am meant to misunderstand him?"

Rumi nodded. "No. To lose your mind so you can gain a new way of knowing."

She paused outside the Kartay Madrasa, considering. She tried to decipher the Arabic inscriptions in the intricate ironwork on the massive front gate, as Rumi traced the calligraphy with his finger.

"The Most Beautiful Names of God," he said.

She leaned in to study the words, wondering if this was a test.

"I thought there was only one name for God."

Rumi took her hand. "God is beyond the limitation of one name. Or how we have come to know the Divine. Follow me, you'll see there are more."

He led her into the building and paused beneath the dome, seeing the huge network of stars made of the traditional turquoise, white and black tiles. The girl gasped, feeling the immensity of the structure. She followed the five Turkish triangles from each corner of the building and the inscription of names she could not read in the highly stylized Kufic script, but she didn't need to understand them to feel their deeper mystery.

The words rose past the star tiles to the opening in the window in the apex where she could see the real stars outside. Rumi led her to the middle of the room and the basin filled with water, glittering with the reflection of the night sky. He reached in and cupped his hand, filled it with water and lifted it for the girl to drink. The water tasted sweet.

She wiped her mouth and turned to him, her face wrought with concern, feeling suddenly too exposed under the open dome with the stars so close she could grab one.

"Why didn't you let me die?"

Rumi let the water drip off his fingers. "Because you have not finished living."

She felt a chill come through the open apex and her lips trembled, remembering Shams' last words, and the instructions to give Rumi the rose oil on his deathbed.

"I can't perform any miracles here, if that is why you kept me alive."

"Your transformation will be the miracle," Rumi reminded her.

She turned to him, her green eyes luminous in the moonlight. "So you don't expect me to give others the ability to see God?"

He shook his head and wiped the tear off her cheek.

"No," he said. "You only have to see yourself."

"What good would that do?"

"So that you can see the blessing and beauty that you are," he said.

Just then, she felt the warmth of the stars and the center of her heart slide open like a door, as if all the hurt hidden through the years had finally been invited to leave.

FIVE

Damascena woke the next morning, finding a headscarf at the foot of the bed. She got up, dressed, and wrapped it around her head, grateful to hide the baldness. If she was supposed to see what was beautiful about herself, it would help to hide what she thought was ugly. Her hair had just begun to grow but was still short and spiky. She did not want to draw any more attention to herself when she walked the streets.

Kerra passed her in the hallway and said, "*Çok güzel*," marveling at the way Damascena's feet and hands had healed so quickly. The rose colored silk brightened the girl's tired green eyes. Damascena nodded, feeling the warmth in her cheeks. She had never seen a woman more beautiful than Rumi's wife, and she was relieved to hear Kerra speak to her. She met her soft gaze and repeated, "*Çok güzel.*" *You are beautiful, too.*

Rumi had finished his ablutions and passed them in the hallway. He did not expect Kerra to accept Damascena as a daughter. He simply wanted his wife to make room for the girl because he had no plans for her to leave anytime soon. He smiled at them but said nothing, grateful for the peace that had finally settled over the house.

Damascena had grown tired of chickpeas, but she did not dare complain. Not after everything Rumi had done to help her. Her blisters had stopped oozing. Her hands and feet had only the slightest markings of burns, aside from the skin fused at her toes. Her hair was growing back. She had even begun to play with the *ney*, the reed flute he'd left by her bed. She liked the instrument. It let her heart speak of things she had no words to say in Turkish or her native tongue. The lamentation filled the house with a measured sorrow that matched that of Rumi's heart. Kerra was the first to notice.

"It is like she knows the whole story of Shams," she whispered.

Rumi only nodded. When Kerra invited the girl to join them for dinner, she confirmed her suspicion. Damascena had been quiet the whole meal. She had avoided Kerra's eyes and followed the protocol of staying silent. She felt awkward sharing a meal with them and would have preferred her own room, where she could feed the visiting nightingales the chickpeas that her stomach could no longer tolerate. She stared at her bowl on the table when it struck her. "We are alike," she said to no one in particular.

Kerra turned quizzically to her husband. "Who?"

Damascena looked down at the chickpeas, then at the scars on her hands from the burns, the only evidence that this was all real.

"We have both become food for the divine," she said and looked up, meeting Rumi's eyes. "We were raw, we were cooked, and we were burned."

Rumi gasped. The girl's proclamation was all he needed to hear. The time had come to take her to Ates-baz's kitchen, where she would burn again, but heal completely.

Anyone wishing to enter the *tekke* would have to observe its kitchen for three days. No exceptions, not even for Damascena, and Rumi had seen a number of potential disciples leave the dervish lodge after just one day. They couldn't handle watching the repetitious activity, in some cases, continuously washing the floor, perceiving it as monotonous nonsense rather than a way of obliterating the ego to purify themselves.

And purification was the point of such pain. Rumi trusted the girl would do well inside the dervish kitchen. She had grown up in a monastery. Order and ritual ran through her blood. Aside from Hosam, the last person he had brought to the kitchen was Shams.

He expected stares. The girl was only fourteen, four years younger than the average aspirant who entered the *tekke* at the age of eighteen. Rumi believed Damascena was mature enough to handle the intensity, and though he was certain she would observe the dervishes with respect, he was uncertain how they would see her now, the girl who'd arrived in a black wool cloak as disheveled as any beggar. Every disciple dreamed of the day when a black cloak would be bestowed on them; only the chosen few would ever wear one. They had to be chosen by a great Sufi master. Rumi had not even draped Hosam's shoulder with a cloak yet. He sensed their jealousy and inner storms, but could not be persuaded to wait four more years. The time was now to initiate Damascena.

Rumi made sure Damascena wore her cloak that night and instructed her to keep her head down and avoid eye contact with anyone who passed them. They walked side by side down narrow, walled streets on the way to the dervish lodge, a simple, square-shaped, multi-domed building made of sandstone that glowed a coppery-pink at sunset.

They had passed the lodge many times, but never entered. Rumi said nothing significant about the place, but Damascena felt warmth in her being and a flutter in her heart whenever they passed it. She experienced shortness of breath and the uncontrollable urge to dance as Rumi had done in her dream. Inspired, she began to twirl in the street, but Rumi reached out and promptly stopped her. It was the only time she felt any force on his behalf, and it startled her. She pressed herself against the alley wall on her left, feeling the warmth of the stones, radiating Konya's heat. A group of young boys ran past them barefoot with puppets in hand, animated, engaged in an imaginary theater.

"Not now," Rumi said, glancing over his shoulder to make sure nobody had seen her or cared to notice. Her form was wrong—rushed, self-conscious. Her right hand pointed down to the earth and the palm of her left hand faced the sky, when it should have been the opposite. He was certain Shams had not taught her *sema* officially.

"But my feet are better. The blisters are gone," she said, confused.

"Your ability to dance has nothing to do with your body," he said, then lowered his voice and pointed to his chest. "It has everything to do with your heart."

"What's wrong with my heart?"

"It is young, that is all," he said. He wanted to say it was also very closed.

"So I must wait to be old to dance? Like Shams—"

He stopped her again, covering her mouth with his hand and she tasted his sweat, the dust of the streets on his skin.

"Please do not mention his name in public places. I beg you, Damascena. For the sake of your life, never mention his name again, or dance *sema*, unless you ask me first."

"*Sema?* Is that the circle dance Shams did?"

"Not here. Please. No one can see."

She studied his face in the moonlight. His sternness spooked her, but she did not want to upset this old man who had done so much to help her recover. She met his gaze, feeling her body tremble.

Rumi softened his grip on the girl.

"No matter who befriends you here. They cannot be trusted to hear about Shams."

"I promise," she said, feeling the furrow in her brows growing deeper. She did not expect Rumi to be so adamant about her refraining from spinning like Shams; and she wondered what Shams had done while he lived in Konya to make Rumi so fearful of her ever mentioning his name. Rumi met her eyes with a ominous stare but said nothing, just pointed to the sand colored building and motioned her to follow him.

She expected to enter through the gate at the front, but Rumi led her to the right side of the building, where a man wearing a long white robe that flared at the bottom walked backward out the door, saluting it with a curious nod.

His long white robe carried the smell of cooked onions and rice. He appeared disoriented and feverish, his face aglow with perspiration, his breath labored as if he had just sprinted to the mosque on the hill. He stumbled, seeing the girl, then paused, seeing Rumi. He saluted him with the same nod and hurried down the street, dabbing his eyes, glancing back every few steps as if he saw an apparition but didn't quite trust his vision.

"What is he doing?" Damascena asked.

"There is a soul in the dervish kitchen," Rumi whispered, adding, "We aim to keep it happy and only enter the monastery when there is something important."

"What is so important?" Damascena asked, feeling her heart sink. Of all the places to visit, she did not wish to enter another monastery.

"You," Rumi asked. "You are ready to enter the kitchen."

She looked at him. She was not hungry. They had just eaten chickpeas.

"We can wait. I do not wish to eat again," she said.

"We have not come to eat. But you will grow a new kind of hunger here."

They approached the door in silence. Rumi gave a nod, lifted the brass door knocker, rubbed smooth by ten thousand touches at least, and murmured, "With Your Leave Holy Dervishes." The door opened slightly and the smell of cooked quail and pilav drifted past them and entered the street, rousing drowsy dogs in doorways.

"*Hu*," Rumi said and looked back at Damascena. She nodded, recognizing this one simple word, meaning *There is only One God and It is He*, but she was not interested in God or kitchens. She simply wanted to dance.

Rumi turned back to the door and continued.

"I bring an initiate with me tonight," he said. "May we enter to observe?"

The senior dervish on duty, Asci Dede, a short, round man with eyes that looked silver in the light, opened the door and fixed his gaze first on Rumi, then at the girl. From the dubious look on his face, he seemed unmoved to open it further.

Damascena did not like the scrutiny. They seemed to stand there for an eternity, exchanging an entire conversation in the silence. She could almost hear the questions.

Does she know anything about cooking? Does she wish to learn? Will she obey the rules? Is she willing to pledge her allegiance?

Did her family give her permission to enter our lodge? Who is her family? What is her reason for being here?

She had no idea why she was there. She was about to turn away when Rumi reached out to hold her hand and spoke.

"When you are scared do not run—" he whispered, when the girl interrupted him.

"*Turn toward yourself,*" she continued, feeling a tingling up her arms, remembering the tanner's last words.

Rumi froze and the dervish at the door asked nothing more of Damascena. Hearing her words, he raised his right hand and brandished it in the air as if it were a flag beckoning the girl to enter the kitchen where her training would commence immediately.

Kazanci Dede met her expectant face with soft eyes and a smile.

"You have come to boil," he said.

Damascena thought she had heard him wrong. Surely his twisted humor was some form of a joke, given she had survived a fire.

SIX

The dervish kitchen was a world of robes, peppered with sweat and purposeful unrest. Men in skirts and a flurry of activity kept the modest, bright kitchen organized and tidy. Natural light fell across cobalt tiles that filled the whole floor, imbuing the space with the qualities of a small pool and endowing it with deep reflection.

Damascena had never seen anyone in the rectory perform such mundane duties like dish washing and floor sweeping with as much exacting intention and intensity. The dervishes seemed content, bent over their station with task in hand, making holy the daily rituals of common men. She sensed it wasn't food they were offering but themselves.

The next morning, she watched them from the *saka postu*, a pelt-covered raised platform constructed of oiled walnut where she was told to sit for three days by the door in silence—to think, reflect and observe the activities in the kitchen. She kneeled down on the pelt, head bowed, as instructed, and would eat what was given to her for the three days. From here, she would be approved or rejected by Kazanci Dede, the Keeper of the Cauldron. His name alone terrified her, let alone the patch he wore on his eye.

She wondered what he would decide about her. She wasn't even sure she wanted his approval or any more cryptic training. Shams had given her enough of that. She had not come to Konya to learn cooking. She already had a trade, gardening, and she longed for the roses, though she felt wrong asking Rumi for seeds. She could at least oblige his request and observe the men he called his brothers. She had been through far worse. Three days in a dervish kitchen were better than forty in a bed.

She focused on the tasks each initiate performed to learn their titles. They all looked similar, wearing simple sleeveless, long tunics and skirts with white, long sleeve shirts rolled up at the elbows. In addition to Asci Dede, General Director, or head chef, and Kazanci dede, Keeper of the Cauldron; she counted fifteen more official positions: Halife Dede, Chief of Religious Matters; Disari Meydanc, The Launderer, and The Dishwasher. There was also The Latrine Cleaner—who carried a foul smelling bucket and dirty rags, and The Stove Kindler, who not only cut and chopped wood, but brought in fuel from the storehouse outside the kitchen, where goats roamed and slept at night. Every time he delivered fuel, he paused at the door to say, "*Bismillahirahmanirrahim.*" Damascena had never heard a longer word in her life, and wondered if perhaps the dervish candidate had a speech impediment or was trying to invoke some kind of magic.

She marveled at the meticulousness of The Master of the Cupboard, otherwise known as the tinsmith, who arranged all the eating utensils. He rubbed his rag over the silver and gold until there was nothing but threads left of the cloth. She sat there for hours, absorbed in his ritual, as if in a trance. It took him all morning just to polish the spoons. Damascena figured he must take a week to work through the full place settings.

When he put away the pots and pans, he flipped them over to use as drums to energize the pace in the kitchen. With the heat so intense, Damascena appreciated that the drumming kept her awake. Sleep was not an option for the first three days. To battle fatigue, Rumi encouraged her to engage with one of the candidates and perform the duty with him in mind. Easy for you to say, she thought, watching Rumi watch her from his seat at the table, content with his coffee and honey-soaked baklava.

She would not be following The Purchaser of Provisions, who went to the market each day. Females were not permitted to walk freely through the streets, though she liked imagining what Konya must be like, smelling the mesquite smoke from grilled meats and other foods being cooked and sold. She had, on occasion, followed the Somatci, who set and cleared the table, but she was not permitted to eat with the dervishes in the dining room and couldn't see what exactly he did.

She found it most difficult to engage with the stern-faced Iceri Meydancisi, Master of Internal Housework, whose only task it seemed was to make coffee and serve it to the novices on Fridays. She sat up taller whenever he passed the platform, wondering if he would turn her shoes away, or place them at the door—an indication that she had been asked to leave the *tekke*. She noticed most of the candidates kept a healthy watch on their shoes, as if they are all waiting for one of them to be turned back out to the world without a chance of obtaining the spiritual growth they desired.

She was least interested in the job of Icieri Kandilicis, Keeper of the Internal Oil Lamps and Tahmicsci, the coffee grinder, who roasted coffee for the Meydan, the large section of the dervish lodge, reserved for the religious ceremonies and *sema*. Damascena was forbidden to enter it without the permission of the Dedes.

She was more familiar with The Bedmaker and The Sweeper, responsible for keeping the floors and grounds clean, but it was The Footman who most compelled her. He appeared ragged from errands he was sent to run each day, but he never complained.

Damascena marveled that none of the initiates objected to the repetition or seemed bored of their tasks. Most of the young men worked with upturned lips and a glimmer in their eye, but their grins vanished whenever The Footman turned her way. She quickly realized that her presence was his most challenging task.

The dervishes did not invite Damascena to meals, and she began to wonder if sitting on the platform was not an invitation to observe them, but to test her endurance. She felt light-headed and dizzy and her mouth watered, watching them prepare soups and stews, roasted meats and pilavs, vegetable boranis, pastries and pancakes that dripped with *pekmez*, a syrup they had made from grapes, and the heavenly *zerdes*, the sweet pudding spiced with saffron. Local dishes, Rumi had explained, loved by the Sultan.

Ates-baz Veli, the Head Chef, offered a dollop on a spoon as if to welcome her with sweetness her first morning. The saffron pudding was the first and last thing she would eat, and she felt her stomach gurgle when the dervishes gathered for meals, once at eleven o'clock and later after evening prayers. They passed the food through a small window to the dining room that she could not see from the platform. She heard only the lowering of a large pot to the floor and the voice of the Kazanci Dedi chanting:

May it be sweet
May God make it plentiful,
By the breath of Hazreti Mevlana,
By the mystery of Ates-baz Veli,
Let us chant Hu.

Whenever she heard the prayer, oddly her hunger ceased and she tasted the sweetness of the pudding as if Ates-baz had just removed the spoon from her mouth. He was the only one in the kitchen who seemed genuinely happy to have her company, and he welcomed her each morning with a cup of tea and fresh *simet*, which she spread with butter and salt. She soon grew fond of this tall, thin man with kind eyes and a curled mustache, who danced around the kitchen with such joy that she longed to join him.

Rumi lavished so much praise on the chef that the girl believed it was his soul that everyone was trying to please in the kitchen. Above every stove was the inscription, "Oh Holy Ates-baz Veli," framed by wisps of steam. He was the only one permitted to talk there, and when he did, the tiled walls met his voice with an ethereal reverberation.

Damascena loved the story about Ates-baz Veli that Rumi told her at home on the second night of her initiation. Though Rumi had not requested the dedes make any exceptions for her, they decided it was not wise for Damascena to sleep on the platform given her fragile health. They instructed Rumi to let her sleep in the bed at his house. He cleaned her burns and applied lavender oil, a ritual that had continued since her arrival.

Rumi smiled as he told the tale of Ates-baz's beginnings.

"When he started in the kitchen as the head chef, he once complained, 'There is no more wood left to light the stove.' The Stove Kindler had failed to show up and perform his duty—apparently his brother's donkey cart full of flour sacks had been overturned by drunk Crusaders passing through town, so I instructed Ates-baz to move toward the stove and put his feet under it. Nothing happened at first."

"Young Ates-baz had stood there barefoot, feeling awkward and humiliated that he could not get his own stove to light. Imagine that kind of impotence! He stood there, stiff-necked and cold. He fumed about the Crusaders and the tragic turn of events. Oh he was so miserable! He cursed the tree that hadn't been chopped, and the dried donkey dung left uncollected. He cursed the weather and he cursed himself, feeling more and more agitated. He was very insulted by my suggestion, and was about to turn away when sparks shot out from his toes and flickered into flames that enabled the stove to light!"

Rumi stood doubled over beside Damascena's bed, wiping his eyes and laughing as he finished the story. Damascena cringed, feeling the heat in her own feet.

"It must have been painful!" she said.

"Painful? Why?"

"Didn't he burn?"

Rumi nodded. "Yes. And that was the point."

"I thought he wanted to light the stove."

Rumi pointed to his chest. "Inside his heart. He was burned for doubting himself."

Damascena looked up and met his gaze in the glow of the lamplight. She drew in a breath, hearing a nightingale sing from the tree outside.

"Is that why I was left to burn?"

Rumi unfolded the blanket at the foot of the bed and pulled it up to the girl's chin.

"You will find out soon enough. First, you must sleep. You've been awake more in the last three days than you have in the last two months here. Rest," Rumi said, letting go of Damascena's hand. He blew out the lantern and walked to the door in the dark.

"Rumi?"

"Yes, Damascena?"

He paused at the threshold, his hand on the cool brass door knob.

"Why do they call everyone in the lodge *Dede*?"

"It means Grandfather. *Dede* is a term of affection," he said.

"Oh," she said, yawning, feeling her eyes grow heavy. "Thank you, *Rumi Dede*."

"For what?" he asked and laughed.

"For not making me eat any more chickpeas."

Rumi smiled in the dark. Nobody in the lodge had ever called him Dede except his grandchildren. His disciples and the people of Konya, including everyone at the Sultan's palace, had bestowed on him the title *Mevlana*, Our Master. He decided against correcting her. It pleased him that her ego did not govern her. He was certain she would not be long on the platform.

"Tell Kazanci Dede my new name tomorrow," he said, just to be sure.

SEVEN

The next morning, Damascena greeted the Kazanci Dede with a smile at the kitchen door, then after waiting for Rumi to enter first, pointed to his back and said, "The real *dede.*"

She had gotten used to the silence over the last two days, but the stillness on the morning of the third gave her pause, and she regretted the words she'd uttered and the accent she could not eliminate. She wondered if she had said something she didn't mean.

Kazanci Dede remained stiff at the door, while Rumi slipped past him, took a seat at the table beside Ates-Baz, and helped himself to coffee and baklava. He sipped his coffee from a thimble-sized cup, his grin as wide as the moon.

Everyone in the kitchen stopped his tasks to watch the fourteen-year-old girl cross the floor to the platform. She felt the leaden stares of the initiates who had already passed this first test. Her legs trembled when she climbed onto the platform to sit alone. The spectacle amused Rumi, and he felt the volley of stares bouncing back and forth between the disciples, waiting for him to signal some appropriate response to the girl's comment. He set his cup of coffee on the table, then bit into the baklava. The silence only amplified the sound of chewing and lip smacking.

Ates-baz finally broke the silence with a bellow so loud and long that coffee spilled from his nostrils and he snorted like a sow rolling in mud. He smiled and the glimmer of his teeth was almost blinding. He turned to Rumi, squeezing his shoulders.

"The real *dede* indeed!" he cried, this time, Rumi howled with him. Both men paused to breathe, then laughed again, this time inviting the dervishes into hysterics and they doubled over, laughing so hard that their tears salted the dishes they were preparing.

Ates-baz walked over to the platform, helped Damascena step down to the floor, and promptly lifted the black wool cloak. She felt immediate relief and lightness in her shoulders, where nothing but a threadbare dress remained. She glanced down, seeing her shoulders through the torn cloth. The skin was pink, stretched tight with scars, and she shuddered, feeling suddenly exposed and anxious without the cloak, as if she no longer had Shams' protection. She thrust her arms toward Ates-baz, reaching for it.

"Please don't take it! It is from my friend."

"What friend is that?" Ates-baz asked and his face had grown serious. He turned to Rumi, following the girl's stricken glance. Rumi had suddenly sobered, too. She remembered what he had told her and she clenched her jaw, locking in the secret.

"No one you know," she said. "Just an old man I met once in a garden."

He paused, studying her in the steamy heat of the kitchen, trying to detect the accuracy of her statement—if he could trust the flawlessness of her face matched that of her words. She was withholding something the way she refused his eyes.

"You will get it back when you prove that you were meant to wear it," he said, handing off the black wool cloak to Kazanci Dede, who folded it stiffly over his right arm then turned abruptly and left the kitchen. Rumi remained at the table but stood behind his chair when Kazanci Dede returned with an armful of clothing, issuing Damascena the requisite robes— the kitchen tenure, the wide-skirted brown garments worn by all the Mevlevi dervishes, and also the wider, white skirts used during the *sema* dance. Then he handed her an *elifi*, a small flat, bell-shaped cap that she would wear at all times.

"You'll never see a dervish wear white in the kitchen," Rumi had told her.

"When do you wear it?" she had asked, recalling the dervish she'd seen run down the street, his wide, white skirt glowing in the darkness.

"You wear the white skirt when you are ready to hold hands with God."

Damascena first told herself that she would never wear it, unable to fathom holding the hand of any deity who let people burn and mothers leave their babies, but the white robe that lay beside her was the most beautiful piece of clothing she had ever seen.

Damascena changed into the kitchen skirt, a durable brown yet scratchy cloth that reminded her of burlap, pulled up a pair of ankle-length britches, covered her head with the light colored hat then began her trial into Sufism under the supervision of Kazanci Dede. They called her "Nev-Niyaz," the undressed novice, and assigned her the role of Foot Runner, petitioning the Sultan to permit her to walk the streets.

"Sufi?" she asked, then turned to Rumi in disbelief. "What is Sufi?"

"The feeling of joy when sudden disappointment comes," he said and laughed, watching the girl's lips flatten and her brow furrow when she emerged from the broom closet where she had changed. The dervishes nodded, all toothy grins, enjoying the spectacle of her initiation. She wanted to cast off the skirt, grab her cloak and run.

"I am no Sufi," she said. "You have all been mistaken."

Rumi shrugged. He expected her to react this way. After all, she had been a reluctant saint, but still performed miracles. She struggled to admit this even to herself. Her resistance was as natural a force as the wind. Most everyone objected to the Path when a great Sufi mystic had chosen it for him. Damascena had simply forgotten her spirit's responsibility in this decision.

He wanted to reach out and press Damascena to his chest, let her hear his heart beating and remind her that they walked the same road as Shams, and that she would be safe. She would begin by walking the streets of Konya in daylight.

She stared at him. "But girls don't walk the streets alone here."

"You will be safe. The Sultan has given you permission to do your work."

She stared at him, incredulous.

"What about my feet and legs? What about my hands?"

Rumi smiled and shrugged, handing her a *pazarci,* two long metal tongs the length of her arm, connected by a metal chain. He tucked them into the *elifinemed,* the sand colored cummerbund, doubled at her thin waist.

"What are those?" she asked, curious. They were not weapons, but heavy.

"*Pazraci?* They are most useful tools. Waive them at the merchants for faster service at the market. It helps them know you come from the *tekke.*"

She pulled one out, feeling the warmth of Rumi's touch on the metal handle.

"You think I am ready for the market?"

Rumi met her eyes and nodded emphatically.

"The blisters are gone. You are healing and ready to walk and learn."

Ates-baz suggested she start as The Launderer instead of the Foot Runner. Rumi objected. She already possessed the patience for cleaning clothes as well as many of the tasks she would eventually come to perform in the kitchen.

"Washing clothes will not advance her learning now," Rumi explained, which is why he arranged with the Sultan to let her in the streets. "She needs to learn endurance."

The Foot Runner stood stunned and speechless at the kitchen door with a sack of sugar balanced on each shoulder. He was an olive-skinned man of seventeen, lean yet broad, long-limbed and threaded with veins. Over his skirt, he wore a loose white tunic that stuck to his back and chest, soaked with sweat. His face also perspired and his salt-encrusted brows belied his age. His hair was a mane of golden curls and he blew a few wisps from his face, catching his breath, looking to his fellow initiates as if a great joke was being played on him when they handed him a sooty lantern and a clean rag.

"But I am only nine days into my service," he said, expecting to fulfill the standard eighteen-day schedule running errands. Not that he was complaining. Lucky for him, he thought, wondering who was taking his place during the hottest days of the year.

In his running around in the heat, he had not paused to study the face on the platform for more than a moment, fearing the initiates would take notice, which they did regardless. He was so compelled by the girl with the wild green eyes standing before him that he lost his balance and dropped a sack of sugar on the floor, piercing the bag on a sharp piece of broken tile. Sugar poured everywhere. He covered his mouth in horror, seeing not white crystals scattered on the floor, but the hard-earned coins of the dervish lodge. Sugar was the most expensive item they could buy at the caravanserai.

"I'm so sorry," he said and turned to Rumi in disbelief, watching the sugar grains fill the grout lines between the tiles. Rumi seemed unfazed and handed him one of the lanterns that had been cleaned and placed on the table.

"Do not be sorry. It is a perfect moment to grow," he said. "You can now be Kazanci Dede, the keeper of the lantern. Thank you, Deniz."

The boy took the lantern, uncertain, and nodded.

"For what, *Mevlana*?"

Rumi beamed.

"For the opportunity you have just given to our newest initiate, Damascena."

The golden-haired young man met the girl's steady gaze, then prostrated immediately to her on the broken bag of sugar. Rumi signaled to Damascena.

"Your first errand," he said. "Is to replace the sugar that we have lost."

She stepped forward, feeling the stares of the initiates at her back. She was perspiring and her lips trembled. She felt as if lightning had shot through her body when she met Deniz's gaze, his face sun-kissed and polished like bronze. To avoid the intensity of his beauty, she dropped immediately to the floor and prostrated beside him, overcome by his scent, the smell of salt, and a sweet sweat, the tang of wet leather from his sandals.

She swallowed what felt like a rock in her throat. She could barely breathe. The room felt suddenly hot, as if all the pots on all the stoves had come to a sudden boil. She felt

Rumi's hand on her shoulder. He gently pulled her up to her feet and whispered.

"Do not be afraid of sweetness."

Damascena felt dread, not joy, entering the caravanserai. Mongol soldiers crowded the courtyard and outnumbered the merchants, and she was uncertain there would be any sugar to buy once they left. She could find no merchant available to engage her in a purchase—and not because she was a girl. With her newly shaved head, cap and dervish clothing, she was able to walk through town undetected; however, she wondered why almost everyone here had gathered in the center of the caravanserai courtyard.

She walked toward the crowd, bathed by the great shaft of light pouring through an arch in the portico. She felt disoriented and lost, no longer a girl at fourteen, not quite a woman, self-conscious of her small breasts as she navigated the throng of onlookers, mostly men and boys who had walked great distances from the looks of their blistered feet. Whatever was being sold that morning had solicited the curiosity of many, including seeing the newest Foot Runner from the *tekke*, a girl taking the job of a man.

She inched forward, feeling the body heat of a group of old men pressed behind her and the wooden prayer beads against her abdomen from the men pressed in front. It seemed like everyone there held small wooden prayer beads, threading them nervously through their fingers. The gravity of the situation made her think someone had died, the way these men sobbed when they pushed their way out of the center of the crowd and emerged, not with sugar but small glass bottles filled with a yellow-green liquid. Their eyes were bloodshot and they stumbled, not grief-stricken, but giddy as young drunks.

At first she thought the liquid they carried was olive oil, which made sense since she'd seen Rumi fill his lanterns with it, but it did not give off a foreign, grassy smell. She recognized the sweetness immediately. Roses—here in the caravanserai.

Damascena staggered, seeing the back of a hooded figure standing in the middle of the crowd. Shams, she thought. At last! He had come for her after all. She felt excitement prick her neck and arms. She would lead him back to Rumi, then leave in the morning to find an empty field and be together again with the roses. She pushed through the crowd and ran toward the hooded man, feeling suddenly free and euphoric. He spun around, sensing her, and she gasped, staring not at the shrunken countenance of Shams but at Ivan Balev, who looked just as startled to see her.

"Ivan!" she cried, seeing the bottles of rose oil at his feet. Hundreds of tiny empty glass bottles filled a wooden box that lay open on the ground. He was filling one, passing it to a man in the crowd, who gave him a sack of coins. Ivan's fingers trembled, carrying the scent of roses, but his body stank of guilt. He refused to look at Damascena.

"What are you doing?" she demanded in rough Turkish, giving herself away with her voice and her accent. A man's voice arched over the crowd.

"What does it look like, girl! He's selling rose oil. Now move so we can buy it!"

"But it is not his to sell," Damascena said and turned to Ivan. "Tell them!"

Ivan shifted his bloodshot eyes to the crowd, panicked. His face had aged a hundred years, a bruised and dried apple shrouded by a hood. He had been reduced to bone and his skin was so tight it looked like parchment paper across his cheeks, but what horrified Damascena most of all was seeing the stump of his tongue waggle when he opened his mouth to speak.

"You tried to kill me for this?" she asked, prying his hands off the bottle.

Ivan opened his mouth and groaned. The Mongols grabbed their scabbards.

"It is not yours, girl!" one man roared. "We own the rose oil. Ivan works for us."

They waved their knives at Damascena. The glint of the blades did not scare her, but Ivan trembled and sputtered something indecipherable.

"Tell them, Ivan Balev! Raise your hand once to tell them the rose oil is mine!"

Ivan stared stone-faced at the bottles, refusing to oblige her. Suddenly, something snapped in Damascena and she lunged toward him, reaching for his throat, but staggered, catching the edge of her skirt on the boot of a customer holding one of the bottles. It slipped and fell to the ground, shattering on a stone, the liquid oozing slowly into the dirt.

The man shrieked and batted the ground with fists, hands raised, ready to fight.

"Idiot girl! Look what you've done!" he shouted. "This cost me a fortune! And now it is gone. Gone! You will pay for your mistake."

Damascena did not hear him, feeling the surge of anger in her body.

"Do you know what this is?" the man bellowed, spittle spraying from his mouth.

Damascena locked eyes with Ivan. "I know," she said. "Because I made it."

Boos. Hisses. A voice cried out. "You are a fraud! Go home, girl!"

She knelt on the ground, dragging her fingers through the spilled rose oil, cutting herself on the shards of glass. She watched her blood mix with the oil and thought if this is sweetness, then the world is a most bitter place. There was no home here or love.

The crowd jeered and booed again, then silence descended on the caravanserai. Ivan turned around, stunned, seeing Rumi step toward Damascena.

"This is no way to welcome your sister," Rumi said, forcing a smile. He had followed her to be sure she was safe in the streets.

The Mongols lowered their blades in the great master's presence. "Great *Mevlana*," they protested. "The girl is a liar and a thief."

"Are you sure? Do you know this in your hearts?"

They balked and babbled. Finally, someone spoke.

"She has no right to claim the rose oil is hers."

Rumi turned in a slow circle, right hand lifted to the sky as if to collect their doubts, then cast them into the hot wind that blew through the caravanserai just then.

"The breath of the divine," he said, grateful for the turn of events. He could have never conjured up such ideal circumstances. Damascena had begun her own fire and the final burning was underway. Her duties as a dervish initiate had officially moved beyond the kitchen now. He spoke loudly so that all could hear.

"The only way to know if the rose oil is the girl's is to let her make some more," he said, locking eyes with her, revealing himself once more with the words she had heard so long ago. "*To go guided by fragrance is a hundred times better than following tracks.*"

PART V

*In the center of the rose
a diamond burns forever
larger than all the worlds
more brilliant than any sun.*

—Jalal al-din Mevlana Rumi

ONE

The mystery surrounding the girl who arrived in a black wool cloak quickly grew to mythic proportions. Though everyone had heard of the girl saint from Rila by now, none could truly attest to her ability to turn roses into oil. The citizens of Konya speculated over the deal Rumi had masterfully struck with the Mongols and Seljuks, wondering into whose safekeeping the rose oil had been entrusted and how long it would remain. No one was to sell another drop, or distribute any profits, until they gave Damascena a chance to prove it was hers. They did not doubt its power, only the girl's power to create it.

"Ah, look closer," Rumi encouraged the naysayers, inviting them to observe. "It is in the garden where she is creating herself, preparing her soul to be food for the divine."

The dervishes badgered Rumi for answers. Had Damascena attained the most important mystical states like Rabi'a al-Adawiyya, the Sufi woman to whom Rumi owed much of his wisdom? Had the girl who claimed to turn roses into oil attained *sidq, muhasaba, sukr, mahabha*, or *ma'rifa*? Was it even possible for a person as young as she to understand the importance of truthfulness, self-criticism, spiritual intoxication, love for God and *gnosis* as a means of spiritual evolution? If it was, they wondered if only age separated them from the very source of truth that was their birthright. They wanted to know why they had forgotten these spiritual truths but were too embarrassed to ask.

Rumi had taught girls before, family members, daughters of friends, even strangers, who had traveled long distances to seek his teaching. It was not uncommon for females to study and earn respect, even to be seen as spiritual masters themselves. But Damascena had arrived in Konya wearing the highly coveted black wool coat, which left most people beguiled and speculating: was the girl taught by a spiritual master, or did she possess such mastery herself? It was the only logic they could apply to Rumi's devotion, still, jealousy bubbled in their blood and felt like sand in their veins.

Ates-baz encouraged the initiates to give Damascena a chance. They continued to perform their tasks in the kitchen, pausing only to stare out the window in disbelief—the girl had even taken over their vegetable garden, now overgrown with roses.

"She's coming here every day?" Hosam asked, one week after a wager was made in the caravanserai. He wished he had been there to protest, and he gasped when Damascena showed up at his house with Rumi. They stared at each other in the doorway.

"Give her access to your land," Rumi said, knowing roses grew well there.

"For what?" Hosam asked, wearing his disdain in the furrow between his eyes.

"Until she has enough cuttings to produce an adequate yield for the oil."

One morning, Damascena demonstrated how to take a cutting for Rumi. The moon was still up and an owl hooted from a tree outside Hosam's house.

"If I push here and they don't give easily, they are too young," she explained, taking only from the stems whose thorns popped off easily in her hands.

Rumi understood. "Yes. Only the mature can leave the stem," he said, recalling Sham's last words before he disappeared. "Just as separation makes a person wise."

She turned to him, squinting in the half-light and smiled. "Shams left you, too?"

Rumi nodded. It was the first time they had spoken directly of their friend for some time and he felt the skin on his neck prickle when Damascena mentioned his name.

"Yes. He was the thorn," he said and laughed softly. "We are the stem. But one day the pain will be transformed."

"Into what?"

"Trust that it will become love. And after that beauty."

They did not speak again of Shams. Damascena resumed her work in silence with a boldness and quiet determination that Rumi had never seen in any of the initiates. It was as if the girl and the roses were engaged in a dialogue that only she could hear; but in the midst of that silent conversation, Rumi heard a woman's voice calling her home.

Damascena worried about lack of rain. The sun beat down on the garden and provided ample light, but the air was too hot and dry. Six hours of sunlight collected in the plot behind the dervish kitchen where only vegetables shared the soil with the roses. Under normal conditions, the soil was rich and healthy, well drained, too, but it had not rained in weeks. These were unbearable conditions for growing roses, considering they needed water at the root level every other day. The roses had already withstood four days without water, the longest she had ever let the roses go in Krun.

Even if the rains came, she doubted water alone would make the roses grow. It was the dance of Shams they needed, and she was determined to master it, even if Rumi had forbidden her. She had not asked him again since the night they stood in the street outside the lodge.

For months, she had stared at the stone wall from the garden, drawn to the rhythms from the *semahane*, the ceremonial hall. It was not the sound of a drum, but something metallic, as if someone was pounding on a large pot. The sound beckoned her, until one day she couldn't take it any longer, and she mustered the courage to climb the large mulberry tree outside the lodge to peer through the narrow slit in the stones that served as a window.

All she could see at first was the Kazanci Dede, bent over a large, cast iron cauldron, beating it with a wooden spoon. His tall conical hat had slid over to one side of his head, revealing matted wisps of hair. He dabbed at the back of his neck with a small towel, pausing every so often to drink water. He had worked up a great sweat keeping the beat for the dervishes who, at first, appeared to be nothing but a black blur as they walked into the great hall and lined up against the wall in their long black robes and conical hats.

She counted nine of them. They knelt on the floor and remained in meditation while another man sang a prayer and a hymn. When he finished, the dervishes slapped the floor with their hands, startling Damascena when a single *ney* began to play. She gripped the tree harder, watching the dervishes rise and walk slowly in a counterclockwise direction three times. It was a curious ritual and she had no idea what it all meant.

The dervishes then paused in front of the *sheikh*, who also kissed each of their long conical hats. One by one, when they reached a post, they turned around and bowed to the dervish following him in the circle—each moving slowly to the flow of the reed flute. The *sheikh* then got up and took a seat at the post, and the dervishes simultaneously removed the black robes, placed them to the side, and began to form a circle again. They held their arms crossed in front of their chests with each hand on opposite shoulders, and every time they passed the *sheihk*'s post, they kissed his right hand one last time and bowed, before spinning in one huge circle around the hall. They slowly gained speed until they appeared to be a blur again, this time all white in the *tennure* skirts, as if the whole point of tossing the black robes was to cast away death and bring light.

Damascena recalled the same white skirt worn by the young man she had seen leave the lodge in a daze one night, the same white skirt Shams had worn that unfurled like a flower when he twirled. She felt a chill. Of course, she thought. This was the dance that made roses grow. The dancers moved in circles, arms outstretched, right hand turned upward, left hand facing the ground, chins steady, eyes focused as if in a trance. They seemed to be held in place by some invisible force, turning, turning, without falling.

No one spoke. The only sound was their breath and the beating of the cauldron, as if to keep them turning at the same pace. It was like Shams was there, she thought, inside each of them. She longed to join the dancers, forbidden or not. She climbed down from the tree and held out her hand, circling it three times, imagining herself inside the hall. She had been issued one white flowering skirt, and she believed she was ready to wear it.

Though *sema* would not be easy, she would dance for the sake of the roses. She would have to wait until after the evening prayers and the last meal, when the dervishes retreated to their cells. Even then, they would check on her from time to time during the night—peering out their windows whenever she chose to sleep in the garden rather than at Rumi's house.

They figured sleeping on the ground was a test Rumi had devised for Damascena, and they were impressed by her endurance, as if the girl had been born to lie in dirt. They believed the fire she survived had made her restless. During dinner, wagers had been made that Damascena would not last three months, let alone three years. She certainly wouldn't make it beyond September, the ninth lunar month that year, but Rumi already exempted her from Ramadan, causing an outrage among the most pious.

Tea and talk turned to quarrels. Was Rumi going mad again? So mad he had exempted someone from the annual month-long purification ritual of fasting, the most important observation in the Muslim calendar? And what was Rumi teaching if he was not teaching Damascena the value of fasting, something he required of himself and all who came to the *tekke* to study with him? How would this girl prove her faith?

Damascena overheard Rumi debating Ates-baz about it. She stood in the garden, hearing their voices through the kitchen door that had been opened to let out the heat from the ovens. The air smelled of toasted cheese and pine nuts from baking borek.

"How do you know she has what it takes to stay on the path?"

"Fasting alone does not illuminate the true character of a person," Rumi said.

Ates-baz choked back a laugh, then slammed a lid on a pot.

"Easy for you to say, *Mevlana*. You're the one who gave her a choice!"

"There is no choice and she knows this," Rumi countered.

"Can't you see? The girl already has faith. Maybe more than most of us, she just doesn't know it yet. The girl has spent her life fasting. And that has been enough to prepare her to stay on this path!"

Damascena did not agree with Rumi. She had no faith. The only thing bubbling inside her was the doubt she had about her ability to make the roses grow without Shams. One more day without rain and the roots would die; but the sixth day of the sixth month was as good a day as any, she thought, to help something live.

Damascena had not mentioned her 15th birthday to anyone and had gone about her duties that day in silence, waiting for the perfect conditions to enter the Meydan. Under the darkness of a new moon, she left her shoes at the door as was the custom in every building in Konya, holy or not, and entered the lodge in her white skirt. It was the first time she had stood in the great hall. The vastness of the space overwhelmed her and she felt even more alone and estranged. She should not be here, she told herself, but her desire to dance was far greater than the shame of her violation.

She flung her arms to her sides and began to turn, expecting the sensation of weightlessness, but the bulk of the skirt made it difficult to move. She could barely turn a full circle without feeling pulled to the floor—finally understanding the purpose of the thick, fifteen centimeter band sewn above the hem on top of the *tenure*. She would have preferred to twirl around a mulberry tree for support. She struggled to keep her shoulders back, and stand tall enough to breathe properly. In all the times she had seen Shams dance, she never once considered the skirt an encumbrance. His movements were so fluid that he appeared to float over the flowers when he twirled.

Her arms flung about awkwardly, legs entangled with the layers of the heavy skirt. When she turned into the light shining on her, she lost her balance and fell.

"Are you hurt?"

She recognized Deniz's voice. The Keeper of the Lantern. His light moved closer.

"My sister, are you hurt?" he asked again, his voice more urgent in the darkness.

The lantern stopped swinging and the light fell on her like a sword. "Damascena?"

She did not like the way he said her name, packing it with accusations. She could not speak and clutched her knees to her chest, feeling the swelling in her wrist. Her lips trembled. She had failed the dance before she even started. She wanted to roll up in a ball and hide forever. She held her hand up, shielding her eyes from the lamplight.

"I'll leave," she said. "I made a mistake. I know I'm not supposed to be here."

"But you are. And you are hurt."

His lantern reflected the shine of her left leg and foot, deformed by the burns, the scar tissue fused at her toes and forming a shallow depression on the side of her thigh.

"I'm fine," she said and pulled her skirt over her leg, then quickly sat back on her feet to hide them from his sight. "I don't know what I was thinking."

"Hopefully nothing if you were you trying to dance *sema*. Were you?"

She sat up, peering past the beam, making out the form of Deniz as he walked slowly toward her. She could smell him and he smelled sweet, of mulberries and musk.

She thought for a moment the light was coming from the center of his chest. He extended his hand to her in the darkness. His fingers were long and smooth and the lamplight illuminated the veins in his hands and forearms like thin blue ribbons.

"Let me help you get up."

She reached out and felt an instant shock the moment they touched. She trembled and he interlaced his fingers with hers and pulled her to her feet.

"If you want to dance, the dance must invite you into it."

She swallowed, overcome by an overwhelming heat in her thighs and chest. She studied him in the darkness, his smooth high cheekbones and slender nose. She had not had a good look at him in the kitchen, but here in the darkness his features seemed more pronounced. She wondered if he could see her cheeks burning.

"So how do I receive the invitation?" she asked.

"No one receives it. Only their hearts. You know you have received the invitation when your heart is ready to risk everything to hold the hand of God. You must be ready—or bold. I know of no one with the courage to dance *sema* uninvited."

"Will you teach me?" she asked.

Deniz studied her in the lamplight. He was new to the dervish lodge, too, and though he had learned the dance, he had not practiced much. He bowed to her, and to his surprise, she bowed back, as if she already understood the ritual.

"I see you are bold *and* ready," he said and set the lamp on the floor.

He rooted around the pocket of his brown skirt and pulled out a large wooden nail, then crouched and stuck it between the first two toes of his left foot. He turned, slowly at first, then faster, arms outstretched, while the nail kept him in place.

"Think of yourself as a rod between heaven and earth. Right palm to the sky to receive heaven, left hand faces the ground to connect the divine to the earth. Your arms are supposed to make the Arabic letters *lam* and *aleph*."

It all looked so organized, she thought. So clean and effortless.

"Is that why you all say *La ilaha illah Allah* before you start the dance?" she asked. He nodded and pulled the nail out, then handed it to her. "Your turn."

She took the nail and placed it between the toes of her right foot, but Deniz swooped down and plucked it out before she could move.

"Left foot. Always," he said, explaining that dervishes use only their left foot to dance and cover the left toes immediately with their right foot upon starting the dance.

"Then how do you move at all?" she asked, unsure of the mechanics of the dance. It had all looked so easy when Shams had performed *sema*.

"Rotate on the left foot with the right foot crossing over the top of the left," he emphasized and then showed her by doing it himself. "You only place the right foot on the left toe at the start of the dance—as a way to honor the Divine."

Damascena was still confused. "I do not understand how that could be."

Deniz shared the beloved tale. "The day Ates-baz kicked the stove in his angst and impatience, he inadvertently burned his left big toe. He was embarrassed by what this revealed about his own doubt, so he tried to hide his burnt toe by covering it with his right foot. It's a gesture we make when dancing *sema*, as a reminder of our faith in God."

"Then I am not sure I should be dancing at all," she said, unwilling to show him her left foot and what remained of her toes. The burn marks left no separation between her big toe and the one beside it, making it impossible to place the wooden nail there.

"That is for you to find out. Only the listener knows what is true for them."

She rubbed her finger along the smooth wooden nail and handed it back.

"I can listen without it," she said.

Deniz nodded. He had never known anyone to dance without a nail to keep them in place. How the girl would turn without it was beyond him, but he did not want to cause her any more humiliation.

"I'm sure there is a way for you," he said as he met her eyes.

She looked away from him. "I really just want to dance. I do not need to listen."

"But we are listening while we dance. *Sema* means listening," he explained, "It is Persian. Surely Rumi taught you that much with all the time he has spent with you."

She shook her head. "No. Mostly we share silence together."

Deniz chuckled. "Now it is my turn to laugh. You have sat with the greatest mystic of all time, possibly one of the best poets, and you tell me you speak of nothing?"

A wave of disappointment surged through her. She felt Deniz's hand firmly on her shoulder and she drew in a sharp breath when he leaned close to her ear and whispered.

"I was afraid of the dance once, too. But I learned to embrace it and the mistakes I would make. Do not turn away from your fear. Turn toward love instead, Damascena. *Sema* will transform you."

TWO

Darkness held Damascena and Deniz that night as it did all subsequent nights when they met to dance *sema*, unseen. Damascena made it clear that she was ready to accept her fate if she got caught; however, she was not yet ready to hold the hand of God, or of Deniz for that matter. When she found herself spinning out of control, she reached for the lion-haired boy, grasping not his fingers, but the thick flesh of his forearms, unable to distinguish the throbbing in his veins from that in her stomach.

"I feel sick," she said, demoralized, and turned to vomit.

Deniz cleaned up the floor and brought her water and a rag to wipe her mouth, wishing someone had done the same for him. The image almost made him laugh. *Sema* was not meant to be easy. It was the work of ardent hearts. He had seen many others suffer the nausea of spinning in the beginning, and often wondered why no one was given any instruction at first, other than the location of the nail to keep them in place.

"First, I will teach you how to spin. The rest of the dance comes later," he told her, just as Kazanci Dede had explained the ancient ritual of turning, paying deference to its Egyptian roots—the Dance of The Stars. He repeated only what he learned about spinning, trying his best to imitate the belligerence and bellowing of Kazanci Dede.

"You dance ... you dance like a girl!" he barked.

"I am a girl."

"The dance is not a flower."

She said nothing, resisting the urge to tell him that was the point. She was doing this for the roses. So why not dance in a manner that evoked their essence?

Deniz stomped his foot on the floor as if he had read her mind.

"No! *Sema* is not about being fragile," he said, recalling Karanci Dede's instruction to him when he was a frail boy who had just lost his father. "The circle dance requires you to be strong. It is a conscious decision for a person to participate in this sacred revolution of all beings. That is why we form a circle. You must move like the universe to become one with it," Deniz said, uncertain the girl understood this when she moved west to east. It made him dizzy watching her turn away from God like that.

"Stop. Stop! You must move in the opposite direction, from birth to death."

She paused and stared at him.

"If there are so many specialized movements, why have you taught me only one?"

"Learning to spin is the only one you're ready to learn," he said.

"Then help! You're the teacher. For days, you've just stood there and watched."

"It is my job to observe you first."

"And what is it you see?" she demanded, hands on hips, lips screwed tight.

He studied her in the darkness, her temples and cheekbones glistening with sweat.

"Everyone's way of spinning reveals more to the observer than it can ever reveal to the dancer at first," he said, recalling how Kazanci Dede had told him the dance would not make him a leader, but would help him overcome his habit of shrinking.

Now this strange beauty who slept in a garden wanted to know what he saw?

He had never met anyone more desperate to learn *sema*, and he was unsure he was the right person to teach her, but something about Damascena suggested she would learn faster than most, even if she had a lot to learn about living larger within herself.

"Go on. Tell me," she urged. "What has my way of dancing revealed to you?"

He cleared his throat, grasped his edge, trying to answer her with authority.

"You spin too fast! You must slow down," he cautioned.

"There is no time," she said, setting the empty glass on the floor and getting up, feeling lightheaded when she crossed to the window overlooking the garden. Deniz followed her, fearing that she would faint. She turned to him.

"Why do you dance?" she asked.

He held onto her gaze, stunned she didn't know. "To meet God."

"I dance to make the roses grow," she said and stared longingly at the garden.

Night after night, she spun and spun, and her whole body pulsed with an energy she had never known. She felt uplifted, as if she were not just remaining in a fixed place, but traveling with each turn. She saw flashes of pearly light, odd colorful forms she could not identify, rainbow prisms, shards of moonlight.

She thought she was seeing fragments of the rose window and the white house. Often she saw the woman of fire and the tanner, wondering if they might meet inside the dance. Although she felt nauseous, she continued to turn even without a wooden nail. The fused toes on her left foot had given her an advantage.

The more she spun, the more she felt at home, as if her feet were growing roots and the dance had become another garden.

She felt Deniz watching her closely in the dark. He kept the rhythm each night by whispering 'hu' so much that she had started to call him Owl, *baykus*. He acted hurt, but his teeth lit up the room when he smiled.

"I am no more an owl than you are a rose trying to will yourself to bloom," he teased. "But speed will not deliver you from what's holding you back."

"And what is that?" she asked, meeting his eyes in the light coming in through the window. It was the second full moon since they had begun her training.

Deniz paused, sensing her challenge, then walked closer and leaned into her, smelling the sweat on her neck. "Fear," he said.

"Of what?"

"Love," he said and swallowed.

"What do you know of love?" she asked and studied his throat.

"It is yours to claim. Do you know why we open our vest with our right hand after the last turn of this dance?"

"Why?"

"To let the world into our heart."

She leaned away from him, uncertain she had the strength to do that when she had not yet let her mother dwell there. She caught his eye, before she began to spin again.

Deniz was pleased with his teaching. The girl looked happier, more radiant and peaceful. He wasn't imagining it. The dervishes also noticed some bigger transformation happening inside Damascena, though they did not suspect it was from dancing *sema*.

She was fifteen and considered an adult. Her hair had grown long again and her eyes had brightened. She was growing taller and she imbued the specialized set of movements with a grace and elegance none of them possessed. It was as if the dance had taken hold of *her* hand.

Deniz could feel the energy pulsing from the middle of her palms whenever he paused to correct her posture. He wanted to know if she believed in life force, if she believed God was coming through her in the form of this energy. Because that's what he believed. Lately, he wanted to know all her thoughts, but mostly what she thought of him.

"You drink too much coffee," she said when they finished dancing.

"How do you know?" he asked. Easier to speak of the mundane in these moments, he thought, than anything that might scare her.

Damascena dabbed the sweat on her brow. Her cheeks pink with the evening heat. "I watch you," she said and took a deep breath, exhaling slowly. "I count."

"You count?"

She nodded. "You drink two cups in the morning, one at night."

He laughed. "Is that right? Tell me more about my preferences."

She held his gaze but not his smile. Her stare sent a rush through his feet, up his legs, grabbed the center of his stomach and pressed the breath out of his lungs. I am not turning, but this is *sema*, Deniz thought, listening to every word, every syllable she spoke as if he had never heard the girl speak. Her voice wrapped around him like spun silk.

"You like stuffed aubergines, but you prefer butternut squash with lamb and onions, and you save all the lamb to eat last, chewing each piece ten times."

"Ten times?"

She nodded and fought a smile. Aside from Rumi, nobody had ever listened to her as closely as this. She whispered and he moved closer. "Chicken borek reminds you of your mother, and you always dab your eyes when a plate of it is set before you. You do not like liver soup or bulgur with yogurt. Your favorite fruit is watermelon, which is why you've named the kitchen cat *Karpusz*. Your favorite dessert is rice pudding and you'll always take one extra piece of baklava and slip it into your robe, then pick out the almonds when Ates-baz has run out of pistachios. You sneeze within three seconds every time you eat anything with mint, and despite the fact that you get a stomach ache," she said and lowered her voice again, barely audible, "You could eat milk and honey sherbet ... every day for the rest of your life."

He stared at her dumbstruck. He could tell her only of the way she held her spoon, and the way her lips looked fuller after she ate a pomegranate.

Fire, she thought, when his lips met hers—I am on fire again. He tasted like lemon and sugar and she licked the salt on his neck, behind his ears, following the ridge of his jaw. The heat surged through her body and blistered her heart with a new kind of soreness after that night, a dull aching when she wasn't in his presence. She felt an inextricable link to him at all times of the day no matter where he was or what he was doing in the *tekke*. For days, she carried the taste of him on her lips.

Her skin glowed. Rumi attributed the girl's radiance to roses and God's beauty.

"The lamp of the light of faith is lit within the glass of the body of the believer," Rumi had told her late one afternoon in the garden at the *tekke*. Damascena paused with the bucket of water she had carried from the well to water the roses. She thought he was referring to Deniz. "The body of the Gnostic through self-abnegation becomes just like a glass through which the light of faith shines," he said, wiping the sweat around his eyes.

"Self-abnegation?" she had asked. Rumi rarely spoke such big words and they didn't sound like his own. He sounded like a professor, which he told her he had been.

"Self-denial," he explained, "My mentor Borhan al-Din believed that fasting leads to detachment from worldly matters. You are doing well here."

She tilted her head, trying to understand. I want to turn the roses into oil, for you, she thought. She was a gardener rooted to the soil, to real things, not thoughts. Her fasting was not voluntary. The transcendent state of being that Rumi and everyone else seemed to be witnessing in her was not a result of her refraining from food.

"I eat between sunrise and sunset. You see me!"

"There are many ways to fast. You are purifying your mind and your heart."

She swallowed, feeling the phantom touch of Deniz's lips on hers.

"Does that mean I will wear the wool cloak again?"

He turned to her. "It means you are on your way to proving the rose oil is yours."

"It will take another year to grow enough for any significant yield."

"Then you are welcome to stay here until you are done."

She stared at him, resisting the urge to stroke the soft white beard.

"You have a lot of faith in me," she said.

"Because God has a lot of faith in you."

She said nothing and resumed her service to the roses. Rumi had attributed her sudden loss of appetite to a detachment from the world, but nothing could be further from the truth. She had lost all self-control and found herself counting the hours, even when tending roses, until she could dance *sema* again and dissolve with Deniz in the darkness.

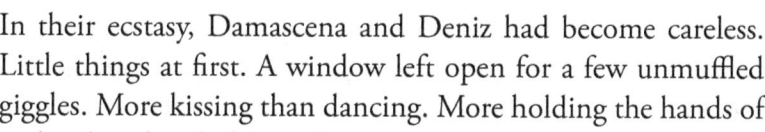

In their ecstasy, Damascena and Deniz had become careless. Little things at first. A window left open for a few unmuffled giggles. More kissing than dancing. More holding the hands of each other than holding the hands of God.

Their passion obliterated any guilt that might have guided them to the right path. First to confess to Rumi, then seek redemption from the rest of the dervishes. Carnal relations were forbidden in the *tekke*, despite rumors of many that had sprung up over the years, even between men.

In the daytime, after the late morning meal, Deniz and Damascena would climb the hills overlooking the peaks of the two distant volcanoes, and kiss in the high grasses with the cicadas and butterflies, their robes open, feeling the heat rising from the plain.

Damascena had been careful to lie on Deniz's left side so that only her right leg touched his. She had been mindful of the robe and wrapped it around her left side to hide the burn marks, but could do nothing about the wind that exposed her that day.

Deniz sat up on his elbow and looked at her for the first time in daylight, his face unable to hide his disbelief and disgust, not at the injury itself, but that she had suffered.

"Who burned you?" he asked, sensing the complexity of the tale, trying to sort out the facts from the rumors he had heard when she first arrived in Konya.

She swallowed, feeling her throat tighten. She had told no one the story. She picked a piece of grass and wrapped it around her finger, debating how much to tell him.

"It does not matter who did it, Deniz. What matters is that I survived."

He locked eyes with her and traced the bones of her face with his finger.

"I am glad you are here."

She nodded, took in a deep breath, fighting the tear that had escaped her and met his lips again, pushing the pain into the kiss and ending their discussion.

On their backs, they pointed to lambs and birds in passing clouds, laughed at the absurdity of their situation, and would kiss again, legs entangled, young bodies pressed against each other, the smell of green wheat and tomatoes in the air, the throaty timbre of distant camel drivers arcing over them. They swam in the river, ran through the long reed beds, playing hide and seek, then chased each other into the streets to eat grilled kebabs and drink fresh juice from the vendors.

She dressed like Deniz and covered her head to disguise herself, but still solicited the admiring, toothless grins and smiling eyes of old women, groups of weavers, barefoot and crouched in the shade carding wool. They received complimentary lemon sherbet from a recently widowed man, who asked them when they were getting married, and if they would like him to provide this refreshing desert to their guests. Family recipe, he emphasized. Loved by Rumi. Deniz laughed. Everyone was trying to claim *Mevlana's* preferences, as if his name alone could sell almost anything in the world. *Buy this silk, Rumi made a pillow out of it. Try on these socks, Mevlana said they were soft. Eat this honey, Rumi's wife uses it in her tea.* But Rumi had no preferences for material things.

Deniz wanted to tell the wispy vendor, "Rumi will probably marry us," but didn't want to excite the man for fear he might drop to the dusty street and die. Deniz liked the vendor's heirloom sherbet and he liked that he gave it to him and Damascena for free, one benefit of being recognized as a dervish. Now he had been recognized as a man, too.

"I have not considered her my future bride until now," he said, feeling suddenly puffed up, sultan-like. He stepped away from the vendor, taking Damascena's hand. He stepped into the street, his fingers laced with hers, and gave her a quick squeeze.

"Will you be my bride?" he asked. She let go and flung her hands to her side as if she'd been stung by a bee, then turned to him, lips parted, wet and icy. She looked like a Greek goddess formed of stone, frozen in the early August heat.

She lowered her voice. "You do not want to marry a girl whose mother abandoned her at birth."

Deniz straightened. "I do not care about that."

"But I do not even know how to love myself."

"I will help you learn," he said, trying to think on his feet.

"Do you think you must teach me everything? Do you really want a wife that is your *student*? Can you not see? I must teach myself!"

He stiffened, stung by her rejection, then cleared his throat in the dusty street, tasting the tartness of lemon and a future without Damascena.

THREE

Damascena followed Deniz back to the *tekke*, where they spoke of new moons, not marriage, and prepared for Ramadan at the end of August. Damascena wanted to participate in the ritual as another way to prove herself to the dervishes who did not see the value in her work with roses. Ramadan seemed to offer one more test of patience, forbearance, and obedience, if her dedication in the garden wasn't enough. She decided refraining from food for a month would be much easier than envisioning herself as Deniz's bride. Fasting would cleanse her thoughts and purify her heart, she thought.

"Are you sure you want to go through with it?" Rumi asked her on the first day, wondering if she had the stamina to last twenty-nine more days of inner housework—clearing out the detritus of one's heart, though everyone knew it was a life-long process.

"Do you know Ramadan comes from the Arabic word *ramida,* meaning intense heat, scorched ground, and therefore, shortness of food?"

Damascena shrugged. "I'm not surprised. Everything around you seems related to burning," she said and glanced at the scars on her hands. "Ates-baz. Even me."

"Then you know the soul work of which I speak. Whether or not we choose to accept that truth depends on our courage.

But life is the work of the spirit trying to have a *human* experience. This being human is a very hard job. And Ramadan is not much easier. I can exempt you again this year, if you prefer."

"Why should I be exempt? I'm fifteen." She was, by society's standards, an adult. She demonstrated her maturity by wanting to participate in this period of slowing down.

"Just get enough rest," he said.

"I will rest."

"Please. Come back to the house often. I don't want you fainting in the sun."

"I won't faint. And I'll be fine sleeping with the roses."

"You must eat both meals, after sunset and before sunrise."

"I will eat."

"Eat the figs. Many figs after sunset. And you will tell me if you don't feel well?"

"Yes, Rumi," she said, refusing to tell him that she did not feel well now.

Deniz's absence was enough to test Damascena's patience and humility. She did not need Ramadan as another trial. She waited for him each night, but he did not come to dance. It had been three weeks since their trip to the market. She wanted to believe he was observing the warnings about physical activity during Ramadan, since drinking water was prohibited during the day. Konya had fallen into a deep sleep, the streets quiet. The shops, closed during normal business hours, burst open with activity only at night. Gone was the safety of dancing in the dark.

On the tenth night of Ramadan, she asked Rumi where Deniz was when the initiates and dervishes met to break the fast after sunset and eat a light meal of fruit and figs. She was surprised Deniz didn't show up for the milk and honey sherbet Ates-baz had made as a treat. She was suddenly panicked.

"He didn't tell you?" Rumi asked.

Damascena lowered her eyes, feeling the stares of the other dervishes who had stopped chewing to listen. Her inquiry about just one of them raised brows.

Rumi lowered his voice and stared at her quizzically.

"He's taken a leave of absence."

"During Ramadan? I didn't think you could do that."

"He had some personal matters to attend to," he said and turned from her, exchanging a knowing look with Ates-baz, who coughed.

"Is he okay?" she asked.

Ates-baz cleared his throat, then walked up behind her and pressed something into her hand. She did not have to look to know what it was. She recognized the smoothness of the wooden nail.

"I don't know. Is he?" Ates-baz asked and met her eye. "He left this."

Stay in the garden. Stay quiet, she told herself, do not bring attention to yourself. She did not speak to the cook again but wondered how much he knew. Ates-baz, like many of the Dedes, was mostly a kind man, but this softness was always proportionate with volatility. Her imagination ran amok when Rumi stopped coming to the garden to visit, and she felt alone and frightened. Even in his absence, The Keeper of the Lantern haunted her. *Sema will transform you.* His words looped in her mind and eclipsed the music of the nightingales. She knew that Ramadan would be a month of reflection, but she had had too much time to think. It struck her that it wasn't just roses she wanted.

She wanted Deniz. She found herself dreaming about his arms, his hands. She wanted to hold him—and smell him. She felt embarrassed. The images she conjured up about Deniz cluttered her head. Surely she would need more than twenty-nine days to purify herself of such desires, but she kept remembering the taste of salt on his neck and chest. She had no way of knowing how he felt about her now, wherever he was. She had left his proposal in the dusty streets of the market, stale as old bread.

On the twenty-third night of Ramadan, Damascena walked ten kilometers to Hosam's, ignoring all warnings to refrain from strenuous exercise. She could see the flicker of an oil lamp and Hosam's shadow on the wall while he prayed, prostrating to Allah. Rumi had warned her not to bother him at this time. Hosam requested solitude during the last ten days of Ramadan, preferring to be closer to nature than sit in the mosque in meditation all day. She knew this was the most intense time of the fast. Rumi told her this was when people got serious about showing God what they were made of, which is why the mosques were so crowded and the town felt deserted.

She agreed to give Hosam space, under the condition that he water the roses. She wanted to trust his word, but something gnawed at her each day she hadn't tended to the roses herself. She thought she would sneak by him, sit with the roses, and leave before sunrise when Hosam resumed his prayers. He wouldn't even know she had come.

Normally, she knocked on his front door to announce herself and say hello, even if he was less than welcoming, but tonight she made her way to the roses alone and lay down in the dirt. She pushed up her sleeves and pulled up her skirt to feel the cool earth on her legs and arms, working her bare heels into the ground to anchor herself to everything that supported her. Ever since the fire, she had stopped praying but tonight, on Laylat Al-Qadr, The Night of Power, she felt the urge to offer gratitude for the roses.

She raked the earth with her fingers, feeling the soil clumped under her nails. This is my union, she thought. These roses whose roots support my spine. The dirt that holds me up.

She did not know how long she had stayed in the rose field. She must have fallen asleep because when she opened her eyes, she saw Hosam standing over her with a small clay oil lamp, the kind in which Kerra believed djinns lived, and it spooked her.

"What are you doing here?" he said, and his voice shook.

Damascena sat up and pulled down her skirt and sleeves to cover herself. The cool night air of mid-September swept down from the mountains and across the plain, delivering the first chill of the season. In the moonlight, the dormant volcanoes in the distance looked like two giant sentries, Hosam standing between them like a gate.

"Did Rumi send you?"

"No."

"But you chose to abuse your privilege coming here tonight of all nights?"

"No, Hosam. I do not wish to abuse anything. I just wanted to—"

"What? What could you possibly want? You have everything. You have Rumi!" he said and swung the lamp over her face. "Do you know what tonight is?"

She nodded, mind racing, trying to make sense of his words. Her lips trembled. "Tonight is Laylat Al-Qadr. The Night of Power. I don't have—"

"The Night of Wisdom," he snapped, correcting her.

She drew in a breath. "I have heard both. What is the difference?"

He mocked her, his voice higher, "*What is the difference?* I'll tell you the difference. This is the night Mohammed received the Qu'ran from the Angel Gabriel. "

She knew and nodded, shrinking in the shadow of the lamplight. He was angry tonight, more disturbed by her presence than usual. She thought to win his favor by reciting the verse from the Qu'ran that Rumi had taught her about Laylat Al-Qadr.

She began slowly, turning her gaze past Hosam to the moon.

We have indeed revealed this (Message)
    in the Night of Power:
And what will explain to thee what the night of power is?
The Night of Power is better than a thousand months.
Therein come down the angels and the Spirit
    and Allah's permission, on every errand: Peace!...
This until the rise of morn!

Hosam's lips parted and she thought at first she had won a smile. He laughed.

"Yes. Exactly, peace until the rise of the morn," he said, looking up at the moon. "So tell me, while there is still peace, why you came."

"I wanted to pray."

"No. Tell me why you came here. To Konya. To Rumi!"

"For the same reason you came to him, Hosam."

She rarely said his name and he took note of the power in her address.

"Why is that?" he said, slowly.

"We've both been contracted."

"Your work is hardly worth a contract. I do not see how the roses serve Rumi ... And Rumi believes you are beyond ego. He is blinded by his love for you."

She swallowed. She did not know what to say about that.

She had not come to Konya seeking Rumi's love or pity. Or anyone's for that matter. Love was not the point and pity was a poor man's pride. She did not need anyone else's love when she had roses.

"I know God wants you to help Rumi write."

He nodded, agitated. "And how did God ask you to serve Rumi?"

"I must grow the roses so that Rumi can go home," she said.

Hosam reached out and wrapped his fingers around her forearm, shaking her.

"Shhh! Don't say that!" he screamed as if she had invoked a curse. "Don't you dare say that tonight! Rumi is home! Here with us on earth!"

Damascena's arm burned. Hosam let go, seeing the imprint of his fingers in the girl's skin. "I'm sorry to upset you, but what I speak is true," she said. She got up to leave and brushed the soil off her clothes, feeling lightheaded. She regretted the distance from here to the *tekke*. If she couldn't make it, she'd sleep along the way. Pray for a donkey or some small mercy. No matter how much she longed to stay with the roses, she did not want to be near Hosam. She could smell his anger and it was fetid and biting like Ivan's.

"So you think you can leave now? Just like that?"

"I have a long walk. I want to go while I can still take water."

"You should have thought about that before," he said and reached out and grabbed the collar of her dress.

She paused, stiffening, hearing the first tear of her dress. Hosam pulled the cloth in half, shoulders to calves, exposing her to the moonlight. She shuddered and when she opened her mouth to scream, he slapped his hand on top of her mouth and whispered.

"Whatever you have come to do, you must let him write. You must promise to let him finish the book!"

She tasted salt and dirt as the tears slid down her nose, then dug her heels into the ground, imagining rose roots shooting out from her feet, grounding her into the darkness.

He lifted his hand off her mouth.

"I cannot," she whispered, pulling the halves of her dress over her naked body.

"What? What do you mean you cannot. You cannot let Rumi die early!"

She met his eyes. "I cannot promise that. I only know what I have been sent to do, like you understand what you have been sent to do. We don't have to be enemies! Don't you see?"

Hosam flung his arms in the air and spit on the ground.

"Allah! Allah," he cried. "You even sound like Rumi! You will drive me mad!"

He lurched forward and grabbed her by the throat, with the impulse to snap it. "Who sent you here! Tell me who put you up to this!"

She struggled to breathe and kicked his shins. "SSSHHHM-MMS." She forced his name. Hosam let go and stepped back with a wild, almost haunted look in his face.

"Who?"

She coughed. Gagged. Spit up blood on her hand. She remembered Rumi's warning not to mention his name but could not help herself. It was her only defense.

"Shams," she said and coughed again, then turned to him and screamed as loud as she could. "SHAMS!" She felt the word come up through her whole being as if the force with which she uttered his name could summon him to the rose fields.

Hosam doubled-over as if he'd been punched in the gut.

"Impossible," he muttered, rubbing his eyes.

"Shams sent me," the girl offered again, hoping he understood.

"I swear on the Qu'ran," she said and shivered. "Shams sent me. He led me away from my burning bed."

"Liar!"

Damascena's bottom lip trembled. Her neck ached.

"He did! You must believe me, Hosam. I am not lying. I cannot tell you the details of it all. I just remember the fire. Shams standing there by the door. It was locked. He lifted me out of the bed and carried me through it. I don't remember much after that. I don't remember the trip, except for hearing the camel drivers sing. Then seeing Rumi when I woke up. Then you. I thought I was dead."

Hosam wiped his neck and stared at her, skeptical. He wiped the sweat out of his eyes, then howled so loud and long that Damascena swore she felt the earth shake.

"You-are-mad-as-Rumi-was-years-ago!" he hiccupped.

"Mad?"

He nodded, smiled, laughed, and cried, then pounded the earth with his fists.

"Don't you see? Shams could not have sent you on this journey or anywhere."

"Why is that?"

"Shams is dead. That is why."

A raven cawed in the distance. Damascena met Hosam's eyes. He nodded, slowly, raising his hand as if to surrender some dark and awful truth into her bewildered face.

She slumped to the ground, gathering the torn dress around her. Her mind raced, arranging the missing parts of the story, weaving in the flashing threads like lightning.

"When did he die?" she asked. No wonder he hadn't written. Aside from the few times he appeared in her dreams, it was no wonder he hadn't come to visit in *two years*.

Hosam's voice shifted and something in it suggested even he was spooked.

"Didn't Rumi tell you?"

"Tell me what?"

Hosam hesitated. He paced and cleared his throat. "Shams died almost twenty-five years ago."

The words sent a shock through Damascena.

"But he *lived* with me."

Hosam lowered his head. "Shams was killed, Damascena."

"Killed?" she asked, detecting an unexpected reverence in his voice.

"Nobody knows how. Some say he was drowned. Others say he was stabbed right outside," he said and choked on the words. "Right outside Rumi's house."

Damascena gasped. The image was too horrible to hold and she flushed it with her tears. "Rumi never told me," she said, wondering why. Her head felt heavy and she felt a hole in her heart. She thought about all the times Shams had refused to go with her to the market, why he insisted she travel alone. No wonder the monks had never seen him. She knew why everyone in Krun called him a phantom teacher and why he had not appeared when the butcher's wife came to take custody of her. Shams was only a spirit.

So no, she never really knew him—or how she had ever come to love him.

PART VI

*There comes a holy and transparent time
when every touch of beauty
opens the heart to tears,
This is the time the Beloved of Heaven
is brought tenderly to earth.
This is the time of the opening of the rose.*

—Hazrat Inayat Khan

ONE

For two days, Damascena sat in the silence of Hosam's rose garden and prayed for a miracle. This is what it is like to feel desperate, she thought. This is what it is like to trust God. All those people who came searching for me, praying for a miracle. Here I am, searching myself to make Shams real.

She prayed for some small sign that he was alive. Old Bird, she said to herself and looked up at the sky, show me your wings. Show me a peach that becomes a feast. Show me a shoe that turns into a knife. Forage in the forest for mushrooms and a fox. Leave footprints in the snow so that I can find you when you spin. Keep spinning. Spin a thousand other riddles, not the one I cannot understand.

If you were never here, where are you now?

She did not feel foolish, but she felt alone; the stars and the moon, the sun and the earth, indifferent to the hole in her heart. She had experienced great pain before, but this burning in her soul was more acute.

She understood Shams differently now. *Do not be afraid of seeing the unseen.* Perhaps this was the awakening of which he spoke. *Trust the unknown.* It was all beginning to make sense. Why he hardly spoke in those first few weeks after they met. Why so much of their time had been spent in silence. The dead do not need mouths to speak. She understood her struggle to glimpse his face beyond the shadows of his hood. The flash of his teeth when he smiled. The flash of lightning in the threads of his robe. Woven with a storm, she once thought, realizing now that she had seen the light of his whole being. Everything else was an illusion. She saw what she needed to see to make him real, his brightest light, his darkest shadows completing the image.

"Where did you go?" she had asked so long ago.

He answered, "Nowhere. I have always been here with you."

But two years later, she was still waiting for him. And while she waited, the miracle waned like a deflated moon, leaking hope like light. She prayed for form. First of Shams. Then of Deniz. She wanted to fold herself into the Keeper of the Lantern and disappear because her own body, that carried her over mountains and lakes, valleys and plains, only served to bring her pain. She prayed and listened, and waited to hear voices that spoke in the darkness and told her that she was not mad, that she did not love a ghost.

She no longer cared if she got caught dancing *sema* during Ramadan, or anytime, and saluted the sun each morning before she began to spin. She wore no shoes in Hosam's rose garden and let the soil collect between her toes, the strips of her dress tied in knots, like some weather-beaten lattice adorning her body, arms outstretched, throat long, mouth open, breathing in the dust of the great Mediterranean plain as it dried beneath her feet.

She spun and prayed and listened. Deniz had told her there were four kinds of listening during *sema*, starting from the most desirable to the least: when the dancer only longed for God, for the formless; second, when the listener longs mostly for God and only a bit of the formed world; the third, which is frowned upon, he explained, having witnessed a dervish kicked out of the *tekke* when he admitted his desire for too much form (a new shop to do his tailoring and a new house); and the forbidden fourth: when the listener longs only for form. Show me your face, she prayed. Meet me here in the rose fields! But after the sixth day of waiting, she stopped moving, though her head spun.

She shuddered, considering the severity of Hosam's recounting of history. She did not know which was worse. That Shams had died or how he had died. She could not understand why anyone would want to kill him.

She broke her silence only once, on the third day, to ask Hosam why when he came to deliver food and water. He met her in the garden carrying a small satchel.

"Jealousy," he said. He looked almost as if he was confessing. "And fear."

"Of what?"

He shrugged, "Speculation has grown like thistles and weeds around the tale. I believe, like many, that Rumi's own son, Ala' ud-Din, killed Shams."

Damascena flinched. "But why? Why on earth would he do that?"

"He was afraid he would get less of Rumi's love."

Damascena laughed.

"Ridiculous! I do not know anyone who has the capacity to love others more."

Hosam nodded, feeling ashamed for the jealousy he had felt in her presence. "It's not that there was less love. It was perhaps misdirected, at least that was the perception. For three years, he cut himself off from his students to be with Shams. That's a long time to go without a teacher. They needed him and he was not there."

"Maybe he was, even when he was with Shams," she said, feeling like in some small way, she was beginning to understand him, and what the tanner had said about her mother's way of teaching. "Rumi really loved Shams," she said.

He nodded.

"Shams loved Rumi. Apparently, Shams asked God to lead him to the person who could receive everything he had to say. People mistook Shams for a vagabond. He showed up in rags. But Rumi could see beyond that. He always sees beyond appearances. Rumi knew from the minute they met he was in the presence of a spiritual master."

"I can see why people would think him disheveled," she said. Some of the most beautiful things are disguised as ugly, she thought. Even the truth.

Hosam chuckled. "He was a vagabond spirit, too?"

"He didn't like to wear shoes and he always complained his feet were hurting."

"Sounds like Shams. You are lucky you met him," he said.

"Lucky?" she asked.

"That he chose you. And you chose him."

"I did not choose him. He just showed up one day."

"Before you were born. When you were both spirits. You had an agreement. Just as Shams sought Rumi. Just as I sought Rumi. I do not believe these things just happen in our lifetimes. We choose our circumstances. You must have sought Shams long ago."

"I do not believe in such things," she said, wondering how she could have ever chosen the circumstances around her own birth.

"I hope you will believe this," he said and gave her the satchel.

Damascena stared at the package, confused. She untied the string and unwrapped the paper, seeing a new dress. She felt a warmth radiate from the middle of her chest, and looked up at Hosam's face, realizing she was no longer his enemy.

He caught her stare and wiped his eyes. "I was once jealous, too," he said.

On the twenty-ninth day of Ramadan, Damascena left Hosam's garden and walked ten kilometers back to town with the thorn of a diktat. In her decree, roses had brought Shams into her life, but they would not bring him back to life. Her legs were sore from spinning for so long and her ankles were swollen. She limped among a litter of kittens the last kilometer, as if they had been summoned to accompany her so that she did not walk alone. She felt as if she had returned from a funeral, depleted, heavy, pulled to the earth with the dead. She wept at her loss, wondering what she would tell Rumi. Ramadan had not purified her heart. She was filthy, covered in dirt.

"What happened?" Rumi said, startled, seeing her face at the door, the dull green eyes more lifeless than when she first opened them in the caravanserai. She was so thin; he held her by the arm and led her into the kitchen where Ates-baz took one look at her and quickly pulled out pots. She held up her hand, refusing. She wanted starvation.

"What happened?" Rumi asked again. "Please, you must speak to me."

She struggled to meet his eyes, wondering how he could have gone for so long without telling her the truth.

"Shams died," she said flatly, as if to announce the weather. There was no telling when the storm in her heart would pass.

Rumi drew in a breath and flicked his hand, ushering Ates-baz into another room. "I have waited twenty-five years to learn the truth. What have you learned?" he asked, his voice quaking with reticence.

She turned to him. "Nothing you do not already know."
He reached out to take her hand but she pulled away from him.
"Damascena? What is it? What happened to you?"
"I danced *sema* at Hosam's."
He stared at her, as if she had shouted an expletive too sensitive for his ears. He drew in a breath, scanning her body, shocked she had subjected herself to such danger. She had depleted herself, and the look on his face suggested he was more worried now than when he watched the infection move through her burns.

"How did you have the energy to dance without food or water?"

"If I danced after a feast, I would be just as tired. I thought *sema* would transform me. But I am still the same bastard girl from the monastery. I know who I am. God knows, too. No wonder he had nothing to say to me."

Rumi looked hurt and scratched his beard.

"My child, what do you mean? God speaks all the time to you."

"Where?"

He looked surprised. "In the beauty that is the rose."

She moaned and grasped her chest.

"My mother said she would be waiting for me in the roses. Where is she now? Where is God? I love the roses because they are real."

"God is real, too, Damascena."

"Then why didn't God tell me the truth?" she asked, eyes spilling with tears, then turned to him with an accusatory look. "Why didn't you?"

Rumi paused to gather his thoughts. "I have been honest with you," he said.

"Why didn't you tell me Shams was dead?" Damascena asked.

"I couldn't believe it myself," he swallowed and began to cry.

"For twenty-five years."

"Allah, Allah," Rumi cried, feeling the release in the repetition. "Shams is dead."

"Yes. Dead. You realize he was killed *before* I was born?" she asked.

Rumi shook. "I am a fool for believing Shams had not passed, that he had just left and gone on to live another life so that I could live the one I needed to live for myself and the rest of the world. He warned me long ago. *Separation makes a person wise. For it is I who will go on a journey for the sake of your development.* Do you know the first time Shams left me, I asked my son to bring him back from Damascus, where he had fled."

"Your son brought him back to kill him?" Damascena asked, horrified.

Rumi turned away from her, refusing to discuss any of his sons' matter in this.

"Shams never returned the second time he left," he said.

Damascena stared at him, realizing Rumi had kept Shams alive, at least in his mind. And after all these years, this spiritual master had still not let go.

"Where did he go?" she asked.

"To you," Rumi said and smiled, nodding, finally seeing Shams' brilliant strategy. No wonder he never came back the second time, he thought. He was always going to you.

"Shams left *you* to come to me?"

Rumi turned back and met Damascena's eyes.

"You share the bloodline of the rose," he said.

"What has that got to do with you and Shams?"

"Everything, my child. We share the same faith."

"What good is faith if I have never met my mother," she said, her voice submerged by disappointment. "I thought I could trust you."

"You can. It is not too late," Rumi said and wiped his eyes. "I am sorry if I hurt you. I did not intend for that, Damascena. I only wanted you to learn."

"I have learned," she said and stood. "To trust myself."

He caught her gaze and brightened, and let her walk to the door.

"Are you leaving then?"

She stared out at the garden, the high walls, the minaret, the hot, dusty streets that smelled of spicy meat and mulberries. Foreign, exotic, hardly familiar.

"This is a strange place," she said, looking down at her body. "It is hard to be here."

Rumi nodded, watching her at the threshold. "I know it has been hard. You are simply a spirit having a human experience. It is never meant to be easy for anyone. You've done well, Damascena."

Damascena laughed, a sad and mellow sound. "Done well? I am filthy and it is the last day of Ramadan. I am no more clean on the inside than I am on the outside."

"Shams would be proud of you, even if you choose to leave now."

"How is that?"

"You have learned to love," he said. "That is all God asks."

"So that permits me to leave? Because I have loved … a lie?"

"If that is what you believe," he said. "Is that your wish?"

She caught his words like a moth in the air and flicked them off her fingers. "My wish is to love what is true," she said and walked out the door—facing forward.

TWO

On the final night of Ramadan, Konya glowed under a moonless sky from the light of a thousand lanterns that hung in the trees and shop windows like colorful birds. Throngs of people filled the streets, dressed in their finest clothes to feed the poor while Konya celebrated the end of its fast, praying only twice that day to thank God for everything they had, for the food, their health, their families, their friends. They scrubbed the tiles on fountains, washed the rugs in the mosques, ensuring the city matched the purity they felt inside themselves. The first chill of fall cleansed the air and laced the ground with frost as if to remind them of the delicate nature of life itself, to honor, preserve, and celebrate it.

Damascena had never seen so much food on display in her life. Large oil cloths had been set on the ground and crowded with platters and dishes, pots full of steaming pilav, grilled meats and vegetables, the summer's last fruit, cakes made of honey and pekmez, grape tea, pails packed with lemon and raspberry sherbet. Helva, stacked like miniature bricks, disappeared into the tiny hands of children, and everywhere generosity filled the air and reminded them of the work they had done for God and each other.

Damascena walked among wealthy families in a clean robe, surprised they reached out with baskets of food, reminding her to eat. She had lost too much weight during the fast, they admonished. She thanked them, but politely declined their offerings, turning to give it to those standing behind her who she believed needed it more. But even the most needy pointed to her bones, the cheeks that looked like two high split pears.

"Eat, sister," they said. "God doesn't want to lose you."

She smiled, gracious, forcing herself to accept the food but could not bear to put any into her body. Couldn't they see? She was not hungry. Sorrow had filled her up with something else. She had lost more than weight. She had lost her sight. She was no longer seeing spirits but she did not trust what she was seeing that night.

Wherever she walked, she saw a thousand versions of herself in everyone and everything she passed in the streets. It was like the world had suddenly become one enormous mirror and no matter who she saw, she saw herself staring back—in the old wealthy women bent over their pots of pilav, in the poor who held out their empty bowls, in the children laughing, trolling the streets in white togas as if they were reenacting some Roman bacchanal. She felt their joy and giddiness. She also felt the hunger in the stomachs of the beggars, the holes in the hearts of broken lovers, the fear in the dogs cowering in doorways, unsure of what to make of the Sultan and his family riding by on horses. She swore the Sultan waved at her, and for a moment, when she saw her face in his, her body mounted on his horse, it struck her that perhaps everyone had the ability to see themselves in others. Even in the rocks. Even in the roses. She felt this inextricable link to all things, living and dead, and she wondered if the wind itself blowing through Konya had always been the breath of spirits.

Rumi told her Eid al-Fitr was the best night of the year. She could not argue. Seeing the city so clean and its people so happy struck her as something from a fairytale. Even the Mongols and Seljuks mingled, offering plates of food, sharing the love of family recipes. In such divided times, she had never seen more people come together.

She was surprised to find herself willing to celebrate—not because she had endured twenty-nine days of fasting and had proven herself to the dervishes or because Hosam had invited her to sit between him and Rumi at the feast, a gesture that did not go unnoticed by Ates-baz or anyone else. That she had forgiven Rumi was another good reason to celebrate, but what she wanted most was to celebrate the vision of the young man who stood in the kitchen door of the *tekke*, older, more mature, with a beard that suggested he'd traveled for days, if not weeks. My God, she said to herself. Deniz.

The sight of him took her breath away. Ates-baz was the first to notice.

"What's wrong, sister? You look like you saw a ghost."

Rumi and Hosam exchanged knowing looks.

"I have," she said and got up from the table, hoping her eyes were not playing tricks on her. She could not bear the pain of seeing the unseen again. She crossed the kitchen to the table, bumping into a new initiate carrying tea. She did not apologize. She wanted to feel the jolt and the awkwardness. She wanted to feel everything that was real.

"I'm sorry, sister," he said, humbly, dabbing at the stain on her robe.

"Do not be sorry, my brother," she said, catching the glimmer in Deniz's eye and the grin he hid beneath his beard. She moved quickly to the door where Deniz pulled her into the star-lit night and led her away, both turning backwards to leave.

❁

They walked in silence, in and out of the crowds, following the spherical dome of the Kartay Madrasa, empty now, silent, swollen with the breath of prayers. A few pairs of tiny shoes lay scattered outside the school, perhaps forgotten by children who had fallen asleep, too tired to walk home with empty bellies. A few birds swooped in to pick at a trail of dried dates that most likely had fallen from their pockets.

When they were alone at last, Damascena led Deniz inside the dome and stood under the huge network of stars. She wrapped her hands around his face and pulled his mouth into hers, sucking his bottom lip, feeling the fullness and softness of the beard. She licked his top lip, slowly, feeling the smoothness of his teeth, drawing the salt off his tongue, his jaw strong in her fingers, devouring everything about him that was real.

When she had enough, she wiped her mouth and caught her breath. "Where have you been?"

"Walking."

It was not what she expected to hear and she laughed, not just because it sounded absurd, it sounded like something Shams would have said. She realized he would have liked Deniz. She laughed again to cover her sorrow. Deniz joined her and their laughter lifted them to the dome and the stars beyond, then floated them back to the floor.

"Walking. Really? For a month?"

"Nearly a fortnight each way. I had only one day when I arrived."

"I hope one day was worth the twenty-nine it took to get there." Deniz nodded.

"I needed to see my mother."

She stared at him. It was the first mention of a family member. Other than the news of his father's passing, he had shared nothing with Damascena about his past.

"You have a family."

He nodded, as if to ask for her permission to acknowledge this in her presence.

"Yes."

"Where is she?"

"Constantinople," he said.

"You walked to Constantinople?"

"Not the whole time. I rode a few horses and camels," he said.

He laughed, trying to bring some levity while he held her close. He had never felt such hardness and softness simultaneously in his own body. It made him want to crawl on top of her and weep. And her eyes. He wanted to disrobe and dive into those deep green pools and float forever. She was so beautiful it hurt. He had turned back twice on his journey, unable to continue without her, feeling the urge to dance *sema* every night.

"You got hurt," she said, seeing the cut above his right eye. She pressed her finger lightly over the wound, seeing a claw mark the length of her thumb. It was infected. She wanted to give him rose oil but all she had was a gentle kiss.

"An hour into my journey, a stork flew straight at my face and scratched my brow bone so hard it stopped me. It was strange. The stork circled until the bleeding stopped, then turned in the direction of my mother! I took it as a sign to keep going."

Shams flies, Damascena thought and smiled. "I am glad you saw the signs."

"Not all of them. My mother died the day after I arrived."

She met his eyes, startled. "I am so sorry, Deniz."

"Do not be sorry. She was ready to meet her beloved."

"I hope she rests in peace," Damascena said, trying hard to hide her disappointment. She would have liked to have met his mother, to have known just one surviving blood relative, and to have felt part of a family for once.

He forced a smile, shrugged. "She picked a good night to leave. Laylat al-Dikr."

"Your mother died on The Night of Power?"

"The Night of Wisdom."

She nodded but did not speak, taken by the coincidence.

"She timed her death perfectly," he said.

Damascena wanted to tell him about her grandmother's letter, but it remained mythic, too large for words now. She wondered if all wise women chose their deaths, if perhaps her grandmother had died on her birthday, the night she received the transmission—if the woman of fire had been her.

"She wanted you to have this," Deniz said and pulled out a small velvet bag the size of his palm.

She opened the drawstring, fingers shaking with the giddiness of receiving a gift. She wanted to slow down time, savor all of this like Rumi drank his coffee and ate baklava in the morning, but she couldn't open the bag fast enough. She dumped the content on her hand. A single gold ring. She looked up at Deniz's smile.

"When I told her about you, she took it off her own hand," he said and wiped his eyes. "She wanted me to give it to you."

Damascena held the gold band in her hand, uncertain. Deniz slid it on her finger.

"I want to keep dancing," he whispered and his breath felt like silk on her skin.

Damascena's mouth quivered, feeling the weight of his intentions.

"What are you asking me?"

"I want to marry you, Damascena. Let's leave this place. Let's start a family."

Family. She covered her mouth, fought the tears, wondering if this was a dream.

"You are fearless!" she cried. "Or foolish."

Deniz shrugged. "I know I'd be a fool to leave you again. I have never felt more certain of anything aside from the day I walked from Constantinople to Konya to meet the great mystic. No matter what happens from here, I can trust life's mysteries. Rumi taught me well."

She wiped her eyes then lifted her hand, lacing her fingers with his, then let go and slid her hand inside his tunic and lifted it off his shoulders, releasing the heat that built up inside. His skin glowed in the darkness and she ran her fingers slowly down his thick arms, traced the sides of his body with her tongue. She shivered when he pulled her to the tunic that lay like a puddle on the floor, feeling his hands on her breasts.

He smelled of honey and earth, fallen leaves starched by the sun, the smell of autumn. The smell of finality. She pulled off her robe. She turned his face toward her, permitting him with her eyes. He leaned in to kiss her cheekbones, the bridge of her nose, lifted her chin to lick her neck and nuzzled her with his beard. She shivered when he wrapped his arms around her shoulders and pulled her closer. She was wet with sweat and he wiped her forehead and kissed her wrist, then the back of her hand.

She pulled him to her mouth again to taste the sweetness as they lay under the tiles bearing the Most Beautiful Names of God. They kissed desperately, passionately, reclaiming the time they had spent apart, turning inside each other until they grew dizzy and broke their fast, filling themselves with love and nothing else.

Damascena thought of Shams the minute she glimpsed the pair of shoes sitting outside the kitchen door of the *tekke*. "Revelation is a subtle thing," he had told her once when she sat impatiently, waiting for the rose buds to bloom. She felt like that young girl again waking into the new day with her hand holding Deniz's. They had slept through sunrise, awakened by the call to prayer and a disheartened old muezzin staring at them, mouth agape, finding the two young lovers unclothed in the school. He swatted at them with his broom and hurled curses, as if Ramadan had never happened.

"Shame on you!" he said as they gathered up their robes and dressed.

Deniz and Damascena laughed, not to spite him, but because they were a jumble of nerves—hurriedly refastening their robes. They did not laugh when they stood before the shoes, recognizing instantly the clothes folded neatly beside them: Deniz's belongings—the first clothes he wore stepping into the *tekke*. The clothes he was not supposed to wear again until he completed his initiation, but the Dedes had decided it was over. They had expelled him. Damascena fell to her knees and gathered his clothes in her arms.

"I'm so sorry," she cried.

Deniz knelt beside her and took his clothes and shoes in his arms.

"You make me proud," he said.

Damascena could not hear him. "What are we going to do?"

He pointed to the door. "You will go back inside. You will finish."

"Why? What is there to finish without you?"

"You must, Damascena. For God."

"But you just got back! Where will you go?"

"To my mother's house. I need time to sell her belongings so that we can start our life together."

He picked up his clothes and stood, resolved, then reached out, offering his hand.

"Do not," Damascena begged, choking on the words. "Do not leave me again."

"I will write."

The words struck her and she cried out. "No! Do not send me letters."

"Why? I promise!"

She told him about her mother. Let the story bubble up like a blister and burst from her mouth hot as flames. He stood and listened and did not move until she finished.

"She's still living?"

"I don't know," she said, feeling a heaviness in her heart.

Deniz caught her eye and pulled her against his chest. Her hair draped her shoulders now, brassy, dark as walnut.

"I would never leave you," he said.

She buried her face against his shoulder. "Rumi said I was to find love here. I found it. I want it. I am ready to leave! Why should I wait another day to be with you?"

"You have one more year. One thousand and one days makes you a dervish."

"I do not care if I am dervish. Titles mean nothing to me. Rumi knows this."

"Rumi knows you have unfinished business. He cares only that you complete it."

"What about you? Are you finished already after everything you did to get here?"

He turned to her, puzzled. He could not say. Only this: "The Dedes put *my* shoes at the door, Damascena. I am no longer welcome. But you? Where are your shoes?"

She wanted to remind him that she once walked barefoot. But that was so long ago. She barely recognized the girl she had left at the monastery.

"I cannot tell you why you are here. Why any of us are here, really. I was a boy. I had a fantasy. I lost my father. I wanted to believe in men who became mystics. And now I do. Maybe I was not meant to be a dervish. Maybe my journey is elsewhere. But I do know this. I came here for a reason, as did you. And maybe that reason was meeting you. I don't regret any of it. Not one day. Not getting caught. Because I love you, Damascena. I love you more than I have loved anyone in my life, but I cannot possess you. Only God has that right, and you are here to serve God, not me. Trust that. Please, trust it and go."

She stared at him, humbled by the revelation yet terrified to walk in the face of her fear. She took a deep breath, said *"Hu,"* opened the door to the *tekke*, and stepped into the kitchen without looking back. She prayed that if there was a God who possessed her, he would deliver Deniz to this door again, waiting for his bride.

THREE

When frost laced the great plain and froze the roses, when the grills were empty and the streets filled with snow, stillness pervaded Konya and stirred Damascena's heart. She had not danced *sema* in half a year and had let the roses lay sleeping all winter. Shams' words haunted her. *Do not despair when the darkness becomes long ... after that the brightness will be long.* Easy words for the dead to say. What did they care about darkness or light?

She did not know whose words to trust anymore, or whom to listen to at the *tekke*. Her nights were long without Deniz, and she had grown restless and unmoored by the loss of Shams, feeling alone in her grief. If what Hosam had said was true, her grief was older than she was, and forgotten by most everyone except Rumi.

She found no comfort among the Dedes, and Rumi had grown distant, entrenched in his poetry with Hosam. She barely saw him anymore, only once each week to share a silent meditation. Even then, he did not ask about Deniz, and she was too ashamed to talk about him or share any heaviness that remained in her heart. She tried to find solace in his poetry, and listened to it on occasion, outside the great hall where Rumi returned to work.

"I read the lovers' story day and night—Now I become a story in my love for you."

The first time she heard this, she wondered if Rumi was making fun of her and Deniz. Did he wish to torment her as a way to teach her a lesson for violating the Kartay Madrasa's Most Beautiful Names of God? She figured her debt was huge to suffer an affliction as heavy as the mass she carried around her heart. She called it the gravity of sorrow, and believed it was the only thing keeping her on the earth—because if she had a choice, she would have left this place long ago, left the sadness and this body that had only filled with pain.

Besides growing roses and hoping she could turn them into oil again, she wondered what else she had to do to leave this place. She worked up the courage to ask Rumi in mid-March when he invited her into the great hall to sit for meditation, the smell of cooked onions and baking phyllo dough drifting in from the kitchen.

"Will you speak the truth to me?"

Rumi nodded. "What is it you want to know?"

"What have I done to deserve this?"

"This?" he asked quizzically. "You act like you are being punished by life."

"Sometimes I think I am. Life can be punishing."

He laughed. "You punish only yourself, Damascena. All of us do."

She stared at the floor, seeing the dimples in the wood where the dervishes held the wooden nails in place, wondering how many Deniz had put there. Not a day passed when she didn't think of him. He had sent no letters and she found herself loitering around the caravanserai day after day, asking travelers from Constantinople if they had seen him. None could identify the golden-haired boy whose veins were threaded with blue silk.

She felt foolish seeking from Rumi what he had never been able to give himself—any reassurance that he'd see his beloved again. Even mystics aren't spared from misery.

"I should go now," she said. "Before Hosam comes."

"Don't go yet. What is it you wish to ask me?"

"I wish I knew what I have done so that I could correct my mistake."

He laughed, twisting his beard. "The only mistake you have made is asking the wrong question. It isn't about what you did wrong. It's what you have not yet done."

"I've done everything I can here. I've been faithful to you and the Dedes. I've fasted during Ramadan. I'm trying my best to grow the roses and God willing, make more oil. I want to be with Deniz, Rumi. I want to leave this place and start a new life."

He reached out, cupped her cheek with his hand, and stared into her eyes.

"You already have. Don't you see? This is your new life."

She shook her head, feeling the first sting of tears.

"I do not trust what I see or have seen in my life."

"Shams was real," he said. "You saw him because you have faith." Rumi pulled out a small tablet of paper he used for taking notes. In the corner, smudged from the tip of a quill, was a poem, the handwriting jagged. He read it to her.

> *There is no salvation for the soul*
> *But to fall in Love*
> *It has to creep and crawl*
> *Among the Lovers first.*
>
> *Only lovers can escape*
> *From these two worlds.*
> *This was written in creation.*

*Only from the Heart
Can you reach the Sky,
The rose of Glory
Can only be raised in the Heart*

"I wrote it this morning, thinking of you. In fact, every poem I have written since you've come has been inspired by your faith. You are what the Greeks call a muse."

She felt the prickle of hair rising on her neck. Faith? In what? she wondered.

He kissed her cheek, pressed his lips to her ear, and told her what she had not done yet, hoping to ignite the final fire in the girl.

The next morning, Damascena knocked on the door of the Meydan and demanded the Dedes let her dance *sema*. "I know how to do it."

"You can't just dance *sema* without being trained," Kazanci Dede protested, his voice echoing off the walls of the great hall.

"I have been trained."

"Hardly. Deniz broke the rules."

"This might be true. But he was a good teacher."

"I was *his* teacher," Kazanci Dede bellowed.

"Then you are a good teacher, too."

Kazanci Dede squinted in the early light. He hadn't seen Damascena this animated since she spent the night in the school with that golden-haired scoundrel.

"Ask Rumi," she pleaded. "He might let me dance."

"Rumi is not the one who decides when an initiate is ready."

"I have been trained since birth. I was born beneath the shadow of this dance."

Kazanci Dede picked at the calluses on the palms of his hands.

"No one *is born* beneath this dance," he said. "This dance gives birth to you."

Maybe it had. Maybe that was the point. The dance had given birth to this fiery young woman who knocked on the door of the great hall each day, though Kazanci Dede refused to invite her inside.

Truth be told, he and the other dervishes simply didn't know how to handle a girl who claimed she could dance *sema*. And for fifty-six minutes straight? This phenomena had turned into a sporting match and wagers had been made, sweetening prior bets about the girl's ability to turn roses into oil that cured lepers, broken wings, broken hearts.

They deliberated for weeks, while Damascena kept knocking and waiting, each time assuring the dervishes she knew what she was doing. Yes. They knew, but they continued to ignore her waiting at the door.

They avoided her during meals even though she stood with the other novices, back against the wall, hands folded over her belly, waiting to serve the disciples. Nobody talked during the meal. Everything was communicated through looks, but the looks Damascena received were not for more food or water. The disciples seemed to be weighing all the arguments against her dancing *sema* but finding none.

Hosam had stayed out of the debate, focusing on Rumi's poetry, but one night, tired of hearing the dervishes talk behind Damascena's back, he simply gestured to her that he needed more water. She stepped forward and carefully filled Hosam's cup.

Hosam kissed the cup and said, "*Bismillahirrahmanirrahim*," then returned the cup to Damascena for her to kiss again, revealing his approval of her. Following the ritual, the others withdrew their hands from the table, then put down their forks and spoons. Nobody had ever asked the girl to refill their cup.

They wished to avoid the intimacy of this tradition with the opposite sex, but Hosam seemed willing to engage her. Rumi noticed, too, and broke the silence with a quiet laugh, then resumed eating.

When everyone had returned their spoons facedown above their place settings, indicating they were finished, Hosam, the most senior dervish among them, folded his hands diagonally, then led them in the prayer of thanks, directed at Damascena.

"*May the morsel we have eaten become light and faith. May our hearts overflow with Divine Love with every breath we take. May our praise and gratitude be eternal.*"

Perhaps it was Hosam's prompting or the earth coming into balance on the first day of spring, but Kazanci Dede was in a considerably charitable mood when he finally allowed Damascena to enter the Meydan the next day.

"You'll need to clean that first," he said, blocking the threshold of the ceremonial hall with his arm.

"What?"

"The dirt on your robe."

She looked down at the white robe, curious. She had been careful to keep it clean and stored it in the broom closet since Deniz had left. She had been proud of the robe's condition, considering how many times she had worn it. Where had the dirt come from? She had never worn it in the garden or walked to Hosam's wearing it, but when she leaned down to inspect the dirt, she realized it was dried blood.

"I'll be back," she said poised.

He nodded tenderly. "We know."

She ran off toward the kitchen, then locked herself in the broom closet with a bucket of water and scrubbed the dried blood, but it only seemed to spread the stain. She could not enter the Meydan with a dirty robe, and when she changed out of it to put on her daily work robe, she followed the dried blood on her thighs and realized she was bleeding. She was horrified at first, panicked, wondering if she would bleed to death before she got to dance *sema*. She ran back to Rumi's to consult with Kerra, but Kerra only smiled and said, "Welcome, sister," and gave her a hug.

"Welcome? To what?" she asked, wiping the tears. "I'm going to die!"

"No. This blood is the blood of life."

The blood of life? The words spooked her and she imagined some kind of sacrifice, hoping nothing like that went on in Konya. Damascena watched Kerra rinse out the stains, but the robe would be too wet to wear today. She sobbed, frustrated.

"I don't want to die today," she cried.

"You will not die," Kerra said, trying to calm the girl. She squeezed a lemon and put it into a glass of water. Damascena guzzled it.

"Then what does it mean?"

Kerra smiled. "It means you have become a woman."

"A woman? I am barely sixteen."

"Yes. But your body is telling you it can bear children."

Damascena looked stricken. "Children? I am not ready for them. I have waited two years for my body to dance *sema*. And Karanci Dede said I could dance today!"

Kerra straightened, wrung out the clothes one more time over a large copper pot she used for washing.

"What should I do? I'm going to miss my chance."

Kerra studied Damascena in the dappled light coming in through the shutters. The girl who had arrived wrapped in a black cloak was now thriving in the white skirt.

"You will go back today and only watch."

"Watch?"

"You will learn more by watching and you will earn their respect by waiting."

Kerra rinsed the skirt one last time and wrung it out, giving Damascena a belt and some old, clean rags to keep the blood from staining anything else.

Kerra handed the skirt to her. "Now go. Hang this up to dry with your tears."

Damascena was bleeding, but she would not die. Not today, at least. I enter with the blood of life flowing through me, she thought. I am alive. And I will dance soon.

She would have to trust the timing of this and sat by the wall in the corner of the great hall where she could watch the dervishes spin without her, the heat from their bodies filling the space like a warm breeze in spring. She marveled at the way the nine men moved together while Kazanci Dede beat the cauldron with his hand.

All those white robes, unfurling on the dance floor, blooming like roses. She wondered what it had been like for Shams, if, in fact, he danced in a group, or if he only shared the dance with Rumi. She felt a cramp in her lower stomach, wondering how anyone who lived here could have killed the man who taught Rumi this ecstatic dance.

The power of spinning was obvious. No wonder it terrified them, she thought, watching the faces of the dervishes, so focused they did not notice the door open in the middle of *sema*. A disheveled beggar stumbled inside, disoriented and obviously drunk the way he staggered, fumbling with the door knob, not knowing which way was out. He pulled it closed behind him then turned, facing the nine men in white robes and gasped, throwing the dervishes into confusion and bringing the dance to a jarring halt.

"Get out, you drunk!" one of the men called.

"How dare you disrespect us," said another.

"Who goes there?"

The man waved his arms, surrendering, unable to speak. He opened his mouth but only a sickening moan crept out. He coughed, vomited, staggered again, angering the men when he fell backward, knocking down Rumi when he walked through the door just then. Rumi struggled, winced, rubbed his eye that had struck the corner of the door and was already swelling, the bruise rising through his skin like a dark blue wave.

"You imbecile!"

"Filthy lout."

"Look what you've done to our master!"

"Are you alright, Mevlana? Can you see?" they cried, desperate to save him from his pain. Rumi nodded. "I am fine. I can see," he said, not mentioning the stars he saw.

Rumi caught the man under the armpits, then slowly lowered him to the floor. He recognized him from the caravanserai. The man was in desperate need of a bath. He pulled back the hood on his head, seeing blood and a hole the size of a coin. He stunk of piss and alcohol, but it wasn't the man that made Rumi bellow, but his own disciples.

"He's the one who drank wine, but you are the ones behaving like dissolute drunks!" Rumi said then turned back to the man. "Tell us your name, brother."

The man gagged, vomited again, but was unable to speak. From the corner where she sat, Damascena saw the palsy in his hand, the way he shrunk when anyone called him brother. He could not speak because he had no tongue. She called out.

"His name is Ivan. Ivan Balev," she said and got up from the corner, crossing the floor, slicing through the circle of dervishes who stepped away in astonishment. The smell of the vomit drifted over them and some fled the room, unable to take in the sour odor that so violently ejected them from their ecstasy.

The man suddenly excreted on the threshold, seeing Damascena wearing a dervish robe and moving toward him with a cloth and rag. Rumi stepped aside and said, "Thank you, sister," then turned back to the dervishes. "Follow her example. Welcome this brother. Anyone looking for friends without faults shall remain friendless."

She crouched down without saying anything and wiped his mouth, then, feeling the eyes of the dervishes and Rumi, held her breath and cleaned the threshold. When she was done, she simply took the dirty rag and Ivan's hand and led him outside to the well.

FOUR

Ivan Balev reached the lowest point of his life when Damascena picked him up off the floor and cleaned vomit off his face. Worse, when she took him to Rumi's house, he had to endure the penetrating stare of his wife, who looked so much like his own mother he cowered in her presence. He felt so shameful that he refused to eat at Kerra's table, and took his meals outside to eat alone, grateful for the nightingale singing from the tree.

The conundrum struck him. No matter what he took in—food, shelter, clothing, he felt so heavy with guilt that nothing tasted good or felt right. A thousand tailors could alter these clothes, he thought, but none would ever fit. I am doomed to a life of despair.

Ivan did not mean to drink both bottles of wine, but he had. And fast. That morning, on his knees, knuckles pressed into the shards of glass that had been bottles of rose oil, he drank and he cried, feeling like an imbecile for trusting the Mongols. They assigned him the job of breaking into the basement of the Sultan's palace, where the rose oil was being held. The Mongols distracted the servants and everyone else living there by threatening to raze the palace with torches. The commotion gathered everyone in the streets well past the final call to prayer. Ivan had no problem carrying out the boxes of bottles. He was stronger than ever. The Mongols had indentured him as a stable hand, and he had spent his days in Konya cleaning horseshit. But instead of selling the rose oil he had reclaimed from the Sultan's palace, they omitted Ivan from the division of profits.

"Play dirty, pay later," they had reminded him when he grunted his dissatisfaction with the business arrangement. When he showed signs of protest—difficult without a tongue, he was reduced to stomping on the floor.

The Mongols laughed.

"You're alive, aren't you? We could have killed you when we discovered you had hidden the rose oil. We kept *our* word and gave you a new life here."

Ivan shrugged, muttering something indecipherable.

"What's that Ivan the Idiot? We don't understand what you're saying."

Ivan threw the first punch, striking the jaw of the Mongol who had sliced out his tongue. The men cheered for each other and a fight broke out, resulting in broken bottles of rose oil. Not a single bottle was spared. Rotten Mongols, he thought, watching them fight like cavemen, pitiful men whose greed and stupidity had ruined his life.

He found solace on the rooftop of Rumi's house and sat there for hours, watching the play of light on the distant mountains, feeling strangely homesick for the monastery and forlorn over the lives he'd ended there. Rumi saw him sitting on his roof one night.

"Do you want to jump?" he asked, seeing Ivan's silhouette in the moonlight.

Ivan shrugged. He wanted to say, Of course. I think about jumping every night.

"The Prophet, peace be upon him, said, *Wherever our religion goes, it doesn't come back without uprooting a person and sweeping his house clean and cleansing him.*"

Ivan stared down at him, trying to understand what the great mystic just said. After three years of working in Konya, Ivan had developed a rough ear for Turkish and could decipher most of what was said, even Persian and Arabic tossed into conversations at any given moment. It had been an unpredictable language and he was relieved that he could not speak at all, for fear of defacing the language and risking more shame.

Rumi hoisted himself up on the courtyard wall, climbed to the flat roof, and walked to Ivan. He sat beside him, knees to chest, admiring the view of the city. The last time he had sat on a roof was with Shams, and he breathed in the memory and smiled.

He turned to Ivan. "My brother, be patient *and* troubled. Eating trouble is an emptying-out. After the emptying, joy appears, a joy that knows no trouble, a rose that has no thorn, a wine that causes no hangovers," he said and laughed, patting his shoulder.

Ivan wanted to understand Rumi's wisdom. He appreciated the man's sincerity and how he never winced in his presence or suggested ways for Ivan to improve himself. He wondered what his life at the monastery would have been like had the abbot been as understanding. He wondered if he would be here at all if his mother could accept him.

Be patient and troubled.

He wanted to tell Rumi he wished that was true. Ivan spit out a curse, shook his fists in the air when he suddenly realized that God *had* answered his prayers long ago. God had sent him a gardener to save his life—and that gardener had been Damascena.

FIVE

Caring for Ivan Balev was the charity Damascena had never given. This was the final test, she thought. Tasting sweetness in her relationship to him. She had spent 740 days with Rumi and had 261 more until her trial ended; even then, she did not know where she would go, or what she would do if Deniz did not come back.

So in the spring of 1273, Damascena surrendered to the dervishes and dove into life in the *tekke*, remaining steadfast by the roses and Ivan.

Shams did not leave when he left his words with Rumi, she thought.

This is not the time to stay at home, but to go out and give yourself to the rose garden. The dawn of joy has arisen, and this is the moment of vision.

Damascena directed Ivan to follow her in the garden each morning with two buckets slung on the end of a long wooden pole he carried across his shoulders. She called him Ivan the Ox and assigned him a new job. The Keeper of the Water.

Ates-baz and Rumi decided it was an appropriate duty. They complimented Damascena on her willingness to give Ivan Balev a purpose at the *tekke*. Some of the newer initiates objected. It pained them to see Rumi's black eye. Nobody had ever struck

Rumi, and though Ivan Balev had not intended to harm their master, he had.

"Do not despair when you see my face," he said.

"But he made you ugly," they protested.

"No. You allowed him to shift your perception of me. You choose to see only the darkness in my eye when you look at my face. I invite you to look more closely so that you see the light, too. Be willing to turn your attention to that which serves you."

"We want to protect you," they said and finally admitted, "We don't trust Ivan."

Rumi tried to explain. "For a dervish, there must be a purpose," he said. "A cause for existence, and inside the cause, a True Human Being. Trust that."

No one imagined Ivan completing 1001 days in the *tekke* and becoming a dervish. His primary purpose, aside from watering roses, was to remind them of the Mystery. He had come as a stranger knocking on their door, and they would welcome him for as long as he stayed. The dervishes finally complied, knowing this was not just Damascena's test; it was their test, too, to remain open and sympathetic to the stranger without a tongue.

The dervishes noticed the ease with which Ivan worked around Damascena. The two danced among the roses, watering the roots, picking dead leaves, fertilizing the soil. At times, Ivan paused to watch her, and the look on his face suggested the regret of an absent father, as if he had known of her his whole life but was only just meeting her.

It was painful watching him communicate. The dervishes had never seen someone struggle so much to express the simplest things. He acted like a child, encouraging them to treat him as such. Ates-baz pureed all his food. Damascena reminded him each day to keep the gash on his head covered, away from the sun. "You don't want to get burned," she told him, missing the irony until she saw tears streaming down Ivan's cheek.

"If you can love all who've betrayed you," Rumi told her the night she brought Ivan back to his house and gave him her bed, "You can taste sweetness in everything."

Rumi had warned her that it would not be easy to love Ivan, but Damascena found interacting with him had never been easier. Without a tongue, he could not criticize her. And he did not dare strike her again. He sulked instead and seemed to sob easily over the simplest gestures of kindness. He broke down at the well, threw himself on the ground and prostrated to Damascena when she led him out of the dance hall that dreadful day.

She had jumped when he kissed her feet. She told him to get up, wondering why he would undo any more dignity that she had tried to restore for him. He was grateful. She knew that by the look in his eyes, the desperate pleading, the apology.

She focused on growing more roses. Keep me busy, she prayed. Keep me so busy I do not have time to think about these harrowing circumstances. Deniz was gone. There was no guarantee he would ever return, not with the Mongols and Crusaders lurking in the night. She had no idea if he was safe, if any of them were safe, including Rumi.

Between the silences she shared with Ivan while they worked in the garden, it struck her that he might be the only person that God intended to keep in her life. He kept showing up and this meant something. She would have to find a way to love him, just as she had found a way to love the roses. She realized this was the invitation to hold the hand of God. Ivan Balev had extended the invitation she needed all along to dance *sema*.

When the bleeding had stopped, Damascena wore the clean white skirt and entered the octagonal floor of the ceremonial hall, draped by a black cape. She did not ask permission to dance, but simply exchanged a look with Kazanci Dede. He nodded.

"Welcome, sister. We have been waiting for you."

He reached behind him and presented her with a *sikke*. Though she now wore the black robe over the white *tennure* skirt, she had never expected to wear a tall conical hat, and stared at it in disbelief. Wearing it would make her an official member of the order.

Kazanci Dede kissed the hat and placed it on her head. "Go with God," he said.

With her head lowered, Damascena humbly entered the circle as the ninth dancer, completing the celestial formation, bowing to the dervishes and Kazanci Dede. They bowed to her and to each other, honoring each other's souls. Then, after removing their black capes, which represented the ego, and receiving the senior dervish's blessing—an attentive gaze, they spun off one by one, counterclockwise on their left foot, unclasping their hands and extending the right upward toward God and the spirit, the left toward the ground, in the direction of the earth, of the material world and mankind.

Rumi and Hosam sat to the left of the orbiting dancers with their heads bowed, long conical hats tilted toward the circle, in deference to Damascena who moved like a star among stars, a heavenly body beyond form. They had never seen anything like the transformation within this girl who had arrived burned and unable to walk, but danced now with grace streaming through her whole body as if she had tapped into the source of surrender itself. She wore a calm smile, beaming joy from every particle of her being.

When the other senior dervishes had stopped after one full hour of spinning, the girl continued to turn. She did not stumble or fall down but floated across the floor of the great hall, transporting not only herself, but also everyone who watched her. The look on her face suggested she was lost to another world. She had let go completely. She had allowed the dance to dissolve her body. She had become one with the unseen.

For the first time, the dance had become a form of prayer, and inside it, she felt free, unburdened by the limitations of form. She had left her body and looked down on herself, turning, turning, arms outstretched, chin lifted ever so slightly, eyes fixed on the air and nothing else while the *ney* and drum played on. She had lost the ability to know where her body started and where it ended or where the outside universe began. And here, she met Shams, who danced with her and did not complain of hurting feet.

The dervishes felt ashamed for doubting her simply because she had no formal training. No one could deny her grace and endurance, but they felt anxious and jealous, considering how long it had taken them to learn how to dance for ten minutes without pausing, not to mention more than an hour. There had been no one in Konya known to dance for more than sixty minutes except Shams. No wonder so many dervishes had come to fear him as much as they wanted to emulate him.

Rumi wanted to get up and join her, but remained transfixed, tears streaming, feeling a peace he had not felt in years. It was as if Damascena's dancing was helping to heal the parts of his heart that had been frayed by Shams' leaving.

I could die now, he thought, and be at peace, but more words came. The girl's dance had triggered a new source of poetry. It was not the time to leave the earth yet.

Damascena danced for three hours straight. At the end of her last turn, she faced Rumi and opened her vest with her right hand, as Deniz had instructed, "to let the world into her heart." Ivan met her at the door when she finished and walked her back to the garden where she collapsed and fell into a deep sleep. He watched over her, hearing the chatter of dervishes who had come to pray over the girl, hoping the dance had not killed her. Ivan wanted to assure them that Damascena was alive. Perhaps more alive than ever.

Rumors circulated through Konya. Damascena had danced *sema* for three hours without a nail. Damascena's dancing had brought them all into a conversation with God. They prayed to keep her healthy. They prayed to see Damascena rise again and dance.

No one could explain how the roses had grown four times their size, not only in the *tekke* garden, but also on Hosam's land. He solicited the help of dervishes and any initiate who expressed interest in tending to the roses. As soon as he assigned them rows to water, the dervishes fled the kitchen to ensure their health, not because Rumi encouraged it, but because they understood caring for the roses was their divine assignment now. Ates-baz had no problem and simply watched, with awe and joy, the transformation taking place among them. Damascena, whose arrival had at first divided them, had invited them into communion—and this was the true path of a Sufi.

On the sixth day of the sixth month in the year 1273, Damascena turned sixteen and stood outside the Meydan where Ivan motioned with wildly gesticulating arms, indicating that something was beyond the door. She heard clapping and turned to look at a group of dervishes emerging from the *tekke* kitchen with Ates-baz, whose smile was so huge she feared his face might crack.

"I don't like surprises," she said, not knowing whom to address. Ates-baz spoke. "You'll like this one."

Ivan opened the door of the great hall, but it was Rumi who stood on the other side and said, "Happy Birthday, Damascena." Behind him, piled floor to ceiling, were thousands of rose petals. She stood, dumbstruck and intoxicated by the scent. Tears streamed down her cheek.

"How did you …?"

Rumi shook his head. "I did not do anything," he said, pointing to Ivan.

She turned to Ivan and knelt beside him, then lifted his hand to her mouth and kissed it once. "Please rise, brother. And dance with me."

Ivan followed her into the great hall filled with rose petals, the picking of which he had supervised during the days that Damascena had fallen into a deep sleep. He knew the dance had caused them to grow. He didn't know how and he didn't need a reason. He simply knew it was his responsibility to save the roses, and this time, save the girl.

Damascena took Ivan's hand, and though she did not perform *sema*, she simply turned around and around in the rose petals. I am the rose dancing with the thorn by my side, she thought and laughed. Ivan laughed, too, and then he cried for everything he had taken from her and everything he had destroyed.

It wasn't only the rose petals undergoing a severe transformation through heat. A fire of words consumed Rumi. The poetry had never come as fast or as furious. Hosam could hardly keep up and assigned other dervishes as scribes while he made sure Rumi was comfortable during the transmission. Hundreds of stanzas poured forth from the mystic's mouth day after day that summer. Hosam joked that for every petal that had fallen off the roses, Rumi had composed another poem. Hosam was deliriously happy.

To go guided by fragrance is a hundred times better than following tracks.

Sitting there in the dim light of the storage house that smelled of wool and roses and felt damp with condensation, Damascena understood the whispered words at last. The dance had distilled *her* and she had become one with the essence of all that is. Some would call it God. Some would call it oneness. She simply felt love, and while she missed Deniz and thought about him every day, especially when she bottled the rose oil—hoping it would have made him proud—she had found her ability to love. She gave Ivan the first bottle.

"For you," she said. "For having the courage to stay with me."

Ivan stood at the threshold with a plate of chicken borek that Ates-baz had prepared for her, studying her quizzically.

"I imagine it was hard for you to receive me when my mother left."

He nodded, feeling the sting in his eye, but he did not cry. He swallowed instead, offering her the plate. She took it.

"Thank you," she said and murmured the Sufi blessing over the food. All he heard was *Ask-olsun* and understood it to mean *may it become love.*

She ate slowly, deliberately, making her meal a meditation. It was almost too much for him to bear, seeing her like this, remembering the way she inhaled the bowl of mash he set before her when she was an infant. He had held her in his arms and wished to hold her again. He marveled at the mystery in her growth, remembering the tiny lips and tiny tongue, the tiny ears and tiny feet, the tiny hands whose fingers were longer than his now, whose bones had grown so long she possessed the elegance of a young queen.

That fall, when the first harvest moon filled the sky over Konya, Rumi fell ill. Most speculated that he was writing himself to death. He had composed more verses in the last six months than he had written in the last six years. He looked frail and sallow. The hairs in his beard had started to fall out and lay scattered on his bed like silver threads. Those who were fortunate to visit him kept one and pocketed it. The hair of our beloved *Mevlana*, they thought, just in case it was the last time they saw him alive.

Hosam, who had been buoyant, slipped into a deep depression. He could not bear to sit with Rumi in his room alone without being reminded of his wife's final days. Even Hosam's own house made him lonely now that the roses had been picked. His field was barren and soggy as the days lost light and the rain soaked the great plain and dusted the mountains with snow. He invited Damascena to join him at Rumi's bedside while he edited the *Mathnawi*, the volume of poetry Rumi had almost completed. He held the manuscript up to the light. Damascena had never seen anything so huge in her life.

"It's thicker than a wall," she said.

Hosam nodded.

"50,000 lines in six books. It is a true masterpiece."

Damascena turned to Rumi, propping up his pillow.

"When did you know you wanted to write poems?"

He paused. "When did you know you wanted to turn roses into oil?"

She smiled. The great mystic, even sick, could not help but teach.

"I did not know," she said and laughed.

"I received a transmission. Just like you. I am simply a vessel. That is all."

"Then where do the words come from?" she asked.

"The same place the roses come from."

She stared at him, vexed.

"Creation," he said. "The act of creation is the dancing of all that has yet to come into existence. The frozen flowers dancing in the winter ground, yearning for form."

"Is that why you dance?"

He nodded. "The dance gives birth to the words."

She held the manuscript, feeling the weight in her arms. She had no idea how many pages. It was simply the largest pile of pages she had ever held. She felt honored, and a bit intimidated by the volume of poetry, and handed it back to Hosam.

"I should like to write some day."

"And what would you write?" Hosam asked.

"A story about roses."

Rumi chuckled and his eyes lit up. It was the first time in weeks that she'd seen him this animated. Hosam looked over at her, sharing his gratitude.

"I think that is a very good idea," Rumi said. "You will write a story that the world will love and remember forever. That would make me very happy indeed."

She smiled at him, playing with the idea. Who knows? It was not impossible.

"Do you know I didn't like roses at first?" she confessed.

He tilted his head on the pillow, sipped some water, put it down.

"How can that be?" he asked.

"Roses reminded me of my mother."

Rumi felt a tingling in his whole body as the girl spoke. Almost three years and she had not opened up to tell him what he had always suspected to be true.

"And why should you not like something that reminds you of your source?"

Damascena got up to refill his glass of water.

"When I was born, she gave Ivan some rose seeds she carried around her neck. She told him to plant them on the first full moon. He never did. I don't know what happened to them. I just know Shams took me to a white house with a field where a rose was growing. It was the first rose I had ever seen, and as much as I wanted to hate it, I could not help but love it. It was so beautiful, it hurt. Everything changed for me then."

Rumi nodded, coughed, gasping for air.

"Yes. Just like the pain of separation that can be beautiful, too."

She exchanged a knowing look with him. He looked at her with a gentle gaze, then yawned. He was tired. It was time for her to leave. She turned to Hosam.

"Thank you for letting me see a masterpiece."

When she got to the door, Rumi called out.

"You," he said.

She turned, watching him struggle to lift his hand and point.

"You are a masterpiece, too."

By October, Rumi refused visitors. Only Kerra was able to enter his room. Ates-baz loped around the *tekke* kitchen, staring at the uneaten baklava, the coffee that he still set out every morning with the hope of seeing Rumi walk through the door again. No one spoke of the likelihood that their master was going to die. Even the dervishes secretly preferred to live in denial that fall. No matter how much Rumi spoke of death being a marriage with the Beloved and something to celebrate, the pain of the separation welled up inside them and made them sad, desperate to hold onto his last words, last acts.

They got busy blowing glass, making enough bottles to hold all the rose oil. If they could not help Rumi directly, they would help Damascena complete her journey.

"What will you do with the rose oil?" they asked.

"I will help others heal."

They nodded. They no longer questioned her, but secretly hoped her rose oil would heal their broken hearts when Rumi died.

By November, Rumi had almost stopped talking altogether and he refused all food. He enjoyed the hallucinations. Seeing Shams almost daily, reliving those moments they shared on the rooftop, dancing in the streets. He laughed out loud remembering some of the outrageous things Shams had told him so long ago. *"I have no business with the common folk of the world; I have not come for their sake. Those people who are guides for the world unto God, I put my finger on their pulse."* He laughed again remembering how Shams had burned his books to teach him that the experience of ecstasy was far more valuable than knowledge. Such brutal lessons. Shams had been rough and abrasive, but just as the sand becomes a pearl, he had refined Rumi. He longed to reunite with him. Soon, he thought, I am coming. Damascena's arrival was proof.

Spring is here.
The rose is dancing with its thorn
Beauties have come from the invisible
To call you home.

He wanted to see Damascena when the first snow fell outside his window and blanketed the streets like the wings of a thousand storks, the veil of a thousand brides.

Damascena looked stricken, seeing him. She breathed in, trying hard not to cry.

"You're ... so sick!" she cried, wishing she could perform a miracle now.

"Do not cry for me," he said.

"What will become of you?"

He rolled his eyes back into his head, then struggling to sit up in bed, recited what Shams had told him. He had written it in his journal and would share this last secret with Damascena. "*The earth is not dust. It is a vessel full of blood. From the blood of lovers. The wound of a checkmate,*" he said.

She shivered. The wind rattled the window and ushered in a cool breeze.

"Nobody wants you to die, Mevlana. You should see the *tekke*. So much sadness!"

"Why do they waste their energy being sad about my returning to God?"

"They love you," she said and swallowed, feeling the lump in her throat.

"I love them. I always will. They will not lose my love when I go."

"They are afraid."

"Afraid?"

"What will become of us?"

"Nothing," he said and smiled, relieved. "No-thing."

"Tell us this is not true! We don't want to become nothing!"

He opened his eyes and stared at her, recalling a poem he heard dancing *sema*.

Why fear disappearance through death?
Next time I shall die
Bring forth wings and feathers like angels:
After that soaring higher than angels—
What you cannot imagine
I shall be that.

Damascena sobbed and he beckoned her to the bed. She sat beside him and instead of taking his hand, he took hers and kissed it.

"Be happy for me, Damascena. I am going home."

"Home? How can you be so happy about your own death?"

He smiled, beaming. "Because I am meeting my Beloved."

She knew. "You are going to meet Shams, aren't you? That's what this has all been about. Not the roses. Shams. Nothing but Shams. I've simply been the bridge."

Rumi nodded.

"To love," he said.

He reached behind him and opened the drawer in the nightstand, taking out a small square box carved of sandalwood. It smelled sweet. He handed it to her.

"I want you to have this."

She took the small box and opened it, finding a single rosehip. She dumped it out on her hand, feeling a surge of heat shoot up her arm into her heart.

"Is it my mother's?" she asked, cautiously. "Did she finally come back for me?"

Rumi looked at her, startled, and shook his head. "That is not from your mother."

She put the rosehip back in the box, felt her heart sink.

"The rosehip is from your grandmother."

Damascena met his eye, feeling breathless, pulled to the center of the earth.

"You know her?" she whispered.

Rumi nodded.

"I knew of her. She lived in my city. We met when I was a boy. She was the most beautiful girl in Balkh, Damascena. Everyone knew about her eyes. She had exquisite green eyes. Like yours. You look almost exactly like her. The resemblance was too uncanny for me to dismiss. The minute you arrived, I knew where you came from."

"You know my people," she said, feeling the shortness of her breath.

"I am your people. We come from the same place," he said.

"Then where is my mother?"

"Where she has always been, sweet child. Waiting for you in the roses. Don't you know? This is why you came. We are in each other's lives to help the other go home," he said, iterating again what he had told her long ago. *"May you go guided by fragrance."*

Earthquakes rocked Konya throughout December. God's warning, the people said, our master is leaving us. They paced. They worried. They prepared for the end of Rumi's life and for the *no-thingness* he and they would become. In secret, bids went out for an architect to erect a tomb worthy of such a mystic and poet, a lover of life, a lover of God.

Meanwhile, the dervishes needed something to occupy their minds and prepared for Damascena's initiation. December 17 marked her 1,001 day at the *tekke*. She had made it to the end. She had become a dervish among them. They wanted to make her ceremony special. Some even spoke of finding Deniz, but none had any luck. Kazanci Dede regretted putting the boy's shoes at the door, shredding the girl's last thread of joy.

Damascena had become reclusive again and joined them only in their solitude and silence, as if something even bigger for her than Rumi's death hovered on the horizon. She seemed preoccupied and no longer danced *sema* or lingered in the garden. She worked around the *tekke* doing odd jobs, finding ways to keep herself busy.

Damascena told Ivan of her plan. They would leave together and return to Krun. He agreed. Her work was finished here. Konya was not home. She did not know what was, but she knew she would never be home without being a part of Ivan's life.

And Ivan fortified their preparations. He ordered new shoes and two new coats: one made of bearskin, one made of sheep, wishing he had more to give to Damascena.

An earthquake awoke Damascena on the morning of December 17, where she lay on the floor beside Rumi's bed, fulfilling her promise to Shams. The earth shook the house and she swayed with the walls. A bookcase collapsed, a chair toppled backwards, and a crumpled ball of paper rolled out from under Rumi's bed. She reached out and opened the crinkled page, not believing it had landed there without a reason. It appeared to be a letter of sorts and when she read it, she knew immediately to whom Rumi had written. Shams. Perhaps his last letter. She held up the letter to the moonlight.

> *Sometimes I wonder, sweetest love, if you*
> *Were a mere dream in a long winter night,*
> *A dream of spring-days, and of golden light*
> *Which sheds its rays upon a frozen heart:*
> *A dream of wine that fills the drunken eye*

And so I wonder, sweetest love, if I
Should drink this ruby wine, or rather weep;
Each tear a bezel with your face engraved,
A rosary to memorize your name ...

There are so many ways to call you back-
Yes, even if you only were a dream.

She watched over him in the dark, listening to his belabored breathing, counting the seconds between breaths as they continued to slow, wondering if she would witness his last breath. She thought of the oblate. She had never seen a person die from natural causes and the rhythms were both lyrical and cacophonous. Part of her wanted to get up and run, but she had come too far to leave as a coward. She had lived the dream of which Rumi spoke, wishing there was a way to call *him* back. When the sun rose that morning, she knew it would only be a matter of hours.

"Good morning, Rumi Dede," she said and smiled.

"Good ... morn ... ing," he said, heaving up the words with wads of phlegm.

He coughed, struggling for air. She gave him water but he refused. He had not taken water in days. Kerra told her not to bother. He was ready, she said. Let him go.

Let him go to where? Where was this home he spoke of? She wanted to be happy for him, but it was hard to sit there knowing this would be the last she would see of him. The last time they would talk. There was no guarantee Rumi would choose to return as a spirit. Unlike Shams, Rumi's business was complete. Hers, however, was not, which is why she had spent the night by his bed. She had something to give him; today, she would complete Sham's final assignment.

"I graduate today," she said. "Can you believe it?"

Rumi gurgled, fluttered open an eye, then shut it again, drifting back to sleep. Damascena reached down and pulled out a small bottle of rose oil from her satchel.

"I've been asked to bring you this," she said. She noticed the nightingale did not wait for the moon to sing last night. It was time. She pulled the cork on the bottle and poured a drop on her finger, then moved toward Rumi and rubbed it between his eyes.

"May it become love," she said.

May it become love. Rumi could make out Damascena's voice. It comforted him to hear her speak his language, though he could no longer see her face. He felt her hands massage his body, rubbing what smelled like a million roses into his aching limbs and muscles, letting the rose oil absorb into every fiber and cell until he had the sensation that his body had broken apart from itself and was floating. All he saw were roses and light, rose petals suspended in the air like butterflies. The smell pulled him upward, through clouds. *To go guided by fragrance is a hundred times better than following tracks.*

The last thing he remembered was feeling lips on his forehead and a simple kiss, and he knew the power of the rose. Damascena had discovered its essence in the oil and in the rose oil, the kiss of God. He had waited his whole life to feel God's kiss. The rose held the secret to love all along.

"It came from The Friend," she said, remembering Shams' instruction. Rumi's lips turned up into a small smile just then, and it was the last expression on his face.

Nobody knew exactly when Rumi left his body. Some time between four o'clock and five o'clock in the afternoon, when his room was empty but filled with light. Some say the sunset on the evening of Rumi's passing was unparalleled in Konya. Painters would try to capture it for the rest of time, wondering if they could detect heaven in such a brilliant display of colors. One thing was certain, *Mevlana* was home at last.

The people of Konya moved in a daze, stone-faced and cold, muttering the mystic's words in the mosque and the markets, inside the steam of the bathhouse, committing them to memory like a song. *Don't be sad, my friend, when the rose's petals all fall. Seek the treasure of God in the devastated heart.* But what treasure could they seek now that Mevlana had left? Jalal–al-din Mevlana Rumi *had* been God's treasure.

Yes, he had left a masterpiece with his poetry that would go unmatched in the world for all of time. But the truth was the truth. Rumi was dead and no human prayers could assuage that devastation. The rose petals had fallen. The sunset burned so brightly that people believed it had absorbed the blood of Rumi.

How a great person dies is often his last teaching, they told each other, smelling the scent of roses for days after he left. People filled the streets, comforting each other, offering food, a good joke for levity, baskets of figs, paper lanterns, kittens, beautiful rugs, combining every holiday they celebrated throughout the year and draping it around Mevlana's death. Some who didn't know how to dance turned in the streets, delirious, giddy, nervous to know what life would be like on the other side of this moment, what life after this life would be like. If their beloved Mevlana believed he was going home, then where had he been in Konya?

Damascena left Konya the morning after Rumi's funeral. She had been unable to sleep, riding the waves of emotions, watching the outpouring of people who had come from all over the world, it seemed, to show their respect to the great teacher. Throngs of people crowded the streets. The caravanserai was overcrowded. People opened their homes to strangers who knocked on their doors. Rumor had it that even the Mongols who had become residents in Konya slept on the cushions of Seljuk royalty and offered their homes to Crusaders. It was an odd and beautiful display of the human spirit shedding its ego. True love, Damascena thought, watching it unfold. Rumi would have been pleased.

A light snow had begun to fall outside the *tekke*, but she was prepared for inclement weather. Ivan had bought a tent from shepherds who worked winters in the Kackar Mountains, guaranteeing their survival on the plains. In a strange way, he was looking forward to returning to a colder climate. He had had enough heat. Enough fire.

He stood beside Damascena and adjusted the saddles on two horses they had purchased with a single ounce of rose oil, securing the rest in a simple leather case used to carry salt. He buried each bottle in the salt, believing that nobody would look there.

"You forgot something," Kazanci Dede said.

Damascena looked at the horse, at Ivan. They had checked and rechecked everything. Ivan had been up for days making sure they had enough provisions to get them to Constantinople. From there, they would stop in a village on the Greek border, then slowly, village by village, climb the Rhodopes into the Thracian Valley and Krun.

"I do not think you should journey far without this."

Kazanci Dede stepped down from the steps of the *tekke* kitchen and presented a clean white skirt.

Damascena smiled. "You think I should take *sema* with me?"

"You don't need to take it anywhere. It will be wherever you go." She took the skirt but looked at him confused.

"Then what is it?"

Kazanci Dede pointed to the door. Standing half in shadow and half in the beam of light slicing through the doorway was Deniz, weathered, shaven this time, and as handsome as she had seen him yet. She felt her lips tremble, shook her head, looked at Kazanci Dede to confirm what she was seeing. He nodded, smiled, hugged her.

"Follow the Path," he whispered and kissed the top of her head. She looked up at him, barely able to make out the words.

"Thank you, Kazanci Dede."

"You're welcome. Be good now. Keep your heart open."

She nodded, eyes blurry, when Deniz stepped between them and took her in his arms, pressing her against his chest, and held her until she stopped trembling. He wore a white sheepskin coat and her tears soaked his lapel. After yesterday, she didn't think she had any more tears to shed. Deniz kissed her cheek, conscious of the *tekke* protocol. When she took his hand, she noticed that he was missing a thumb.

"I'll explain," Deniz said, conscious of her stare. "I'm coming with you."

A million questions whirled through her head but she asked only one.

"Do you know where you're going?"

"I know that if I follow you I am going where there is love."

She nodded, feeling a warmth in her whole body.

"One more thing before you leave," Kazanci Dede said and motioned for Hosam who stood just inside the door, waiting with the other dervishes, initiates, and Ates-baz to bid the girl farewell. Hosam carried the black wool cloak and draped it over Damascena.

In the aftermath of Rumi's death, she had forgotten about it completely.

"You have earned back the right to wear it," he said. "Do you claim it as yours?"

Damascena nodded, feeling the weight, smelling Shams in the wool.

"Yes. I claim it as mine."

"Do you claim the rose oil as yours?"

"Yes. And I have not forgotten it," she said and laughed.

Hosam's eyes lit up. "Very well, then. We would like to bless you."

Damascena felt embarrassed, being the center of the dervishes in the black wool cloak. They circled her in their robes and hats but it felt odd not to turn with them.

"For many years, we have called this The Prayer of Completion," Hosam continued, "But after hours of deliberations, we changed the name, in your honor."

"My honor?" she asked, feeling Deniz squeeze her hand.

"We are calling it the Rose Prayer. Because, thanks to you, dear sister, we all now know the rose is the symbol of the soul's completion. Brothers, please join hands."

Damascena bowed her head, listening to Hosam:

May this moment be blessed
May goodness be opened and may evil be dispelled.
May our humble plea
be accepted in the Court of Honor;
may the Most Glorious God purify and fill our hearts
with the Light of His Greatest Name.
May the hearts of the lovers be opened.
May our moments and joy be resplendent.
by the breath of our master Mevlana,

by the secret of Shams and Weled,
by the holy light of Muhammad,
by the generosity of Imam Ali,
And the intercession of Muhammad,
The unlettered prophet, mercy to all the worlds.
May we say Hu.

When he finished, Hosam kissed her hand.

"Thank you, sister. We will think of you when we see a rose and when we dance."

They walked in silence for days, digesting the turn of events, trying their best to organize the details of their fate. How Deniz had been mistaken as a thief when he arrived at his mother's house to sell her belongings. It was only by chance that a monk, who had come to pray for an ailing inmate, noticed Deniz, threadbare and shivering in the corner of the prison cell. The monk related his story and the jailers immediately removed the golden-haired boy, stricken by their mistake. They apologized profusely.

Deniz forgave them, following the Sufi way. *Feel joy in the midst of great disappointment,* he kept telling himself again and again. He had begged to write to Damascena but they cut off his right thumb. Now, when he held her hand, he felt the twitch, but realized a man does not need a thumb to hold love in his hands.

He followed her. That is all he could do with Ivan behind them, so very dumb but devoted. When Ivan slept, Damascena told him the story and Deniz listened, incredulous, staring into the fire they had made to keep Ivan warm. How can he sleep, he thought, wondering how many ghosts haunted him each night.

He was not surprised when one spring morning, in a village on the border of Greece, the strange man without a tongue did not awake. They nudged him, held the rose oil under his nose, trying to bring him back with scent. Ivan Balev lay stiff with a crooked smile. Confused? At peace? At home? They buried him there, as close to the sea as possible. Near the sailor. With his beloved.

Damascena did not cry. She simply put Ivan Balev in the ground, blessed him with the rose oil, then buried him, as if she was making a bed.

"He had a hard life," she said. "May he rest in peace."

"You think he will go to hell for what he's done?"

Damascena shook her head. "For raising me? I don't think so."

Deniz marveled at Damascena's fortitude and how she negotiated the mountains as if no obstacle were too big for her to overcome now. There they were, gaining altitude with the birds. She was stronger than he thought, and the higher they climbed, the more easily she seemed to breathe, as if the mountain peak itself was the closest she could get to God without dancing. At night, she burrowed her body against Deniz and dreamed. They made love in the middle of the night, in the darkest hours, when Damascena awoke to the shadow of the dance that circled the tent, wondering if Shams was with them.

But there was no evidence of him anywhere, other than the stork that met them the morning they crossed into the Thracian Valley and made their way to Krun, following the same path that Shams had shown her so long ago.

She should have been exhausted, but the closer she got to the white house, the lighter she felt, as if she could run. It was only the horses they had to wait for now. She practically had to push the animals toward the edge of the property the morning they arrived. Dawn had broken and dusted the June sky with bands of lavender and rose.

She could see the thatched roof in the distance, surprised the property had not overgrown. She motioned for Deniz's hand, seeing rose fields, feeling the flutter in her stomach. She moved forward, half walking, half skipping, half running through the field to the shadow of the stork flying over the roses.

"Shams," she cried. "Shams!"

Deniz could hardly keep up with her while the horses stood at the edge of the woods, bearing witness. Damascena chased the shadow of the stork until it suddenly disappeared. She paused, stricken, and searched the sky but did not see a bird anywhere.

"Shams? Where are you?"

She looked back at the field and where there was a shadow of wings, she saw a woman crouched in the roses, taking a cutting. Hearing the girl's voice, the woman stood. Her green eyes glinted in the early light and spilled with tears.

"Damascena," she said in disbelief.

The woman's voice was familiar, the same voice that had called out to her in the market the day she walked away from her inquisitors. She tingled and gasped.

She squeezed Deniz's hand and swallowed and was about to turn away when the woman said, "Wait." Damascena felt her heart move into her throat. Even if she turned and ran now, she knew this was the moment of vision she had waited for her whole life.

This is my fortune, she thought, watching the woman walk slowly toward her, retracing the path of the stork. It took only one glimpse of the woman's eyes to see that she was staring into her own. One glimpse to see the long fingers holding the rose cutting and the knife and know they matched hers. One glimpse to know that what she saw was her mother and that her mother was waiting for her in the roses. The love was everywhere and hers to claim.

THE END

ACKNOWLEDGEMENTS

No book is created entirely alone. I am grateful for the collaboration, encouragement, and suggestions from the following people who contributed to the creation and refinement of *Rose Girl* over the years. Thank you for your time, commitment, and open hearts.

Masie Cochran, for your superior editorial skills and years of steadfast faith, thank you for reading every single draft; and Joaquin Lowe, whose keen eye helped shape the final draft.

Albena Stoyanova, my translator and intrepid guide in Bulgaria—thank you for the adventure of a lifetime picking roses on a full moon, Susan Black for guiding my initial research on rose oil, and for the rose pickers of Kazanluk, Bulgaria, thank you for opening your homes and hearts.

To my readers and friends, thank you for your encouragement and contributions to the refinement of this story: Diana Cohn, Elizabeth Rose Raphael, Lisen Stromberg, Petek Kent, Dr. Kimberly Green, Joann Lustig, and Kimberly Bartlo, Adrienne Hall Lindholm, the late Hilary Hamilton, Barbara Transue, Donna Laemmlen, Ushi Patel, Lee Kravetz, David Ewing Duncan, Eleshiva Hart, Mariam Baker, Cigdem Duysal, Barbara Hubbard, Dorothy Woessner, Ellen Brookhart, Louise Henriksen, George Grenley, Deirdre

Gleason, Christopher Beaver, the late Tom Clarke and the late Karin Hemple, Steven Meloan, and Dmitry Tartakovsky, PhD Slavic Reference Service and the International and Area Studies Library at University of Illinois at Urbana-Champaign.

Dr. Francesca McCartney and MIM 27, for holding space for the transformation and healing.

Tom Joyce. Your insights, generosity of spirit, editorial notes and steadfast commitment to the birth and rebirth of this book make you a dear friend for life. Rumi gave us friendship. Books sustain it.

The Rose Girls of Carmel. Bonnie Bufkin, Kim Gilbreath, Meg Grundy, Jamie Roth, Tara Ryan, Kathryn Morrisey, Amy Somers, and all who gathered in the barn. Thank you for inviting me into your hearts. Hilary was the seed for the sisterhood we share.

My daughter, Gracelyn Rose, my brightest light, my greatest teacher, thank you for coming into the world for me to love. And Scott Larson, for loving all of me and gently guiding me forward.

A REQUEST TO SHARE THE LOVE...

Thank you so much for taking the time to read *Rose Girl*. Without readers like you, my role as a storyteller is futile. You complete the writing process, and your opinions matter to me and other authors. Your reviews and recommendations to friends help support authors and allow us to keep giving you deeply satisfying reading experiences.

As I raise my daughter to love and respect books, I hope that her generation and those to come continue to expand their minds with the very human activity of reading and connecting with others about the books that touch and change their lives. My greatest hope is that *Rose Girl* gave you something you needed or wanted, inspired, intrigued you, or surprised you in a good way.

Here's three easy ways you can support me and all your favorite authors:

1. Please leave a review on Amazon and any of your favorite platforms that connect readers.
2. Follow me @ hollylynnpayne on Instagram, Facebook and Twitter.
3. Sign up for my monthly newsletter at www.hollylynnpayne.com to get updates and the latest episode from the Page One Podcast and hear from the world's master storytellers.

Books really do get discovered by word of mouth, so thank you for your help. Please stay in touch! I love hearing from you and would be happy to meet with your bookclub.

In service with love,

holly

@hollylynnpayne on Instagram, Facebook, Twitter
www.hollylynnpayne.com

HOLLY LYNN PAYNE is the critically acclaimed author of four books of adult historical fiction in the U.S. and ten countries, with her debut, *The Virgin's Knot* (Dutton), selected for B&N's Discover Great New Writers. She founded the software company Booxby to aid book discovery after serving on the faculty of Stanford, the Academy of Art University, California College of the Arts, and San Francisco State. She currently produces the Page One Podcast with master storytellers and is a private writing coach. She lives in the San Francisco Bay Area with her family and beloved dog and can be found getting dirty on a mountain bike. You can find her at hollylynnpayne.com and follow her on Instagram, Facebook and Twitter @hollylynnpayne.